the

heartbreaker

SP♠DE
HOTEL

the
heartbreaker

SP♠DE
HOTEL

USA TODAY BESTSELLING AUTHOR
MARNI MANN

Entangled Publishing, LLC
644 Shrewsbury Commons Ave., STE 181
Shrewsbury, PA 17361
rights@entangledpublishing.com

Amara is an imprint of Entangled Publishing, LLC.

Visit our website at www.entangledpublishing.com.

Edited by Jovana Shirley/Unforeseen Editing
Cover art and design by Hang Le/By Hang Le
Interior design by Britt Marczak

ISBN 978-1-64937-870-5

Manufactured in the United States of America
First Edition September 2024

10 9 8 7 6 5 4 3 2 1

ALSO BY MARNI MANN

Some men will burn down the world for you. Some will get on their knees for you. Some will take you by the hand and bring you to a Taylor concert, where your inner princess reigns. Ladies... Ridge is all three. He is the perfect amount of sizzling sex appeal, swoons, and single daddy.

Playlist

"Horns"—Bryce Fox

"Dirty Love"—Mt. Joy

"Fire"—Barns Courtney

"World on Fire"—Nate Smith

"Half of forever"—Henrik

"Closer"—Nine Inch Nails

"She"—Jelly Roll

"You're on Your Own, Kid"—Taylor Swift

"Miss Americana & The Heartbreak Prince"—Taylor Swift

Chapter One

RIDGE

"I don't want to let you go."

Those were the words I said to my father as I held his hand while he lay in bed.

During the moments when neither of us said anything, the quietness of the room taking hold of me, I memorized every inch of him. His skin was so pale, almost gray, compared to the constant tan he'd rocked for as long as I could remember. His eyes were hollow. His grip was weak as his thumb clasped the back of my hand.

Ray Cole was one hell of a fighter. He'd held on longer than we'd anticipated, but cancer ended up being stronger than his will and the medicines combined. Rather than going into the hospital, he opted to stay home under hospice care. A hospital bed had been moved into his bedroom, where he now spent all his time, and he had around-the-clock care until he took his last breath.

We'd been told that would be within the next few hours.

My siblings and I were each spending some alone time with him. Rowan, my sister, had gone first. Rhett, my oldest brother, had gone second. My father had asked me to come in last, and I now sat on the side of his bed, grasping his fingers, feeling the iciness coming off his palm.

I didn't know what else to say.

As the emotion churned inside my chest, Dad's breathing came out in shallow pants.

My time was running out, and, fuck, that hurt.

Because this moment, these last few minutes, was a memory I'd replay forever.

"You're not letting go, son. I'm letting go." He cleared his throat. "It's my time." He spoke slowly, and I could tell how much energy it took for him to form each syllable.

My poor father.

Always the pillar of strength for our family—a role that was now mine. Rhett had been through enough; he would never willingly want to shoulder that burden. Rowan was a daddy's girl, hanging on by a thread, the tears worsening since she'd had her daughter, Rayner. Rowan wanted Dad in her daughter's life. She wanted trips to Disney and grandfather-and-granddaughter dates and holidays with all of us together.

I understood.

I wanted that as well for my daughter, Daisy.

But Daisy was lucky enough to have spent the six years of her life with him, where Rayner was still a baby and far too young to remember any of this.

"Dad..." My face fell forward, the agony tearing through my chest.

There were so many kinds of pain.

I would take physical over the emotional heaviness of this any day.

"Son, I want you to promise me something." His hand was now on the top of my head.

"Anything."

"I want you to promise that you're going to love big. Love hard. Love unapologetically. Because being in love is the greatest blessing in this world."

Out of all the things he could have said, that was where he'd gone. A part of my life I'd given no time or attention to since things had ended with my daughter's mother.

As my head lifted, his hand lowered to my cheek, a place he'd held when I was a kid, and then it went to my chin.

"Don't be alone like me," he continued.

"You're not alone, Dad." I squeezed his hand, not wanting that thought to even enter his brain. Not now, not at the point where he was at. "You have us—"

"I'm alone." He attempted to clear his throat again. This time, he choked, the air wheezing through his lips until he stopped coughing. Once he was settled, he added, "I can tell you it would be a different kind of feeling from the one I have now if the love of my life were holding my other hand." As his hand left my face, it hit the mattress and stayed disconnected, balled up, as though he were reminding himself that only he could hold those fingers. "Ridge, I have so many regrets when it comes to love. Don't do love that way. Live your life with it, don't regret that you don't have it."

Growing up, when my parents had still been married, I couldn't recall a single time when they enjoyed being in each other's presence. The hate was evident—I could sense it, even at an early age. The tipping point was when my mother caught him cheating. That was when the paperwork was filed to officially end things, and she kicked him out.

The reality was that my parents just didn't love each other. I wasn't sure if they ever did. They'd stayed together because of us kids when they should have divorced long before the cheating started.

Was it a detriment that I hadn't witnessed love in my parents' houses? That I had a promiscuous father?

Maybe.

But neither of those points was the reason I was single.

When Jana, Daisy's mother, and I had broken up, I'd made the choice not to have women come in and out of my daughter's life. Rather than focus on anything serious, I had fun. I worked my ass off. I gave every bit of my attention to my daughter.

Love wasn't a priority.

And as I looked at the deep grooves in my father's face that I knew weren't from smiling and the quietness in the bedroom and the vacant spot on the other side of his bed, I realized he hadn't made it a priority either.

Since his divorce, approximately twenty-five years ago, he never lived with anyone.

He never introduced his kids to anyone.

He never spoke to us about anyone.

But we still knew that women came and went, just like the hospice nurses who covered each of the twelve-hour shifts at his home.

I searched for something to say that would alleviate the loneliness he was feeling, and before I could voice anything, he whispered, "Promise me, Ridge. Promise me that you won't end up like me."

A statement I couldn't wrap my head around.

My father had an incredible life. He traveled the world. He'd built one of the most successful hospitality brands. The only one that was larger—the Spade Hotels—we had now merged with. He had three children, who had taken over the reins of his business, and he had more money than he could ever spend in ten lifetimes.

Ending up like him wouldn't be such a bad thing.

"Ridge"—he shook my hand—"promise me."

I nodded. "All right, Dad. I promise."

A contentment passed through his glossy eyes. "I need you to be the leader of this family. Make sure Cooper never hurts your sister, and you treat Rayner like she's your own."

There was a knot in the back of my throat. One that was building larger, denser as the seconds passed.

"Done."

"And your brother. I need you to care for him. That boy"—he stopped to take a breath, the wind he inhaled too much for his throat—"has been lost and doesn't want to be found. Find him, Ridge. Help him."

His last requests hit my chest in a way where it felt impossible to speak.

I didn't want my father to see emotion as the last look on my face.

I wanted him to know I could handle the position he'd just given to me.

So, I swallowed the tears threatening to pool and the trembling inside my body and the aching not just in my chest, but in every joint and muscle.

"I will," I said softly. Since that didn't feel like enough, I said, "I promise."

He gave a slight nod and brushed his thumb past the peaks of my knuckles.

A movement that I knew, deep in my fucking heart, would be his last.

"You've always made me proud, my son." His cough thickened. "I love you, and I love Daisy."

Chapter One

Ridge

Three Months Later

Out of all the places I'd expected to end up tonight, a strip club wasn't one of them. Shit, I wasn't complaining. Spending an evening looking at naked women wasn't exactly a bad time in my book. Especially when the ladies left the stage and pranced topless around the lounge, where all the patrons, including myself, were sitting. That gave me an up-close-and-personal look at their bodies. Asses that were covered by only a thin, usually sparkly thong. Nipples so hard that it was as though they'd been rubbed with ice. Eyes that taunted as they locked with mine and skin so heavily perfumed that their scents lingered long after they passed me.

I wasn't a virgin when it came to strip clubs. I'd visited my fair share over the years, so I knew that inside these walls was nothing more than a fantasy. The strippers were saleswomen. The nods and smiles and words exchanged were all selling tactics.

The only real thing that came out of a place like this was a fucking hard-on.

That was why, earlier tonight, when the thirty or so of us had packed into a party bus, celebrating Brady Spade and Lily Roy's joint bachelor and bachelorette party, and Brady announced this was our next stop, I hadn't been excited. Brady was one of the executives at Cole and Spade Hotels, our company, and the last of the Spades to settle down—something I'd never, in my lifetime, thought would happen with a reputation like his.

But he'd proven everyone wrong—and by everyone, I meant all of California and probably half of the West Coast.

Rhett looked about as amused as me, so I rested my arm across his shoulders and said, "I never thought I'd say this, but I'd rather be at a club right now."

"That sounds as insufferable as this," he replied.

I wasn't surprised by my brother's answer. The last three months had been tough on all of us. As the leader, I encouraged my siblings to keep living, to keep enjoying—that was what Dad would have wanted. What would make him roll over in his grave was if we stopped living because of his death.

Rowan was trying her best. She didn't like to leave Rayner, but since it was a joint party and her boyfriend, Cooper, was Brady's brother, she was here. She was smiling. Drinking. There was a look of happiness on her face as she mingled with the girlfriends of the Spade brothers and the Daltons, their best friends.

But that wasn't the way Rhett looked at all, slumped in the chair next to mine. His expression told me he was going to hit something. Not just punch it. He wanted to pulverize it.

"You all right, brother? I know the last few months—"

"Don't talk to me about the last few months. Not here." His expression turned grim. "Not now."

"I hear you. My bad." I squeezed the spot I was holding. "But is that what's bothering you? Dad?"

He rubbed his thumb and forefinger together as though he was getting ready to lock them into a fist. "I shouldn't be here."

"Why?"

I wasn't sure who was about to roar the loudest, Rhett or the lion tattooed on his thumb.

"You know why." His teeth ground together.

I circled back to our father as the reason he was acting this way. Work could be another cause. My brother had been putting in some serious hours lately, and maybe he was feeling guilty that he'd taken the whole weekend off.

Or, hell, maybe it was something else.

"How about you help me out and just tell me the reason, so I don't have to keep racking my brain—"

"The date, Ridge." His head shook in a way that told me he was disappointed. "What's the fucking date?"

The date.

The date.

And then, like a bolt of goddamn lightning across the back of the head, it hit me.

Fuck.

I gave him a solid squeeze, rubbing his muscle back and forth.

How could I have forgotten?

"Do you want to talk about it?" I asked him.

"No."

His answer didn't shock me in the least bit. Rhett never wanted to talk about anything. He kept it all buried in the furthest, deepest part of him until he exploded. Those explosions always looked different, but in this case, I wouldn't be surprised if he disappeared for a few days.

Still, I pushed and said, "Are you sure?"

He swished out some air. "Yeah, I'm fucking sure." He stood. "I need another drink."

I wasn't positive if that was code for something else, like he was calling a rideshare to get out of here, so I asked, "Are you going to take off?"

"If I do, don't come looking for me." He disappeared toward the bar.

Damn it. One sibling was keeping it together while the other was falling apart.

I tried not to think about Rhett while I turned toward the crew. The couples all seemed to be having a blast, the women far more engaged with the strippers than their men. The only singles part of the gang, aside from Rhett and me, were the Westons. A family of five siblings—four men and a woman—who owned high-end restaurants and clubs across the world, many of those located in our hotels. Although Eden couldn't attend—she was away on business—the four brothers were here. Since the merger, I'd gotten the opportunity to work with them, even hang out outside of normal business hours, and I would consider them friends.

Which was why I knew things were about to get rowdy.

If there was one thing this group did well together—the Coles, Spades, Daltons, and Westons—it was having a good time.

And it seemed like everyone was.

That was all the more reason to shake Rhett out of my head and focus on the party. Especially considering this was my first time out in a while. Daisy's mother was back in town after a long stint on the road, and she had Daisy for the next week. Knowing my daughter was safe and in good hands gave me a chance to let loose and unwind. I wanted nothing more than to laugh my ass off, catch a buzz, and go for a long run in the morning to sweat out all the excess booze.

But before this night was over, I needed to make sure I had enough material to razz up the guys during our next executive meeting. After a night of debauchery, I fucking loved rousing the fellas on all the shenanigans that had gone down.

One way to ensure that was more alcohol.

There wasn't a waitress anywhere near our tables, nor was there any walking around the VIP area. So, I turned around to scan the other side of the lounge, looking for someone capable of taking an order of shots, and that was when I saw her.

A woman so fucking beautiful that my eyes wouldn't leave her.

Even if there was a reason to drag my stare away, I wouldn't.

I couldn't.

She was that breathtaking.

That gorgeous.

That enticing.

I pushed myself to the end of my seat, knowing I was about to get up at any second because I needed to talk to hear her voice. I needed to talk to her. I needed to be closer to her than I was now.

That was how drawn I was to her.

And while I stayed here, somewhat frozen, I took in the details I'd missed when my eyes first landed on her. I certainly couldn't have ignored her red hair. That was what had initially mesmerized me. But the more I looked at the long waves, strands that hung down her back and over her shoulders and hugged the sides of her face, I realized it wasn't just a deep auburn. The color reminded me of a burnt fall sunset.

Her face was a combination of soft features that even individually screamed of a level of beauty I'd never seen before. Lips that were plump and glossy. A small button-like nose. Smooth, sun-kissed skin. Eyes that I couldn't see the color of from here, but I could feel how alluring they were.

And then there was her body.

A chest that was the perfect size for her petite frame, hips and a waist that dipped in just right, and an ass with the amount of thickness I desired.

She didn't run in a straight line from head to toe.

She had curves.

Curves I wanted to fucking devour.

There had been a dullness in my chest when I walked into this strip club tonight.

Now, I was on fire.

And there was no way I could let another second pass without buying her a drink.

"Going to grab a cocktail?" Beck Weston asked as I stood, his chair directly next to mine. "Do you mind grabbing one for me too?" The NHL star was loving his offseason life, freeing up his time to attend things like this.

"I'm not headed to the bar."

He chuckled. "Where else would you be going? The restroom?"

I nodded toward the redhead, watching Beck's stare land on her.

"Enough said." He pounded my fist. "Go get her, my man."

I took off before anyone else could distract me and delay me even more, and I walked out of the VIP area and into the general lounge, stopping at the base of the stage where she was standing.

Now that I was nearer, I could fill in all the blanks, like the color of her eyes, which was the lightest brown. A dusting of freckles that ran down the middle of her nose. Skin that wasn't just smooth, but silky and creamy. Thighs that had the faintest definition of muscle.

And, *goddamn it*, nipples that were the lightest pink.

I didn't care that she was standing on a stage with only a thong covering her. I sure as hell didn't care that she was a stripper. Nor did I care that every fucking man in this room had his eyes on her.

What I cared about was that as soon as she stepped onto the floor, I grasped every bit of her attention.

Despite this being an imaginary playhouse, I was about to find the authenticity in this room.

And I was going to show her that in me.

Luckily, I didn't have to wait long. The song was ending, and she was making her way to the steps, holding her bra and the cash she'd collected from the stage. A bouncer helped her down the short staircase where I waited for her.

As he moved away, helping the next stripper onto the stage, I said, "Hi," just loud enough that she could hear me over the music.

Her smile tugged from the side and lifted. "Hi."

"You were incredible up there."

She knew how to shake her body, how to use the pole, how to squat with her legs spread wide while her hair whipped across her face.

"Thank you."

I kept my eyes fixed on hers, not allowing them to dip even though I wanted them to. "Can I buy you a drink?"

She slipped her arms through her bra straps, wrapping the lace around her tits before she clasped the hook behind her back. "Why would you want to do that?"

"I was watching you from the VIP lounge and hauled my ass over here to talk to you."

"Aren't you charming?" She batted what I assumed were fake lashes, considering how long they were. "There's a stage in there too. Was the dancer not entertaining enough?"

My hands were at my sides, but I wanted them on her waist, so I could feel just how velvety her skin was. And while I was there, I wanted to wrap her legs around me and carry her somewhere quiet. "She's not you."

She laughed, showing teeth that were white and beautifully straight. "I'm not sure what to say to that."

"Say you'll have a drink with me."

"You're cute—you know that?"

"Follow me," I instructed.

She stayed planted. "I think you're forgetting where we are."

"I know exactly where we are."

She combined all her hair and laid it over one shoulder. "Then, you know I can't join you. It's not that I don't want to. I'm just not allowed. If I'm not up there"—she pointed behind her at the stage—"then my job is to roam the room until I book a private dance."

"What does that entail?"

"The private dances?" When I nodded, she continued, "You've never had one?"

I chuckled at the way she was looking at me. "Why does that surprise you? You know nothing about me…" I gave her a wink.

"I just assume most people who come here are knowledgeable about the services that are offered. If I'm being honest, I'm glad a guy as handsome as you isn't a regular here."

She thought I was handsome.

Finally, I felt like I was getting somewhere.

"Because?" I questioned.

"Regulars can be a little creepy…if you know what I mean."

I crossed my arms over my chest. "Trust me, I'm not that."

She laughed again as she shifted her weight, the sky-high heels bringing the top of her head to my throat.

"I don't mean any disrespect when I say this, but I don't make it a habit to come here." I kept my voice gentle. "My friends and I are celebrating a bachelor and bachelorette party and ended up here."

Her brows rose. "Is it your bachelor party?"

An appropriate question.

I whistled out a mouthful of air. "Fuck no."

It seemed my answer registered through her before she nodded toward the VIP area. "Back there, there are private rooms. You can rent them for a dance, two dances, three dances—however many you want."

The more I spoke to her, the more I realized there was no way I could have left here without talking to her.

I would have regretted it for the rest of my life.

Because looking at her from where I'd been sitting with the group wasn't nearly enough.

Neither was this conversation.

Whoever she was, however her story unraveled—I wanted to know both.

"I'd like to rent a private room for the entire night."

Her eyes widened. "Really?"

"If that's the only way I'll get to spend time with you, then yes. Take me there."

The shock was evident on her face. "I think there are some logistical things we have to work out first."

I reached into my pocket, took out my wallet, and grabbed the wad of cash from inside. I didn't need to count it; I knew just how much was there, and I placed it in her hand. "That should more than cover it."

She slowly glanced down at the stack. Her chest rising and falling several times. "You're giving all of this to me?"

"Pay the house or whatever you have to do to cover your bases. The rest is for you."

Her head shook, giving me the impression she didn't want to take it.

That gesture, that modesty, made me want her even more.

"Are you sure?" she asked.

I almost laughed.

A greedy person would take the money and immediately lead me toward the private rooms. She wasn't greedy at all. And something told me the redhead was a lot different from most of the people in this establishment.

"I'm positive," I told her.

She nodded. "Okay. Come with me."

I followed her through the main lounge and past the VIP section, where she stopped at a window. I kept my distance, giving her the privacy she needed while she spoke to the cashier. She counted out an amount I could vaguely see and palmed the rest. When she made eye contact with me, waving me forward, I moved in beside her, and we entered a small room.

With the walls, ceiling, and floor all black, it was difficult to see with just a single dim spotlight above. But it gave off enough of a glow that her skin sparkled and the whites of her eyes and teeth really stood out.

"Why don't you sit here?" She stood at the side of an armless chair.

There were two in the room, and they were identical, placed a few feet apart.

As I got comfortable in the seat, she made her way to the front of me and put her hands on my shoulders.

The stage, where I'd met her, had been too congested with scents, so I couldn't detect hers. But now that she was in this position, I knew why I hadn't been able to smell her. Her perfume was too light. But in here, the subtleness of her vanilla-latte aroma was just right.

"Just so you know, there are cameras in here." The ends of her hair dangled in my face. "My manager can see everything we're doing."

A warning I didn't need.

"Are you saying that for your protection?"

She stilled. "I would say that to anyone I brought in here."

"I realize you really don't know me, but I didn't bring you in here to touch you or do something that would cause your manager to be alarmed."

"Why did you bring me in here, then?" She spoke so quietly.

"Let me clarify something first because I don't want to be misleading." I rubbed my hands together before I set them on my legs. "Touching a body like yours would be a fucking dream, and I'd love nothing more, but that's not my motive. I want to get to know you. That's why I wanted to buy you a drink, and that's why we're in here."

She said nothing.

"What's your name?" I was met with more silence. "I'm Ridge."

I could feel the hesitation before she voiced, "Addy."

"Addy"—I lifted her hands off my shoulders and escorted her to the other chair—"why don't you sit? That'll make it easier to talk."

"You're sure you don't want a dance?"

If we were anywhere else, this would have gone so differently.

I wouldn't know that her fucking nipples were the lightest shade of pink. I wouldn't know that she had a patch of freckles, like her nose, that ran up one of her ass cheeks. And I wouldn't have to move her to the chair next to mine since the chances of her straddling me right away would be slim.

"We're just talking, remember?" I waited until she sat. "I'm one of the good guys. I know you don't believe that, but you will before the night is through."

"How good?"

I chuckled. "Fuck, you must meet some real assholes in here if you have to ask that question."

She turned the chair to face me and moved it closer, her knees briefly rubbing against mine as she crossed her legs. "I don't know if I should admit this or not, but this is only my third shift and my very first time bringing a guest in here. So, to answer your question, I'm sure there are lots of assholes, but I'm not seasoned enough to know just how spicy they can get."

For some reason, I really liked hearing that she was new and inexperienced.

"Third day on the job and your first private booking. Is it safe to assume you weren't a stripper before you took the job here?"

She let out a burst of air that sounded like it came from her nose. "No."

"New profession, then."

Her head dropped. "New and very temporary." She wrapped her arms around her stomach.

"Can I ask you a personal question?"

Her eyes lifted. "You've already seen my boobs, Ridge. I think we're past personal, don't you?"

I laughed. "This question digs in a bit."

She shrugged. "Try me."

"What makes one decide to strip?" My hand went in the air. "I'm not knocking the profession—I want to make that clear. I'm just curious what made you choose this path."

"Ah, that." She sighed. "It's a very good question. I think everyone in here probably has a different reason." She glanced toward the door, which was closed, her arms appearing to tighten around her. "I'm not even going to lie. I almost chickened out before my first shift, wondering if I would survive and trying to come up with another option. But I figure I can do it for a couple of months—or however long it takes—and be done. It won't be the hardest thing I ever overcome in my life—that's for sure."

"If it's any consolation, you happen to be really good at it."

"Oh, Ridge," she exhaled, "I don't know if I should laugh or cry from that statement."

"Laugh. Always laugh." I winked at her.

Her head shook. "I picked the wrong profession. My parents had warned me when I declared a major, and I didn't listen. I went with my heart instead of my bank account. Wrong move, I guess."

"And which profession is that?"

She smiled. "One that pays like shit."

She wasn't ready to open up. I could understand that.

The environment, I was sure, had something to do with it.

"Or maybe I should say, it's a profession that doesn't pay as well as this," she clarified.

"Listen, there's no shame in hustling. We all have to do it at some point or another, and that hustle looks different for everyone." I was tempted to take out my phone and show her a picture of Daisy, but I kept it planted in my pocket. "I've got a little girl. I can tell you right now, there isn't anything I wouldn't do to provide for her. She's my priority. She's the reason I work as hard as I do."

"How old?"

"She's six, going on twenty-five. Smart as a whip. Hell of a lot smarter than me."

She nodded, grinning. "And her mom?"

My head tilted as I took in Addy's stunning face. "If her mom were in the picture, I wouldn't be in this room right now. Remember… I'm one of the good ones."

Her smile stayed wide.

"I want to go back for a second." Because it was a question she'd danced around. "I told you my daughter is my reason and she's what motivates me. What's your reason?"

Whatever her answer was, was her breaking point. And I knew, without even hearing it, that it would teach me so much about who she was and what her life looked like.

One thing I knew for certain: this job wasn't for the weak. It took serious balls to walk in that door and accept a position that came with the requirements she faced.

So, whatever drove her, it made her one unique woman.

She leaned forward, resting her arms on her thighs. "You really want to know me, don't you?"

"You could say I'm interested."

"In what?"

"You." I cleared my throat. "All of you."

She released a small noise that didn't sound like a sigh or a moan. "Ridge…"

"You're not asking me why I'm interested. Or how I'm interested. Or when I became interested."

"I don't have to—because we're in a private room of a strip club and you saw my moves on the stage, courtesy of high school and college cheerleading, and thought to yourself, *She'd be a good lay.*" She chewed her lip. "Am I right?"

"Addy, you're not giving yourself nearly enough credit." I paused. "Were your moves noticed? Sure, they were. Was your body appreciated? Fuck yes. But I would have appreciated your body if we'd been in a bar, and you were in jeans and a T-shirt, and my imagination was filling in the blanks. Being in here and what you're wearing"—I nodded toward her—"have nothing to do with my opinion. I would have reacted the same way regardless of where we'd met." I crossed my legs. "I could have paid you for a dance in the VIP room. I could have let you dance topless on top of me when we came in here. I told you, that's not what I want or what I'm looking for."

"Tell me, then, Ridge, why are you interested?"

Chapter Two

ADDISON

I wanted a cardigan. No, I wanted an oversize hoodie and a pair of sweats and my hair in a messy knot on the top of my head while digging into a bowl of steaming hot ramen because the salad I'd scarfed down a few hours ago wasn't nearly enough to hold me over. And while I slurped up the piping hot soup, I wanted to listen to Ridge talk. I wanted to feel his gaze on my face.

I wanted to smile and have him tell me there was a green onion dangling on my lip and have the two of us laugh about it.

In a perfect world, all of that would be coming true.

What I didn't want was to be practically naked while I sat in front of him, the air-conditioning making my nipples hard, the room so dark and uncomfortable that it felt like I was in a straitjacket and there were bars between us.

The only thing that made it better was his eyes.

My God, Ridge had kind eyes. They were the first thing I'd noticed when he met me at the bottom of the stage. They were a cobalt blue with navy flecks around the outer edge.

A combo of shades that was so rare together.

I wished I could see the color of them now while he shifted in his seat, getting ready to answer the question I'd just asked.

A question I was dying to hear the answer to.

"Why am I interested?" he said. "Telling you you're the most beautiful woman I've ever seen is easy. That's the obvious answer, but it's not my answer even though it's true."

His charm went beyond his appearance despite him being the handsomest man I'd ever seen. It went deeper than his words.

It was his gentleness I could feel.

A tenderness that I wouldn't have expected in a man like him.

"Keep going," I encouraged.

"You know, it's one thing to find you attractive, it's a whole other thing to want to know your story. To look at you and wonder how you take your coffee and what you order for breakfast. To want to know what type of outfit makes you feel the sexiest—not what I find the sexiest on you. To want to know what you do when you crawl into bed at night, whether you read from a tablet, or scroll your phone, or shut it all off and cover your eyes with a mask." He moved his arms to his chest. "It took only a second of looking at you, and that's what I was thinking. To know there was something far deeper in those light-brown eyes than what I was seeing on the surface." He paused. "That's the how. That's the why. And that's the when."

A response that completely took me off guard.

Most guys my age would have stopped at the beautiful part and would have used *hot* instead. But I had a feeling Ridge was older, somewhere in his thirties, not his mid-twenties, like me.

"If you learned all of that about me," I said, "what would it tell you?"

He shook his head. "It's not what it would tell me. It's what it would show me." He set his hands on his thighs, clenching them for a second before they lay flat. "I'm not looking to change you, Addy. I just want to get to know you better."

Another shocker.

As though I were an end piece with straight edges and a dip in the middle and he was the next row, measuring to see if his bubbled-out piece fit with mine.

But why?

That was what I couldn't understand.

I was an actress onstage, and he was paying for a show. How did he know he would even like what was beneath those light-brown eyes?

Still, I had to give him an applause for creativity. "You're more than just a handsome face, Ridge. Has anyone ever told you that before?"

He laughed.

Not just a chuckle. He really laughed. And the sound was so sweet that it made me laugh.

"I like you."

His admission came when we were both almost silent.

"You can't like me in a place like this. Feelings are forbidden."

"I'll like you when we're outside of this place. In fact, I'm positive I'll like you even more."

My hair fell into my eyes, and I didn't push it back. "I doubt that."

"Why don't we leave and find out?"

I stared at him, at the little parts of his face that I could make out in the faint light. Ash-brown hair that was longer and messy on the top, like I'd just run my hands through it. Scruff that fell past his jawline and onto his neck. He hadn't taken the time to shave that part before he went out, which told me he didn't care enough. He hadn't come here to meet a woman; he'd come to celebrate with his friends, so shaving wasn't exactly needed. Below his face was an outline of muscle that I could see through his clothes, a style that was more Malibu than LA.

And his scent, I couldn't get enough. It was uncommon, like his eyes. An aroma that reminded me of a place where the trees met the waterline. A little earthy, a little salty, and a little spicy.

What Ridge was showing me was that he was everything I looked for in a man…if I was looking for one.

I needed to get through this season of my life, the next couple of months being the most complicated with everything I had going on—starting with the fact that I was working here—and then maybe I could consider dating.

Intrigued? Yes.

Enjoying myself? Absolutely.

Mentally prepared for something? That was where things became muddy.

"I can't leave," I told him. "I'm scheduled to work until closing."

"But I paid for the entire night, which means you're not on the stage and you're not out on the floor. In your boss's eyes, they've already lost you for this shift. Why would it matter if you left?"

He had a point. It wouldn't matter, especially because I would technically be spending the rest of the evening in here with him and the club had already gotten their cut of what Ridge had paid me.

But could I really leave with him?

Did I want to?

"Where would we go?" I glanced down my body. "When I'm dressed like this?"

"Did you wear that to work?"

Another point.

Of course I hadn't worn this. I'd changed after I arrived.

I didn't know what I was thinking. He somehow got my brain all twisted around—and I wasn't thinking.

"All I have with me are workout clothes. Yoga pants. A tank top. A zip-up sweatshirt—"

"Since I'm assuming you don't want to come back to my place—even though I make one hell of a mac and cheese"—he laughed—"we can go to this little hole-in-the-wall restaurant that's not far from here. They have the best ramen I've ever had in my life."

My eyes bugged, my mouth hanging open for several seconds before I voiced, "Did you just say ramen?"

"I did."

Out of all the food choices, he had gone with one of my favorites and just what I was craving.

How did he know?

Was he somehow inside my head?

"Sigh," I drew out. "It's impossible for me to turn down a good bowl of ramen."

"It's like I read your mind…"

• • •

The only things missing were the sweatpants, although yoga pants were just as cozy, and the messy knot—I'd opted to leave my hair down even though it reeked of the strip club. There was so much perfume sprayed in the back room where we all got ready that when I left each shift, I smelled like I worked at a scent shop. Everything else—the company, the ramen, the iced green tea—was beyond perfect.

Maybe too perfect.

Which was why I hadn't kept my eyes off Ridge, stealing glances at him at every red light while I'd driven us to the restaurant and the whole time we'd been here.

Where were this man's flaws?

What was off about him? Because something had to be off. He couldn't be this fabulous…*could he?*

"My daughter loves it here," he told me, twirling some sun noodles around his chopsticks. "We come almost every Sunday. We've tried different ramen places around town, but this is her favorite."

"She has good taste. The ramen is incredible." I savored the soft-boiled egg, my eyes closing as I chewed. "I'd want to come here every Sunday too."

He smiled, running his thumb across his lips.

Why was that simple movement—that pure, innocent swipe—so sexy?

"That's our day-date day—that's what she calls it. We go to the park, we come here for lunch, and then we go to the horse barn."

I recrossed my legs, my knee briefly grazing his. "She rides?"

"She recently got into it. Little did I know, when she first started, it would take up so much time. Gymnastics was a few hours a week—tops. Swimming was the same. But my little one doesn't want to just ride, she wants to help bathe the horses and brush them and feed them, and we end up being there until dinner." His finger stilled by the corner of his mouth. "*Daddy, they need my tender touch, or they can't do their horsey-riding things,* she tells me." He shook his head, smiling. "How can I say no to that? She has a soft spot for animals, and I have a soft spot for her cuteness."

As though my heart hadn't already been pounding, it was now on the verge of exploding. Not just from the voice he used when he imitated her, but his whole demeanor.

"I don't mean to talk about her." His hand touched my arm, the warmth of his skin almost a shock compared to how cool it was in the restaurant. However, it wasn't the temperature that sent vibrations through me. "I know it must be boring to hear about someone else's kid."

I knew he'd made a statement that I needed to respond to. I just couldn't yet.

There was something besides words that was taking over my body.

A feeling that had come out of nowhere.

It started in the spot that he'd held for only a second and traveled. To my chest.

To my stomach.

To—*oh God*—that throbbing place between my legs.

"It's not boring at all," I whispered.

"Do you have kids?" He held the porcelain spoon on top of the soup, waiting for my answer.

"No. I'm only twenty-four. That's not to say I'm too young for kids—I'm certainly not—but I'd like to be closer to my late twenties before it happens. And I want it to happen. I want lots of kids."

He chuckled. "How many is lots?"

I finished a bamboo shoot and gave him a grimace with lots of teeth. "Four to five. I've always wanted to be a mom, and I want a giant family."

"That's a hefty range all right."

I wiped the corners of my mouth and returned my napkin to my lap. "It was just my sister and me growing up. We're six years apart, so by the time I hit middle school, she had already graduated and was off for premed. Even though we're super close, the age gap gave me only-child vibes. I guess it had its perks, but I want something different for my kids."

He moved his spoon around, but didn't take a bite. "Did you grow up around here?"

"I'm from the Bay area."

"And what brought you south?"

"College brought me, and the weather made me stay. Let's face it, the beaches are far better here."

"Does that mean you surf?"

I exhaled. "I like to. I'm just not very good. But I'm game for anything on the water—paddleboarding, boating, Jet Skiing, parasailing. Put me near an ocean and give me lots of sun, and I'm a happy girl."

His head bounced to a silent beat. "I like that."

"Why are you so tan? Did you just travel somewhere exotic, or do you like the beach as much as I do?"

He set his spoon down. "I used to travel a lot, and then I became a father, and that changed, mostly because my daughter's mother has a job that takes her out of town more often than she's home. And then my dad got sick, and I didn't want to go too far in case something happened. So, no, I haven't recently been anywhere exotic, unless you count Malibu, and in that case, I'm there all the time."

"Do you go there to surf?"

"No." He clasped his hands by the side of his bowl. "I go there for work."

I couldn't even guess what kind of employment that would be. He wore a nice watch, but I couldn't tell if his clothes were designer or if he'd bought them from Target. And since he and his friends had taken a party bus to the club, I had no idea what he drove.

Curiosity got the best of me, and I said, "What do you do?"

He chuckled. "Something that pays me plenty."

I laughed with him. "I suppose I deserve that answer."

"I work in the hospitality industry."

I could probably push and get an exact explanation and title, but that would require me to open myself up a bit more. Now that we were outside the club, I found it easier to be myself, to say the things I wouldn't have while we were in that private room. There, I needed to keep things as impersonal as possible. But here—here felt different. It felt weirdly natural. It felt easy with a heavy side of spark.

"How's your dad now?" I raised my hand. "And if you don't want to go into it, it's okay, I get it."

He was silent for a moment. "He's gone."

I could hear the pain in his voice.

"Ridge, I'm so sorry." My hand found its way to the top of his arm. "I feel awful that I asked. I didn't mean to make you talk about it."

"Don't feel awful. If I didn't want to talk about it, I would have danced around the question—something I'm learning you're very good at." He winked.

But even with a gesture as cute as the one he'd just made, I could see how much the loss of his dad upset him.

"The good news is that he's no longer in pain," he continued. "Now, my siblings and I are just finding our own way of dealing with it. It happened three months ago, so it's still fresh."

"I can't even imagine," I said softly. "The thought…" I lowered my head. "I can't even go there."

"It's rough."

"How many siblings do you have?"

My hand left his arm when he took a drink of his iced green tea. "A younger sister and an older brother."

"Do they live around here?"

I was surprised by how many questions I was asking. It seemed, once I got a taste, I needed more.

Like this ramen.

But where the soup had started to cool, Ridge was scalding hot.

"Their houses are less than a mile from mine, and we're coworkers. Time spent together is something we're not lacking in my family. We're close in many ways."

"I'm jealous. My sister lives in Dallas, and I don't get to see her nearly enough. One day, I'm hoping she'll transfer hospitals and come here to work—or at least somewhere in California so she'd be easier to get to."

The waitress refilled our glasses, and as soon as she was gone, he asked, "What kind of medicine?"

"She's an anesthesiologist, and let me tell you, she sees some wild shit."

His hands unhooked, and he lifted his spoon, taking a mouthful of the broth. "How wild?"

There was only one other couple in the restaurant, so I didn't really have to keep my voice down, but I lowered it while I said, "There's a woman who's addicted to swallowing batteries. Every month or so, she ends up in the emergency department with a battery or two or four"—my eyes widened—"in her stomach. And the thing is, she knows it requires surgery to get them out, yet she still swallows them."

"Man"—he took a bite of a noodle and covered his mouth with his hand—"I can't understand why she would swallow something so dangerous."

"From there, things get a little spicier."

"Like?"

I chewed my lip. "Broken light bulbs."

"You're telling me someone swallows a broken light bulb?"

I giggled. "No, I'm telling you someone uses a light bulb to get off and it happens to break in the process."

He went silent. "You're fucking kidding."

"And the pieces of glass have to be surgically removed."

"Dude, no."

I devoured some fried nori. "But it gets worse—kinda. Because what I didn't know—and maybe you don't either—is that the butt acts like a suction cup, so once something is in there and the end is lost, you can't go searching for it. Once it's gone, it's gone."

"Surgery is the only way to get it out?"

I slowly nodded. "Yep." I stirred the rest of the broth with my chopsticks. "This one lady had that happen during a vacation in Bali. She didn't want to go to the hospital there, so she flew home—all of those hours sitting on a plane and probably having a layover and going through customs—with a dildo up her tush."

"Jesus Christ." He couldn't stop laughing.

"I'll stick with my job that pays like shit because *no, thank you.* Between the super-sad cases and the wild cases, I don't know how she does it."

"Whatever her reason is, I'm glad she does. We need people like her."

"We do." I quieted for a moment while I finished the last of my soup. "Bet you didn't think we'd be discussing *that* tonight."

"I didn't anticipate tonight looking anything like this." His hand landed on top of mine. "But I'm glad it did."

His eyes were telling a much deeper story.

A story that didn't just hit me at every angle.

It wrapped around me and squeezed the shit out of me.

"Ridge…"

"Tell me you're not having fun. Tell me you haven't laughed your ass off. Tell me I'm nothing like the man you assumed I was."

I took a deep breath, taking in the blue of his eyes. Why did they have to be so beautiful? "I'm definitely having fun. I've most definitely laughed my ass off."

I tried to force myself to look away, and I couldn't. There was something drawing me to him, and I didn't know what it was. His sweetness? His patience? The way he spoke about his daughter? His good looks? All of it?

"And you're right, I don't know what I assumed, but this wasn't it."

The table we were sitting at was tiny, a high-top that couldn't have been more than a foot and a half wide, so it was easy for him to lift his hand and put it on my cheek. His thumb stroked my lips the same way he'd done to himself earlier. And each swipe sent a fire through me.

But that fire wasn't burning; it was igniting, and those tingles were shooting straight through me.

"If you tell me there's a green onion on my mouth, I might die," I admitted.

"There isn't."

I should have felt relief in hearing that.

But I didn't.

I was too worked up.

Too turned on.

Too…wet for this man.

My eyes closed for a second as a sensation passed through my body, one that was more intense than any kind of jolt I'd ever experienced before.

"What was that?" he asked when my lids opened. "I felt a shiver move through you."

My head shook, but his hand stayed. "My way of reminding myself that I need to breathe."

His chuckle was deep. Sexy. Gritty. But comforting at the same time. "You want me to kiss you. That's why you're having a hard time breathing."

I was sure my face was reddening. "I never said those words."

"You didn't have to…"

Chapter Three

RIDGE

I was a gentleman, but I was also a fucking man. The entire time we'd been sitting at this table, I could sense what was brewing inside of Addy, and I wanted to put out those flames with my tongue. I knew how she was feeling based on the way her stare changed as she looked at me. The way her lips stayed parted and her tongue licked the inside of them, like she was thinking about lapping the edge of my dick. How my words—regardless of what I said—would cause her skin to redden or her body to turn fidgety or for her to go from spoon to chopsticks, spoon to chopsticks, and not take a bite.

She was feeling me.

So, when I told her she was having a hard time breathing because she wanted me to kiss her, I wasn't kidding. Based on the desire in her eyes, I was only speaking the truth.

Desire I also saw in her cheeks.

In her lips.

In her body.

A body that needed to be satisfied by me.

"Come here," I ordered.

She didn't move. She just stared at me from the other side of the tiny table. The distance was so narrow that I could smell her vanilla-latte scent, almost feel the heat from her skin.

She took a breath, and when the air panted through her lips, she inhaled again. "Why?"

"Addy…" I shook my head, laughing. "I'm going to kiss you."

"Here?" She glanced around the nearly vacant restaurant.

"Yes."

Her brows slowly rose. "Now?"

"Unless you say no or give me a solid reason not to."

She smiled, and it came with a small laugh. "We just met?"

"Are you asking me or telling me? Because it sounds like you're asking, and my answer to that is, we're both grown adults, and I don't think a timeline of events is relevant."

"But what's relevant is where you met me…"

I let that response really hit and sink in. "That obviously really bothers you." I didn't wait for her to say anything else before I continued, "It shouldn't. But I do realize money was exchanged tonight. For the record, I don't look at it that way at all. It was part of the deal to get you alone, and I don't regret it, and neither should you. Besides, you wouldn't be here unless you wanted to be, nor would you have driven me here and taken the risk of being alone with me." I studied her eyes. "There was a reason you agreed to come, and it wasn't only because you were hungry. Something about me interests you." I smiled. "Is it my lips?"

"They are sexy—I can't lie."

I fucking loved her honesty.

"Come here, Addy."

"First, tell me this…why do you want to kiss me?"

There had only been one other time in my life when I looked at a woman and I could see tomorrow. I could see next week. I could see next year.

That was all it had taken—one look.

Since Jana, I hadn't been looking.

But what Dad had said to me was in my head. It was in my heart. And, goddamn it, I hadn't anticipated looking at the strip club since I hadn't even expected to be there, but once I'd spotted her, I wasn't going to lose the opportunity, even if there was a chance she'd turn me down.

"I have this feeling," I said. "I want to see if I'm right."

"And a kiss will confirm that?"

"You do know the power of a kiss, don't you?" I waited and got nothing. "It's not just lips on lips. It's the most intimate, telling act two people can share. And it's going to confirm if what I'm feeling is real."

"Or if I'm just a beautiful redhead who danced on top of a stage and knew how to move my body."

My tongue folded over my top lip for a second. "I wouldn't have put it that way. But, yes, not everyone is meant to be."

"And you think we are?"

She was smiling.

Which made me grin harder. "I have very little doubt…but you're asking some heavy questions that come with a lot of pressure."

She placed both arms on the table, confirming she was staying put for the moment. "Listen, mister, if you want my lips, you're going to have to earn them."

"With words."

"Only with words," she replied.

"What if my words are lies?"

"They're not." Her stare intensified.

"You still don't believe I'm one of the good guys, so how do you know if I'm telling the truth?"

"That job that I spoke about—the one that pays me shit— it's taught me a lot about people. Especially their eyes. And when someone speaks to me, of course I can't see directly through them, but I get a good read and whether they're just talking to hear their own voice or if there's meaning behind what they're saying."

"What have you learned from me?"

Her head bobbed to the music that was playing. But it wasn't a dance. It was a stall. "In theory, you've probably earned that kiss."

I laughed. "But in reality?"

"Playing hard to get is so fun."

More honesty.

I couldn't get enough.

"Here's the thing, Ridge." She focused on the table instead of meeting my stare. "Regardless of how steamy things can get between us"—she finally glanced up—"I'm in a tough place, like I told you. There are so many things happening in my life. You need to know that—and I need to remind myself of that."

The latter seemed the most important of the two.

And it was a reminder because I was sure she was feeling the same way as me.

All this banter only proved it.

"What I'm hearing is that you want me to give you as many orgasms as possible."

"Ridge—"

"Don't worry, I'll treat your pussy better than it's ever felt."

"Ridge!"

I chuckled. "I hear you. Your request has been noted." I watched her struggle to breathe. "Admit it, you've never met anyone like me."

"That's easy to admit."

"Had I been just a regular dude, this right here"—I pointed to her and then me—"would look a lot different." I held out my hand. "Come here."

She didn't immediately set her palm in mine, but when she did, I waited until her feet were on the ground and led her to my chair, sliding so she could stand between my legs. Once she was positioned in front of me, our eyes locked, my fingers fanned over her cheeks, and I tilted her head back. During those few seconds of silence, I searched her stare for the truth—a truth that was buried behind the beautiful light brown of her eyes and long lashes and dark makeup.

"Do you want to know something?" My voice was soft.

"Yes."

"I'm getting a good read on you."

"And?"

"You want this just as much as me." I traced my thumb over her top lip before moving to the bottom, slowly inching my way across the plumpness.

Fuck, she felt good—to have her this close, to have my hands on her, to smell her in the air without having to search for her scent.

"And in your head right now, you're thinking about what I'm going to feel like, what I'm going to taste like, if the sensation inside your body is going to dull or get stronger." I leaned my face into her neck, taking a long, deep whiff of her perfume, and dragged the end of my nose up to her ear, where I placed my mouth right over the shell and whispered, "You're already getting that answer, aren't you?" I shifted to the front of her. "You're surprised by how hard your heart is pounding—and I know it is, I can feel it. Mine is too. And that you're still finding it so difficult to breathe, just like I am. And how the build-up is driving you absolutely fucking wild, like it's doing to me."

"Yes."

"To what?"

"To all of it, Ridge—"

I couldn't wait. Not a second longer.

But instead of slamming us together, which I wanted to do, I drew her closer, letting her experience just how bold the wait and anticipation could be, and I met her somewhere in the middle. I halted when there was just the tiniest slice of distance between us.

And from there, I let the pulse lengthen, making her pussy beat even fucking harder.

"Tell me you want this kiss," I commanded.

Her eyes were already closed.

"Tell me, Addy."

I didn't need the confirmation—I already had it. I just wanted her simmering to the point where one touch would send her over the goddamn edge.

"I want it." Her voice wasn't tender; it was needy as hell.

Just the way I desired it to be.

I gave her lips one final stroke and aligned our mouths and melded us together.

My dick was already hard. It had been since I'd touched her. The feel of her alone had sent all the blood to my tip, and I was throbbing.

But now…*shit*. Now, I was aching to the point where it hurt.

Because what I'd learned in these last few seconds, what this intimate moment had really shown me, was that this wasn't just a kiss.

This was a beginning.

And this gorgeous woman tasted as good as she smelled, fitting perfectly against me. Not just in the way we embraced, but in the way her body collapsed against mine, where there wasn't even air separating us.

My hands stayed on her face, my tongue dipping in, circling, massaging.

There was no training needed. She knew just how to move her mouth, how to accept my tongue, how to work with me rather than against me.

When I'd called her over, I'd thought this would be enough.

The feel of her.

The taste.

But the longer my lips stayed on hers, all it did was goad me into wanting more.

My hands moved to her waist when I felt her weaken, taking the rest of her weight. I wasn't gentle in the way I gripped her curves. I wanted her to feel me. I wanted her to know the strength I could bear. I wanted her to know there was zero possibility that I would let her fall.

What that earned me was her arms. They wrapped around my shoulders, her hands diving into the back of my hair. And as our kiss deepened, her back arched, and her fingers slid down my neck and onto my chest, the tiniest moan coming from her throat.

That sound told me it was time to ask an extremely important question.

As I pulled away, I watched her eyes gradually open and her breath come out in quick exhales.

But I didn't let go.

If anything, I held her harder.

"Did that give you *your* answer?" I said.

She didn't immediately reply. "That you're one of the good guys?" She let out a single laugh. "Or that your mouth is the most addictive thing I've ever tasted?"

A response that couldn't have been more perfect.

I chuckled. "That leaves only one more question, then, Addy." My hand rose to her face, palming a cheek that was flaming red. "Do you really want this night to end?"

"What are you asking?"

I touched her lips again, reminding me of just how good that kiss had been. "You're the one with the car. So, do you take me back to the club to meet up with my friends—if they're even still there—or do you leave me here to order a rideshare"—my other hand lifted to her side, stopping in the middle of her navel—"or do you come home with me?"

Chapter Four

ADDISON

"You're coming inside…aren't you?" Ridge asked.

Once I shifted into park, he was looking at me from the passenger seat of my car. The engine idling in his driveway, my finger now hovering over the button to turn off the ignition.

If that kiss in the restaurant hadn't completely blown me away, I wouldn't be here.

I wouldn't be staring into his eyes.

I wouldn't have been so turned on by the thought of what those lips were going to do to me that I'd agreed to something as foolish as going home with him. But here I was, sending all the wrong messages, going against all the promises I'd made myself.

Who am I right now?

I didn't know, but I was just going to go with it until my gut started to tell me not to, and so far, during the drive to his mansion, it hadn't whispered a word.

I hit the button, and the engine turned off. "Yes, I'm coming inside."

I unbuckled my seat belt and followed him to the front door. His thumbprint pressed against the tablet on the side of the lock, which got us into the foyer, where I immediately glanced up to the ceiling. A height that seemed at least several stories tall. A grand black staircase wrapped around the back side of the entryway, a glass catwalk across the middle, and pendant lighting highlighted several pieces of art and sections of the stairs to make them focal points. As my stare lowered, I could see to the other side of the house, where the windows overlooked a pool, the water lit up a bright blue. This was probably only a tenth of his home, and I was already completely blown away.

Our eyes locked, and I asked, "What kind of job did you say you have that pays you so well?"

He was smiling, laughing even. "I didn't say." His hand went to my lower back. "Let's get you a drink." He led me into a big, beautiful kitchen, decorated in a dark emerald green with gold and black accents.

Whatever this man did, he did it very well.

"Wine? Beer? Alcohol? What's your thing?"

"Rosé." I didn't know what to do with my hands, so I tucked them in the pockets of my sweatshirt. "But I'm guessing you don't have any, so I'll go with white." I grabbed his arm as he went to take a step. "If you don't have an open bottle, please don't open one for me. I'll honestly drink whatever."

"How about I open a bottle of white for the both of us?"

"You drink white wine?"

Most of the guys I knew wouldn't touch wine—red if it was a must, but never white.

"I do tonight."

As he walked into the living room, where there was a wet bar along the side, I continued to look around, and that was when I noticed his daughter's stuff. The stack of coloring books on the corner of the counter. The small pink chair next to the oversize sectional. The box of toys on the opposite wall of the wet bar. Her drawings taped to the fridge. The pink stuffed horse on the couch. The cookie jar by the stovetop with pink sprinkle cookies inside.

Details that were positively adorable.

"I picked up this bottle during my last trip to Napa. Let's see if it's any good," he said, returning to the kitchen, where he unscrewed the top and poured some of the wine into two glasses. He handed me one and held up his. "To our first date." The most seductive look came across his face, and it made me blush. "Cheers."

"Cheers." I took a drink, the wine tart and crisp, just how I liked it. As I swallowed, I peeked at the staircase, wondering if I needed to keep my voice down. "Is your daughter here?"

He huffed. "No. She's with her mom this week."

"So, you have all the time and freedom to get in all kinds of trouble, just like you have tonight." I winked.

"You call this trouble?" He grazed my waist, and it was enough pressure that it sent a spark right through me.

"What would you call it, then?"

"I'd call this tame. But remember, I haven't touched you yet, Addy. When and if I do, that's not the description I'd use."

As though it was the most natural thing, he licked across his lips, and my mind went straight to the movement of his tongue.

"I'm not really the trouble-finding type of guy, if I'm being honest." He set his wine down and lifted me onto the counter, placing me along the edge of the large island, and he stood in front of me. "You're assuming I do this a lot, I'm guessing, and I don't. Do I hook up with women? Sure. I'm certainly not celibate. But compared to my friends, I'm nothing like them. Don't forget, my ex is on the road more often than she's not, so I have my daughter about three weeks a month."

I was surprised by how easily he had lifted me, how light I'd felt in his arms even though he only held me for a few seconds. And I was just as shocked that when his hands left me, when one returned to his glass and the other flattened on the counter beside me, I missed them.

Because they felt so much better on me than off me.

"That must be a hard balance for her and your daughter—I know, if I were a mom, I'd want to be with my little one every night."

He nodded. "My ex has a great job, and she loves it. She's a celebrity makeup artist. She wouldn't make the same kind of money if she was stationed just in LA. It's hard for her, for sure, but it works for us, and they FaceTime several times a day, so even though she's gone, they see each other constantly."

"That's a cool gig."

"You know how your sister has these wild stories from the emergency department? You should hear the shit my ex tells me about celebrities." He gripped the back of his neck. "She sees and hears some of the craziest stuff."

"I'm impressed you even listen to her stories."

He laughed. "What is that supposed to mean?"

I kicked my legs into the air. "From my experience, men aren't the best listeners, and as far as retaining, forget about it. In one ear and out the other."

He laughed even harder. "Damn, you're tough."

"It's the truth."

"Quiz me," he demanded.

"On what?"

"On anything you've told me tonight. I'll prove to you I was listening." He wiped his lips even though nothing was there.

The thing was, I hadn't really told him much about myself. I'd done that intentionally. I didn't want to get in too deep—yet I was at his house, sitting on his counter, and he was standing between my legs. So, my entire plan had gone to hell.

"*Hmm.*" I did a mental scan of our entire evening together. "I ordered an extra ingredient in my ramen. What was it?"

"Cilantro."

I took a drink of wine, floored that he'd gotten that one right. "I mentioned that I cheered. Was it in high school or college?"

"Both." He placed his hand on my thigh. "Come on. You're being too easy on me."

"How many shifts have I worked at the strip club?"

"This would be the end of your third." He moved in a little closer. "You want four to five kids. You're from the Bay area. You came to LA for college and didn't leave because you love the weather. Get you by the ocean with some sun, and you're a happy girl. You want me to keep going?" His brows stayed high, and so did his grin.

Why was that smile so addictive? A perfect set of straight teeth and thick lips, surrounded by scruff that had felt so soft during our kiss.

"Showoff." I sighed.

"I told you, I listen."

"You're running out of boxes to check off on the I'm-one-of-the-good-guys list."

"It's not intentional, it's just who I am."

I didn't know why, but there was a tightness in the back of my throat. "I like that about you."

"Yeah?"

I shrugged. "It's refreshing to know my words are being heard since my past is filled with guys who are on the asshole list."

And those assholes hadn't heard anything I ever said. They didn't bother to listen. And they had done very little to make me happy.

That was what I got for being attracted to the bad boys.

"It wasn't always a strength, but it became important when I had my little girl. I want her to grow up knowing we're not all the same. And when she's old enough to date—God fucking help me—I want to be a good role model for what she looks for in a guy."

A man who had reshaped himself to be the best example for his daughter.

There was literally nothing hotter.

My God.

I took a couple of deep breaths to cool myself down. "I get the sense you're an amazing dad."

He bit the side of his lip. "What makes you say that?"

I was around a lot of fathers. I knew the difference between amazing and emotionally absent. It took a lot more than just talking about your daughter—something he'd done very early on in the night—for me to form that opinion. It was something I could see in his eyes, by listening to the activities that he had her involved in and the way he joined her, how he'd described his priorities, how he had almost full custody, and how there were signs of his little one everywhere I looked.

"It's just a hunch, combined with the way you look whenever you bring her up."

He exhaled. "I talk about her too much, don't I?"

I put my hand on his shoulder. "It doesn't bother me at all—I actually love it."

"Tell me, Addy, from the little that you know, what else do you love about me?" He paused, his stare narrowing. "There's a reason you agreed to come home with me. I want to know what that reason is."

I could feel the heat move across my cheeks. "The way you kissed me. That's one."

"You liked the way my mouth felt on yours." His voice was deepening, almost becoming grittier.

"And the way you touched me."

"I barely did that. I only touched your face"—his hand grazed my cheek—"and your waist." He lowered and held the center of my side. "Are you wondering what else these fingers are capable of?"

As his thumb stroked my stomach, I sucked in a deep breath. "Along with a curiosity of what it would be like to be with an older man."

That made him laugh. "Just how old do you think I am?"

"Early thirties, which is older than me, considering I'm only twenty-four. Most of the guys my age, at least the ones I've dated, are only into themselves. I want to experience something different. Because, I swear, if I see one more mirror selfie, I legit might scream."

His laugh didn't fade at all. "I'm thirty-one, and I assure you, you will never get one of those from me." He was stroking my mouth with the pad of his finger. "So, experience turns you on."

It hadn't until our kiss. It hadn't even been on my radar.

But now—now was a whole other story.

And I knew I shouldn't even put my brain in either place, but I was too far deep to pull back at this point.

"The idea of it, yes," I replied.

"You know, if I was going to send you any kind of selfie, I'd need to have your number." With his other hand, he cupped the base of my neck.

"Numbers really complicate things." I smiled.

His mouth wasn't far from mine, but his head tilted. "Let me get this straight. You'd give me your body, but you wouldn't give me your number?"

"You have to earn it."

"Make it make sense, Addy."

For the briefest of seconds, my mind went there—to my plate not just being full, but overflowing with everything I had going on in my life—and I started to spiral.

"I'm just trying to get through today, Ridge. I honestly can't even think about tomorrow, or I'll start stressing even more. And stress is what I'm trying to avoid. That's why I'm here. I'm drowning in you instead of treading in all of that."

His teeth grazed his lip. "You're telling me you want an escape—is that what I'm hearing?"

I swirled some wine around in my mouth before I answered, "It's been nice to shut it all off and get on this ride and see where it takes me."

"What kind of ride are you looking for?" He gripped my ass and slid me to the very edge of the counter, so my legs were forced to straddle him. A move that made me even wetter. "Do you want it rough? Do you want it soft and slow? Or do you want it somewhere in between?"

My eyes closed as my neck tilted back, and his lips were instantly on my throat.

"Whatever is going to make me scream the loudest."

"It sounds like you're leaving that decision up to me." He kissed the base of my neck just as I was swallowing and inched up to the center. "I can read your body, and I'm listening to what it's telling me. There's just one problem…" His hands lifted to my ribs, directly below my breasts, the tease enough to make me moan.

"What is it?"

"You're wearing too many clothes."

Chapter Five

RIDGE

I dropped the last piece of Addy's clothing on the floor of my kitchen and backed up a few inches to take a real good look at her. Of course, I'd already seen a majority of her body when she was onstage; the only things hidden had been the top and lips of her pussy and the small part of her ass that hadn't been covered by the thong.

But as she sat under one of the lights, leaning back on her arms, she looked entirely different than earlier this evening.

She was even more breathtakingly beautiful. Every inch of her body was fucking incredible. And here, with her posture relaxed, the edges of her had softened. Her sun-kissed skin was even smoother. Her tits bounced with each breath, shaped like perfect teardrops, with pink nipples that were achingly hard. A rod with a pink gem at the top was pierced through her belly button. And below sat one sexy pussy, her clit hidden beneath tight, hairless folds.

How the hell did I get so lucky?

"Fuck," I groaned, unable to look at her face just yet. Not when I still had so much of her body to take in, not when I was finally making tonight's dream come true.

In my house, she wasn't posing. She wasn't putting on an act.

She was showing every honest, raw curve.

And I wanted to lick each one.

"You're looking at me like you haven't already seen most of my body."

Reluctantly, my eyes rose to hers. "I feel as though I haven't."

"How can you say that?"

I closed the distance between us, rubbing my hands over her legs. My pressure wasn't like a massage; this was lighter. "The woman I saw at the club isn't the same woman who's in my kitchen now." My face leaned in closer. "What I saw there was a screen. A filter. You might as well have been dressed in a fucking snowsuit." I traced the bottom of her jaw. "Here, I'm seeing you for the first time, and, my God, Addy, I've never seen anything so gorgeous."

"It's like I've never heard those words before—that's how powerful you make them feel."

I caged her between my arms. "And knowing that body is going to be mine tonight—you have no idea what that's doing to me."

"Tell me."

I hovered my lips over hers. "I want to fucking worship you. Starting with your hair that I want wrapped around my fist, moving to your skin that I want to lick and suck. Bite. And when I can't take another second of not being inside of you, I'm going to slide into your hot, wet pussy. A pussy that's so wet because of what my tongue plans to do to it."

I kissed her.

Not just a parting of lips and the exchange of breath.

This was a kiss that she'd remember. One that tilted her face at a new angle, that gripped her cheek, that had my tongue slipping into her mouth, that had her inhaling my air.

And when I pulled back, she let out a long, deep pant. "Wow."

Her eyes were wide, feral.

Starving.

"I don't know what's been spoken to you before. I can only tell you that even though that's the best I've got, that statement isn't nearly strong enough. Because nothing I said even comes close to describing what I'm looking at right now."

Her hand went to my cheek, holding it while she gazed into my eyes. The silence from her was louder than anything I'd ever heard.

What she wasn't saying, what I'd sensed from our previous conversation, was that Addy hadn't been appreciated the way she deserved and what I gave her was something she hadn't anticipated.

She was here for an escape. That was all she'd admit to.

For now.

But she was getting much more, and she'd continue to until she walked out my door.

"There's nothing like you," I whispered.

That was confirmed the more I talked to her, the more I learned, the bit by bit she unraveled.

She scanned my eyes, from right to left, and then a slower sweep, reversing the pattern. "What are you doing to me?"

"Nothing yet."

Her head shook. "That's not true."

"You came to my house for my lips…it's time you get them."

Her finger pressed against the center of my mouth as though she were quieting me.

I knew she wasn't.

"Regardless of what I came for, you're giving me much more than just these."

I said nothing, not because her finger was in the way—that certainly wouldn't have stopped me—but because I let my eyes do all the talking instead.

After several seconds of a hard, rabid stare, I reached behind her back and pulled her fully against me, making sure her legs were wrapped around me before I lifted her into the air.

"This is the longest walk of my life," I said against her lips.

"Because I'm heavy?" Her hair tickled my face before she flicked it away. "You can put me down—"

"You're not even close to being heavy." Her assumption earned her a chuckle. "It's just...the longer it takes to get you into my bedroom, the longer I have to wait to taste you."

"That's right, you're going to...taste me," she breathed.

"Yes."

"Don't hate me when I ask this—I know the timing is awful and random, and this question is probably coming out of the blue."

I halted in the center of the living room.

"Could we make a pit stop at the shower?" Her arms crossed behind my neck. "I only need a few minutes in there, but washing off this night is honestly very necessary—along with all this perfume."

A request I could handle, unlike some of the others that had come to mind.

"I'll make a deal with you," I voiced.

"We're negotiating?"

I smiled. "We can stop in the shower as long as I can take one with you."

"Deal."

When I walked us into the wing of my bedroom, I turned toward the en suite, reaching inside the large walk-in shower to turn on the water and setting her on the bench opposite the multiple showerheads.

"Don't move." While I left her there, I went into my bedroom and into my closet, grabbing a condom from the drawer where I hid them under my boxers—a place Daisy wasn't tall enough to reach yet.

And as I made my way back to the bathroom, I stripped off my clothes. By the time I reached her, I only had my boxer briefs left.

"Good Lord," she sang.

My hands stilled on the elastic waist. "What?"

"I knew you were hiding something special under those clothes, but *that*?" Her eyes weren't on mine; they were on my body, just like mine hadn't been on hers once I got her naked. "*That* I didn't see coming."

Damn, I loved the heat from her stare.

And I loved that she liked what she saw.

I stroked my abs and lifted to one of my pecs, rubbing my hand across it before I let my boxers fall.

"And I'm dead."

I pumped my dick several times, my hard-on raging. "It's yours tonight, Addy. But you can't die on me, at least not until I have you."

She slowly looked up at me. "You mean, until I have you."

"You wanted experience, you're getting it."

"With that"—she nodded toward my cock—"I'm getting a lot more than just experience."

I joined her in the shower and set the condom on one of the shampoo ledges. "Come here."

I lifted her onto her feet, positioning her in a way where the overhead faucet would flow against her hair and the side jet would hit her back.

"This is going to be the best shower you've ever taken." To prove that point even further, I dumped some shampoo in my palm and rubbed it over my fingers before I slipped my hands into her hair, spreading the suds over her long locks.

"It already is," she moaned. "This feels so good."

Once I got each strand coated, I did the same with the shampoo and moved on to the soap, lathering some of the body wash between my hands and rubbing the liquid over her shoulders.

"*Mmm.* The earthy scent."

I dipped to her upper back and around to her sides. "The… *what*?"

"I smelled a combination of scents on you."

While the water was beading over her long lashes, she put some soap in her hand and stuck her face under the stream, scrubbing off the makeup. When she glanced at me, her eyes were free of all the black, and she looked even more beautiful in this raw form.

"I didn't realize one was from your soap," she said. "The other two must be from your cologne."

"Which are?"

She smiled. "A little salty and a little sassy."

I laughed and added more body wash to my hand, slowly making my way up to her navel. "I know we're both naked, and I know what I'm about to do to you, and I know that's the whole reason we're in this shower, but the good guy in me wants to ask if it's all right to touch you." My hands froze at her ribs.

"So, so sweet." She stood up on her tiptoes and kissed me, her arms locking around my neck. "What if I said no?"

"I'd let you wash yourself, and I'd hand you a towel when you were done. That doesn't mean I wouldn't watch you—fuck, I'd have the best seat in the house."

"You want a show?"

My hands went higher, sitting just below her tits. "I already had that tonight. It's my turn to give you a show."

"How do you plan to do that?"

"I want you to watch me while I touch you." I pressed my lips against the far side of her cheek. "And when I'm on my knees, licking your pussy, I want you to watch that too."

She let out a quivering exhale, a sound that told me she was ready for whatever I wanted to give her.

"Every time my tongue laps your cunt, Addy, I want your eyes fixed on me."

"Yes," she dragged out, tugging my hair. "What are you waiting for?"

"You haven't given me your permission."

"Touch me, Ridge. Please." She drew in some air. "Now."

When she'd wrapped her arms around me and pulled me close, she made it difficult to touch her chest, but I still squeezed my fingers between our bodies and rubbed the bubbles across her nipples. I pulled at the small buds, pinching them just enough to make her arch.

"God. That feels so good."

My lips left hers and went to her neck, kissing up to her ear and across her cheek, and when I reached the other side, I went down her collarbone. My hands, drenched with more soap, were moving at the same time, gradually making my way to her stomach until I reached her pussy.

"Oh!"

"You want more?" I asked.

"Yes. Whatever you do, don't stop."

My soapy thumb went to her clit, the pad brushing circles around it while the rest of my hand dived through her lips and around her pussy, washing her off before one of my fingers plunged inside her. "Am I still so sweet?"

"Fuck." Her nails were stabbing the back of my neck. "It's not going to take much more of that to make me come."

It didn't matter that I'd washed her with my soap and that her hair was now soaked and unscented; I could still smell the vanilla-latte aroma, and I wondered if the scent would be on her cunt.

If I'd be able to taste it.

If it would be running down my throat when I swallowed her.

"What about when I do this?" I added a second finger and turned my wrist, aiming toward her G-spot.

"Ridge!" She gasped in a mouthful of air, her lips on mine, so I could feel her inhale and her chest pressing against me when it puffed out.

"Does this still make me the sweetest?" My hand began to move faster, deeper.

And, damn it, all it did was tease me. I was envious of my fingers since they were getting to feel her tightness and wetness before my dick. A hard-on that was fucking pounding to be inside her.

"You're veering toward naughty." She added, "Very, very naughty," when I increased the pressure.

I pulled my way out of her locked arms and squatted to the floor, gazing up at her while I replaced my thumb with my tongue. While I gave her a long swipe, I breathed her in, filling my nose and mouth with vanilla.

A flavor that was suddenly explosive.

"And now?" I asked.

"Oh. My. God."

I didn't lick like her clit was the tip of a soft-serve ice cream and I was sampling the flavor. I licked like I was taking my first bite, like I couldn't wait to eat, like I needed her covering my fucking tongue.

Like her orgasm was the one thing I was after.

Because it was.

I wanted to feel her shudders vibrate across my mouth. I wanted to taste her cum in the back of my throat on its way down. I wanted to hear her moans as they echoed through the steam in my shower.

"Your tongue...damn." Her eyes were closed, but they found mine. "How are you so good at this?" She reached for my hair, twisting the locks.

I was focused on the top of her clit. But that was with my tongue. With my fingers, I worked up to a speed that was driving her straight to the edge.

I could see it in her face.

I could sense it in her voice.

I could feel it by the way her hips were rocking forward and how her clit was hardening.

I didn't want to stop. I could lick her cunt all night.

But there were other parts of me that wanted to experience her pussy. That wanted to sink into her wetness. And that was what I thought of when my tongue and fingers synced up and went faster.

"Ridge!"

There was nothing hotter, more satisfying than hearing a woman moan my name.

The only thing that came close was watching her come.

And that was about to happen.

Right fucking now.

"Ah!" she shouted.

Her hands flattened against my head as I sucked her clit into my mouth, holding the back with my teeth and flicking the very end. I didn't need to add a third finger. Two was enough for her body and plenty to push her toward the peak.

A peak that was coming on strong, her stomach still, her thighs frozen—until they weren't. And when that happened, spasms shook both parts of her body, her screams the only thing I could hear.

What a sound that was.

What a sight.

What a feel, especially as my teeth released her and her pussy turned even wetter.

"Fuck! Me!" She was grinding against my mouth, using my head for balance, her wet hair a curtain as she stared down at me, her expression showing that she couldn't believe what she was feeling.

If she only knew...this was just the beginning. I wasn't just a man dreaming about tomorrow. I was a man dreaming about doing this day after day after day.

Feasting on a pussy like this would be enough for me.

"I can't...breathe." Her eyes closed. "Ridge, shit!"

Even though she was on her way down and I'd slowed, my movements were still strong, lightening a little more with each pass, waiting for her stillness as the signal to stop.

When I got it, I gave her a final lick, making sure I caught every drop of her cum on my tongue before I rose to my feet. "Addy, your pussy—it's fucking beautiful."

She gazed at me like she was in awe. "You…"

I smiled, thumbing her off my lips. "What about me?"

"When I come up with the right words, I'll blurt them out. But right now, I think you've licked the sense out of me."

I chuckled. "That's fair." I grabbed the condom from the shelf and tore off the corner, returning the foil next to the shampoo and holding the latex.

"Are we getting out?" she asked.

"Hell no."

She skimmed her bottom lip with her teeth. "Good, because it's my turn." She held my hand and walked me over to the bench, where she took a seat, facing me, and aimed the tip of my cock to her mouth.

"Yes," I rumbled. "I like how you think."

"It's only fair to know how you taste too."

Her eyes widened as she took in my crown, her hand circling the bottom of my shaft, pumping toward the middle while she lowered.

"Yes," I whistled again. "Just like that."

I didn't need to guide her; she knew what she was doing. What speed to use, how much tongue to press against me, how far she could go before she gagged. But I still held the side of her face, encouraging deepness and a faster tempo.

"Addy…"

My balls were already fucking tingling. That was how good she was, bobbing to the center, suctioning her lips as though she was trying to force me to empty myself.

If she wasn't careful, that would happen.

But coming in her mouth wasn't the way I wanted to get off—at least not right away.

So, after a few more dives, I popped my dick out and rolled the condom over my tip and down my base until it wouldn't go any further.

Once my hand was free, I lifted her, holding her in my arms, leaning her back against one of the walls of the shower, and I positioned her over my tip.

"You make me feel weightless." Her fingers found my shoulders.

"That's because you are." My tip pushed into her wetness, and I inched my way in, slowly allowing her to get used to my size before I hit her with any power, breathing through the desire of taking her all at once. There wasn't any rush—I needed to remember that. There was just nothing that felt like her. "Fuck, you're even tighter than I thought."

"And you're bigger. Much, much bigger."

If I wasn't so turned on, I'd chuckle. But that gesture was so far from my mind and chest and lips because, right now, all I could do was moan.

From how fucking good this felt.

From how narrow her pussy was, fitting so snug around my shaft.

And then there was her wetness, guiding me right in, steering me toward that soft, sensitive end.

My head tilted back, meeting the water. "Addy..."

"Yes." Her voice was like a song, the word lasting several syllables. "I wish you knew how incredible this feels."

I met her eyes. "But I do."

With that, I reared my hips back, going as far as my crown, and stroked in. I didn't stop at one thrust, nor did I continue with the same speed.

Everything became faster.

Harder.

"Ridge!"

Her pussy was squeezing me from the inside. Pulsing. Beating every time I slammed into her.

And with each plunge, her breathing became more audible, her moaning got louder.

"Fuck," I exhaled. "Fuck," I repeated, but this time even grittier.

She left my shoulders and stretched her arms up the wall, palms flat against the marble. There was nothing for her to hold on to; all she could do was slide during each pump and lower when I bucked back, a constant teeter of motion.

One that was full of friction and my strength.

And she took it, every drive, every rotation of my hips, every grind, ravishing her in a way that was leading us both toward an orgasm.

But hers was coming on faster.

I heard it build each time she screamed, "Yes!" And when she gasped in some air, her pussy clenching in even more. "Don't stop!"

It would take a fucking miracle to make that happen at this point.

But what I did do was pull her off the wall, bouncing her over my dick as I walked us to the bench and took a seat. The new position had her straddling my waist, her knees on either side of me, her tits right in my face.

"This is where you want me, huh?"

"To get to look at your body, to get to touch every inch of it—yes." I took a nipple into my mouth, gnawing the end before I demanded, "Now, ride me." I gave the hard bud a quick flick with my tongue. "I want to come, watching you come."

She set her feet on the stone and her arms by my neck, and she rose to the highest part of me, circling before she dropped. And while I was fully plunged, she moved her hips forward and back, hitting spots that I hadn't reached yet tonight.

Spots that rubbed my tip and gripped the sides of my cock, like her pussy was begging for my cum.

"Fuck." I banged my head against the wall, pounding it to spread some of the pleasure. "Addy…fuck."

"Your dick…"

"You want it to get you off?"

"Yes."

"Are you obsessed with it?"

"Oh my God, yes," she cried.

I put my thumb on her clit, stroking it while she rocked against me. "How about when I do this to you? Does that change everything?"

"Oh!" She swallowed. "Ah!" Her eyes closed. "I can't control it... I'm going to come."

I was tempted to take back the control, to charge into her with all the quickness I had and even more pressure than she was using.

But I wanted to watch her fall apart all on her own. I wanted to experience just what she was willing to give me.

Because I could pound any woman. But not just any woman could ride me hard enough to time up our orgasms.

Addy could.

And she was.

"Ridge!"

That sound, the pitch in which she screamed my name, gave me a few seconds of warning. So, while the spark began to work its way through my balls, spreading across my body, it also loaded into my shaft.

And while I was heading straight for the summit, my eyes memorized the sight in front of me.

The pursing of her lips.

The pebbling of her nipples.

The flush of her skin.

Man, she was something.

Something striking.

Something sensational.

"Fuck me," I commanded at the very last moment.

She didn't need that direction; she already had it handled.

Within a couple more swivels of her hips, my orgasm was shooting through me, emptying into the condom.

"Addy!"

She was hugging me to her body, slapping our waists together, shouting, "Ridge! Fuck! Yes!"

My chin dipped into her cleavage, my forehead kissed her lips, my nose filled with that tantalizing vanilla scent, and my ears became full of her sounds.

She was overloading every one of my senses.

And with that came an intensity, a paralyzing catapult of passion.

There was nothing better.

What followed was a mix of shudders—some that came from her, some from me—until we turned completely still.

By then, fully emptied, I held her face, hovering my mouth over hers. "Do not move."

I couldn't handle it. Not yet. I needed to fucking breathe it out first.

"I'm right there with you," she admitted. "I've never felt this sensitive in my life."

"Addy...your fucking pussy." I pressed her cheeks with my thumbs. "I don't know what it just did to me." I paused. "But I need you to kiss me."

There was no hesitation. She instantly connected our lips, her tongue finding mine at the same time I searched for hers.

Our embrace was unhurried.

Deep, passionate.

A tug of lips and pants.

By the time she pulled away, I was ready to work my way out of her, lifting her from the bench and placing her under the water. I added soap to my hand and carefully rubbed it around her pussy, cleaning it from the condom, soothing it from the roughness of tonight.

I gave my own body a quick wash, and I turned off the water, leading us out of the shower, where I wrapped a towel around her before I tucked one over my waist.

At the edge of the counter, between the two sinks, I pulled her into my arms, holding her quietly, taking in the details of her face under this light. "You can stay."

"The night, you mean?"

I nodded.

She was silent for a few moments. "I shouldn't. I have to work early in the morning."

In the morning?

"The strip club opens early?" I asked.

The sound wasn't a laugh, but it wasn't an exhale either. It was a combination of the two. "No, at the job that pays me like shit. I have to go in and get some things done. You know, working for free on a Saturday since I'm a salaried employee."

I dived my fingers into her hair. "I know the feeling."

"With a house like this, I don't think you know the feeling at all. But it's kinda cute that you're trying to relate." She smiled.

This wasn't the right time to discuss work.

This was the time to discuss tomorrow.

"I want to see you again."

"Ridge…"

"There's no reason to say no. Not after tonight. Not after what just went down." I held her chin, tilting her face up at me. "You can tell me you didn't feel it, but I won't believe you. I saw it in your eyes, and I felt it in your body." I lowered my lips to hers. "So, do you want to lie and tell me that didn't just rock your whole fucking world?"

Chapter Six

ADDISON

Whenever I was in my car, I always flipped through the radio stations until I found a song with lyrics I knew and could sing to or one with a solid beat where I could dance. As soon as the song ended, I'd scan the stations until I found another that met the same criteria. If, for some reason, the music wasn't holding my attention, I'd listen to an audiobook.

But tonight, those same rules didn't apply.

Because when I left Ridge's house, my hair still dripping from the shower, my skin a little damp from putting my clothes on too soon, I turned off the radio and simmered in the silence the entire drive to my apartment.

Ridge had given me an escape. A few hours where nothing was eating away at me, but the commute home reminded me that the break had only been temporary. I needed to sit in these thoughts, and I needed to come back down to reality and face the next couple of weeks of my life.

But that break, *whoa*, it hadn't been expected when I went in for my shift. Not even a little. And even though the club was where

I'd met Ridge, I couldn't continue having evenings like this. Nights where I found a patron so utterly and unbelievably attractive that I made careless and reckless decisions.

Leaving with him, sleeping with him—*what was I even thinking*?

His charm had captured me. His good looks had sealed the deal.

And hearing he was one of the good guys had literally turned me into a pool of goo because I was just so tired of dealing with assholes.

But the whole point of me being at the club was to make as much money as possible so I wouldn't have to work there anymore. I wasn't there to find a man. To date one. Or to even get close to going home with one.

Tonight was wrong on every level.

Ridge was all the extra I hadn't been looking for, yet once he touched me, I realized he was all that I needed.

I could still feel his hands on my body, his lips on my skin, his tongue between my legs.

My God, he was perfection. I couldn't find a single inch of him that I didn't desire.

The mere thought of him made me instantly wet again.

Which made Ridge the most dangerous man in the world.

And someone I needed to stop thinking about.

So, I forced myself to as I parked my car and walked up the steps to our second-floor apartment, quietly opening the door so I wouldn't wake up Leah, my roommate and best friend. But as soon as I got inside, the lights in the living room were on, the TV was playing, and Leah was tucked into the corner of the couch with a glass of wine in her hand.

"You're home late," she said. "I thought you'd get in around two, and it's"—she looked at her watch—"past three."

I sighed. "It's a long story." I grabbed a glass from the cabinet and found her bottle of rosé in the fridge, pouring myself some before I joined her in the living room. I snagged some of the blanket she was using and hugged one of the pillows to my chest, sitting on the opposite side of the couch.

"Wet hair?"

I took a long drink of the wine. "Like I said…long-ass story."

She held the side of her long blonde hair that was twisted into a high knot. "It's a good thing I'm not tired. I want to hear all of it." She tucked her legs beneath her. "But before you get into it, tell me, how was tonight?" She muted the TV. "Was your third shift as bad as the first and second?"

"Different. Much different. But not as bad."

"Babe"—she offered a consoling smile—"you're getting used to it. Good thing is, you'll be done before you know it."

"That, yes." I leaned my head on the cushion behind me. "Along with the fact that I only had to do two stage dances before I was hired to go into a private room."

"You were?" Her eyes perked up and widened. "It finally happened. Yay! How much did you make?"

When the need for extra money had come into play, Leah had helped me come up with a plan. Plan A was a loan. The bank looked at my student loans, my car loan, and credit card debt and denied me. Plan B was an OnlyFans account dedicated to my feet. Something I didn't want to do either, but feet were better than full-body shots, and I wouldn't ever have to show my face. After a week of opening my OF account, cross-promoting on the other social media sites, I still had no subscribers. That was a full seven days of posting and commenting and trying to encourage men to subscribe to my channel, and I'd earned nothing. It was going to take far too long to build an audience on that platform and generate a steady stream of income.

I didn't have time.

Which left me with only one other option.

Plan C—to strip. I convinced myself it was like the years I'd spent cheering in college, minus the top and bra.

But it was a decision that hadn't come easy for Leah or me. What it was, was a fast solution that wouldn't last more than a few months.

"I earned over nine hundred," I told her.

"Holy shit." She pulled at her hair knot to tighten it. "I didn't realize you could make that much for one dance!"

I'd heard many different amounts could be made in those private rooms. There were even scenarios when the cameras were mysteriously shut off.

The girls didn't brag in the dressing room when I was in there with them, changing my outfit or freshening my makeup, but they talked enough that I got the drift. It just depended on how much the manager was tipped and how big of a whale the patron was.

I'd spare my bestie those details since I would never be in a situation where the cameras needed to be shut off.

Even though I'd basically done that tonight—I'd just gone back to his house instead.

Did that make it any better?

Or worse?

Damn.

I finished the rest of my wine and went into the kitchen to pour myself more, talking loud enough that Leah could still hear. "For just one dance, I wouldn't have come close to making that." I filled my glass to the top and returned to the couch.

"Then, how did you?"

Do I really want to get into this?

Leah was such a lover. Since I'd met her, all she talked about was marriage and kids. The second I mentioned Ridge, she'd be sending me wedding dresses and love memes.

I also couldn't lie.

So, I said, "He hired me for the whole night."

"*Whaaa?* Details, girl. I have no idea what that means."

I put my feet on the ottoman, kicking off my shoes, wiggling my bare toes. "Normally, it means dance after dance until the club closes. But Ridge didn't want me to dance for him. He just wanted to talk… and get to know me."

"This sounds kinda…serious?"

I hugged a pillow close to my chest. "He saw me onstage, and the second I was done, when I was walking down the steps, he approached and asked if we could get a drink."

She inched forward, her arm going to mine. "And?"

"Well, I couldn't get a drink with him—it's against club rules—so he opted for the private room."

"And?"

I didn't know why I found it so hard to breathe. Especially since I was only recapping events that had just happened, but the more I spoke, the more constricted my throat got.

"And we went in there," I said. "He wasn't interested in a dance, like I told you, so we talked. He wasn't just going through the motions, he was actually listening to me, soaking in everything I was willing to divulge. The best listener—besides you—I've ever come across." My eyes closed for just the briefest of moments, a heat moving straight through my body. "He was hot, Leah. I'm talking a ten."

"Tell me more."

"He has a six-year-old little girl, who he spoke about nonstop. He works in the hospitality industry and is quite well off—I mean rich, not above average. And his smile"—I shook my head—"it was everything and then some."

"I'm obsessed with every word you're saying." Her fingers squeezed me. "Addy, it doesn't sound like this dude just wanted some hot girl bouncing on top of him—I say that with love, you know I do. It sounds like he likes you. Like really likes you."

I filled my lungs, holding in the air before I said, "Which is probably why he asked me to leave the club and join him for some ramen."

"Stop it!" When I stayed silent, she said, "Keep going."

I explained how Ridge was there for a bachelor party and didn't have a car, so I drove us to the restaurant and that there was only one other table, leaving us basically alone and on a semi-date.

"So, you're eating your favorite food with a guy who's semi-seen you half naked—"

"A point that really kills the vibe for me—I'm not going to lie."

She rubbed the spot she'd been squeezing. "So, you're eating your favorite food with a hottie who's clearly into you," she corrected. "What happens next?"

"He tells me he doesn't want the night to end."

A smile moved up her face. "Smart man."

"But remember, I drove us there, so I could either leave him at the restaurant, take him back to the club where his friends were—if they hadn't left yet—or take him home."

"You went home with him." Her big blue eyes didn't blink once as she stared at me.

"Yep."

"And the wet hair?"

My head dropped, the embarrassment causing every part of me to not only stay hot but flushed. "I used his shower."

"You mean, you took a shower with him, and you guys did the dirty while you were in there." When I said nothing and still didn't look at her, she slapped my arm. "Oh my God, I'm right, aren't I?"

"In my defense, he was irresistible—"

"Why are you defending yourself, Addy? You did absolutely nothing wrong." She moved even closer, running her fingers through the side of my hair. "Babe, look at me."

The feelings and emotions began to settle inside me. "Why does it feel so wrong?"

"Because you slept with him? Something you legit never do, which I wish you'd do more of." She paused. "I don't get what's upsetting you."

"Because I met him at a strip club, where he semi-saw me half naked." I used a mix of her words so it would make sense. "I don't know…for some reason, that's eating at me."

"You're saying it would have been better if you'd met him somewhere else? Like a pool party, where your nipples and your vag were covered—although, honestly, I don't see the difference."

I shrugged. "But wouldn't that be better?"

"Are you asking me?"

My head started shaking again. "I don't know."

"How did you guys end things? You obviously didn't stay the night since you're home."

That was the part I'd tried not to think about during my drive home. That I'd tried not to second-guess.

When I had been at his house, in a towel, standing between the two sinks in his bathroom, with his arms around me, he told me he wanted to see me again.

I'd reacted quickly, without really thinking.

And I didn't know if I'd made the right choice.

"He gave me his number." I reached inside my pocket for the small piece of paper he'd written it on. "I'd left my phone in the car, so I couldn't program it into my Contacts."

"Why didn't he just text you so you'd have it?"

I mashed my lips together, remembering I was holding wine, and that was when I started to guzzle, swallowing to say, "I didn't give him my number."

"What? Why?"

I set the half-empty glass on the table next to the couch. "Everything was happening, and I was unsure about it all, and being in control of the situation felt like the right move. I figured, if I had his number, I could decide if it was best to see him again. But if he had mine and reached out, I might have a hard time saying no."

"Would you want to say no?"

"Ugh, Leah, I don't know. I'm a mess."

"And he was okay with not getting your number and leaving the ball in your court?"

"I told him I'd be in touch really soon. I'm sure he believed me."

"Even though you weren't exactly telling him the truth." She focused on my eyes, and I could tell she was trying to read them. "I don't get it. Did you have a bad time?"

"No." I adjusted my position, folding my legs beside me. "It was, hands down, the best sex I've ever had in my life. He was"—my chest felt like it was on the verge of exploding—"so perfect that I could cry."

"Then, call him, Addy. Or better yet, text him right now and tell him you had a great time and you want to see him."

"It's too soon."

"It's never too soon." Her hand moved to my shoulder when I made no effort to get my phone from my purse, which was somewhere in the kitchen, where I'd left it. "Are you really all that hung up on where you guys met? Is that the thing that's holding you back?"

"Maybe." I took the last sip and returned my glass to the table. "And the timing of all this—I'm just in a place that's so emotionally, physically, and financially draining. Working two jobs is literally going to kick my ass soon. And I want to make smart decisions, you know? I want to have a clear head. I surely can't get involved with someone while I'm straddling other men and putting my boobs in their faces."

"That's a fair point." She moved some hair out of my eyes. "But I want you to remember that Ridge never wanted you to dance for him. He wanted to get to know you. And he wanted to get you out of the club, probably sensing that the scenery made you uncomfortable. That says a lot about him, and that's not the kind of guy you want to lose."

She'd made a fair point.

But would he want the woman he was dating to be working at a strip club?

The questions, the scenarios—they seemed endless.

"I know," I whispered. "If I don't get myself out of this situation, I will just continue to spiral and drown, and that's not going to take me to a positive place. So, once I don't have to work at the club and my life is more in order, I'll be the person he's looking for. You didn't see him, Leah. He has everything together. You should see his house. I don't want him to see the hot mess that I am."

"I know you better than anyone in this world, therefore, I know you look for reasons not to do things. After your last breakup and the way that dick treated you, you said you were going to take a long break from men. Six months is a long time, babe. Don't rule things out just because you're a mess. We're all a mess—don't forget that. And if Ridge has a six-year-old, I suspect he's somewhat of a mess too."

I nodded. "I hear you."

"You'd better." She winked.

I swayed over the cushion, reminding myself that I needed to be responsible in the morning and that meant I had to get at least a little sleep. "I'm going to go crash. I have to be up in five hours."

"Is there anything I can do to help?"

I smiled and got up from the couch after giving her a quick hug. "If you happen to pass a store or a bakery during your morning walk, buy me everything that's chocolate. That way, when I get home, I can shove my face full of all the sweets before another shift at the club tomorrow night."

She laughed. "Done."

I went into the kitchen and grabbed my purse, setting the glass in the sink, and on my way through the living room, as I headed for my bedroom, Leah said, "Hey, Addy, I'm proud of you."

"For what?"

"For finishing your third shift and what will be your fourth one tomorrow. You've got this, babe."

I formed a heart with my hands and continued to my room, closing the door behind me.

I took the money out of my purse and opened my panty drawer, where I kept an envelope. The cash went inside. And on the outside of the envelope, I wrote the new total—a running tab from all my previous shifts.

Man, I still had such a long way to go.

I quickly got undressed, putting on an oversize T-shirt, and climbed onto my bed, holding my phone and Ridge's number in my hands.

There were several notifications on my screen. One was a text from my sister.

Morgan: *Hi! I'm not trying to rush you—please don't think that— but the first deposit is due in a week. Will you have the money?*

Me: *Yep, I'll have it.*

Because of Ridge's contribution tonight...I would have it.

I exited out of my texts and pulled up my Contacts, typing in Ridge's name and number and saving it. My thumb hovered over the button to text him. Leah's voice was in my head, telling me to do it.

But I couldn't yet.

At least not right now—not when I still smelled like him. Not when all I could feel was him.

I was too vulnerable. Too wrapped up, and I'd end up saying the wrong thing, and before I knew it, I'd be driving to his house.

Ridge had made me break many promises tonight.

I wasn't about to break another by texting him.

Chapter Seven

RIDGE

"What do you want?"

That was the way Rhett answered my call. His voice snappy, loud, and extremely angry as it came through the speakers of my car.

I quickly checked the time as I slowed down for the red light. It was seven thirty in the morning, but most of the executive team didn't roll into the office until past eight or closer to nine. Rhett was an early riser, so I knew he was awake. Most nights, he barely slept at all, and from the sound of his tone, I guessed it had been one of those evenings.

"I've been texting you since you left the strip club on Friday night," I said. "Since you didn't write me back, I wanted to make sure you were still alive."

"It's only Monday."

"Which is too long to go without hearing from you. Are you doing all right?"

I was met with silence. A sound that didn't surprise me.

Rhett wasn't going to tell me how he was feeling. He wasn't going to talk about the things—or in this case, the thing—bothering him. He was just going to go quiet on me, like he'd done since the joint bachelor and bachelorette party. At least he'd answered my call. At this time last year, he'd disappeared for a week and gone completely radio silent despite Dad being sick as hell.

"How about I ask this instead: do you need anything?" I inquired.

"I need a lot of fucking things."

I let out a deep exhale. "Rhett—"

"Unless you're a magician, then don't fucking ask."

Sometimes, when it came to my older brother, it wasn't like walking on glass. It was like walking on the tips of knives.

"How about we meet up for a drink later—"

"Are you on your way to the office?"

I turned at the Stop sign and began to slow as I made my way down Jana's street. "I'm headed to Jana's."

"To pick up Daisy? What, are you bringing her into the office?"

"We're bringing her to school together."

He huffed. "Aren't you just the perfect parents?" He paused the sarcasm. "It's too bad she has school. I wouldn't mind ditching work and spending the day with my girl."

Daisy was the light in my brother's life. For as much of an asshole he was, he turned into a softy around her. And when Daisy looked at him, she didn't see the darkness or his constant state of rage. All she saw was a man she admired and loved.

"I get her back this weekend. Why don't you swing by on Saturday morning and take her out for the day?"

"How about I bring her back on Sunday morning? You cool with that?"

The only reason he'd ask for a sleepover was if he really needed her.

Some people got emotional support dogs. Rhett escaped by hanging out with my kid, taking her to Disney or the movies or for

Putt-Putt—a place where he could be a kid, bringing him back to a time when his life had been much easier.

"I'm cool with that."

"I'll see you when you get to the office," he said and hung up.

Once I got through Jana's gate, I parked in the driveway and used my code to get in through the garage. We had an unwritten rule that when we came to each other's house for anything related to Daisy and the other person was waiting and expecting our arrival, we let ourselves in. Any exceptions to that unwritten rule, we rang the doorbell.

I made my way inside, through the laundry room and living room, hearing the girls in the kitchen. When there was a second of lull in the chatter, I said, "Where's my baby?"

I was just passing the couch, so neither of them could see me yet.

But I heard, "Daddy," along with the pattering of bare feet on the hardwood floor.

Daisy's greeting hadn't changed since she had been big enough and capable of running into my arms. One day, I knew I wouldn't get that kind of entrance, and my heart wasn't ready for it.

This morning, what came darting at me was a blur of pink and curls—an outfit and hairstyle I was sure had been changed multiple times before settling on this one since both were so important to my daughter.

"There she is. Don't you look beautiful?" I lifted her into the air, holding her against my chest, hugging her little body against mine. "I missed you, baby."

"Missed you, Daddy." She giggled. "Daddy, the scruffies. Owie."

My lips left her cheek, giving her skin a break from my beard. "Did you have a good weekend with Mommy?" I carried her into the kitchen, where Jana was sipping from a large cup of coffee.

"Yes!" Daisy sang. "We played with puppies!"

I eyed up Jana, who knew taking our daughter to play with dogs would result in one thing. "You did, did you?"

"Golden ones, Daddy. With big paws. Paws the size of my hand. And I got licks—on the face! They were wet and slimy, and I *loooved* them!"

Jana was laughing.

We'd talked about getting a dog, but not until Daisy was old enough to be fully responsible for the animal. With Jana's job constantly taking her out of town, I would end up caring for the pup a majority of the time. Even though I wanted a dog and Daisy did, too, I didn't need to care for anything aside from my little one.

"Playing with fire, I see," I said to Jana.

Jana took another sip and crossed her arms, showing off her full sleeve of daisy tattoos. "Daisy, why don't you tell your father why we were playing with the puppies?"

Daisy's hand went to my beard, combing through my whiskers. "I volunteered, Daddy, 'cause the doggies needed me. I scooped poop! And one of the doggies peed on my leg. She didn't mean to, and she was very sorry, but she chewed on my fingers, so I don't think she was *really* sorry." She let out a long, loud giggle.

"One of my clients just opened a rescue center and needed a few extra hands," Jana explained. "I thought it would be a good opportunity for Daisy to learn about giving back."

I gave Jana a nod, showing my approval. "That was really nice of you to help with the dogs, baby." I kissed the side of her hair. "How many puppies were there?"

"Six! They were so cute and little, and their tails looked like those hot dogs you sometimes make me with barbeque sauce."

I smiled. "So, Mom put you to work. I like it."

Daisy leaned into my ear and whispered, "Mommy told me no doggies when it was time to go home. 'Cause I wanted to bring them all home, Daddy. And I cried forever and ever."

I rubbed my hand across her back. "Sounds like Mommy laid

down the law." I winked at Jana, appreciating that she'd done the heavy lifting on this one.

"Meanie." Daisy pouted.

"Maybe in a couple of years, mean Mommy will change her mind."

Jana scrunched her face, a look that defined her new nickname. "Mommy would have happily adopted the Saint Bernard that was available. Maybe I should rethink that plan and—"

"You're funny."

"Aren't I?" Jana chuckled and set down her mug. "Daisy, we need to get ready to leave. Are your teeth brushed?"

"*Ughhh*," my daughter moaned. "The bubblegum is gonna taste yucky with the syrup."

"I don't care. You have to go brush them," Jana said. "And is your backpack ready to go?"

"Yep!"

"And have you brought your dish to the sink?"

She wiggled for me to put her down, and once her feet hit the floor, she grabbed her breakfast plate from the table and brought it over to the sink, running for the stairs.

"Don't run," Jana told her. She shook her head and began washing Daisy's dish. "How was the bachelor and bachelorette party?"

"Eventful as hell."

I leaned my arms onto the island across from her, thinking of the star attraction.

Addy.

A woman who had been haunting my every thought since she'd left my house a few evenings ago.

Shit, I needed more of her—at the very least, a repeat of everything that had gone down between us. But I hadn't heard from her, and it was eating away at me.

Why the hell hadn't she reached out?

Was it work? Had she really been that busy the last few days? Or was it something else?

Because when she'd left my house, I had been positive she'd text me the next morning.

That afternoon.

Or, fuck, that evening.

But silence was all I got.

And I wasn't happy.

I wasn't going to mention any of this to Jana since there was really nothing to talk about, even though I could tell her without an issue.

Jana and I had been broken up for three years, but we'd remained good friends and discussed the people we dated. We agreed that if a relationship became serious, on either side, they could be introduced to Daisy. Until anyone reached that point, our daughter wasn't to meet them. Within that span, Jana had only introduced one man to our daughter—a relationship that had recently ended. And with Jana being the last woman I'd been serious with, Daisy hadn't met anyone I dated.

"Rhett was in a mood," I continued.

"When is he not?" She gave me a look of concern before something seemed to click through her eyes. "Oh shit—the date. It was last week, wasn't it?"

I nodded. "You always remember."

"Rowan and Rhett will be my family until the day I die. Nothing will ever change that."

"You know I appreciate that." Because the better Jana and I were, the better our daughter was. "Rhett's going to take Daisy on Saturday, and she's going to spend the night with him."

She sighed. "I'm relieved to hear that. He needs her, Ridge."

"I know."

"I'm *reaaady*!" Daisy shouted from the top of the steps, followed by thump after thump as she jumped down each of the stairs, breathless by the time she reached the bottom. "Let's go to school."

"Do I need to smell your breath, or do you promise you brushed your teeth?"

Daisy gave a big smile, showing her missing front tooth that she'd lost last week. The tooth fairy had made a very expensive stop at my house. "Promise, Mommy."

"And you haven't forgotten anything in your room?" I asked. "Everything is in your backpack?"

"Yep! And I brought my colored pencils because if we get to color something like the golden puppies and I don't have the right color, I want to have the right color for the doggies, and I have every color."

Jana put Daisy's lunch box into the backpack, and after zipping it closed, she lifted the top, measuring the weight of it. "Daisy, are you sure this won't be too heavy for you to carry?"

"Nope. I'm so strong." She made a muscle. "Just like Daddy. Haw!"

"That's my girl," I said.

Jana leaned down in Daisy's face, fixing her ponytail since it had gotten messy from all the stair jumping. "Just so you know, Mommy is very strong too. I gave birth to you. Do you know how much strength that takes?"

"More strength than I have," I said to Daisy. "Because I can tell you right now, I wouldn't have survived what Mommy did." Especially without an epidural, which had blown my mind, but she'd gone into labor so fast that she didn't have time to get one.

I checked the time and said to Jana, "We have to go."

Jana hung Daisy's bag over her shoulder. "Do you mind bringing me back here so we can drive together?"

"Of course not." I nodded toward the front of the house. "Come on."

Daisy took off to the backseat of my Range Rover—what I normally drove when I was with my daughter, given that it was safer than the Bugatti—and Jana followed. I locked up the house before slipping into the driver's seat, making sure Daisy was fully secure before I even started the engine.

"Daddy, I wanna hear Taylor. Play my favorite song, *pleeease*."

I scrolled through the playlists on my dashboard until I found Daisy's favorite song, and "You're on Your Own, Kid" instantly came through my speakers.

"I can't believe you're playing this for her too," Jana said, keeping her voice down. Not that Daisy was even listening. She was singing too loud to hear us. "I thought I was the only one who had caved."

"It's Rowan's fault she even knows who Taylor is. She took her shopping with Rayner, and Daisy heard this song in the car and the part of the lyrics where Taylor sings about Daisy May, and there was no turning back. She thinks Taylor wrote the song for her."

"Oh my God, of course she does." Jana laughed. "Has Daisy asked you to take her to Taylor's concert?"

I chuckled, weaving down the narrow, tree-lined streets. "No less than twice a day."

"Ridge, I don't know how I feel about it. The tickets are outrageously expensive, and I know that's not a deal-breaker for you— because, knowing you, you'd probably get her backstage passes—but I just don't want her to be spoiled rotten."

"You mean more spoiled than she already is?"

"Exactly." She paused. "She comes from a family who can give her the moon and stars, but I want her to know the value of that sky and what it takes to earn it and the meaning of hard work."

"She's six," I said gently.

"There still has to be a balance."

"I don't disagree."

"What if we make her work for the tickets? We can assign her a few jobs around our houses. Use a notebook to keep track of all the hours she puts in and have her chip away at the goal. The concert isn't for a while. That'll give her plenty of time to earn the money."

I slowed at the light, the song changing so there was a bit of quietness in the SUV before Daisy started belting out the lyrics of the new song.

"I'm sure I can have the housekeeper assign a few of her tasks to Daisy."

Jana rolled her eyes, laughing. "Such a bougie answer."

"I'm bougie." I chuckled. "Says the woman who lives in a three-million-dollar house and employs the same housekeeper as me." My smile told her I was just teasing.

"A house you insisted on buying for us because you wanted your daughter to have the best in both homes. I would have been perfectly happy in the two-bedroom condo I'd bought before we got together."

"My daughter and *you*," I said. "Jana, you're the mother of my baby. I want the both of you to have the best. That's nonnegotiable. And I'm not saying the condo wasn't nice—it was—but it's not like the house you two live in."

"You're such a good guy, Ridge." As she inhaled, she briefly closed her eyes. "But you're going to be the reason our daughter gets everything with the snap of pink-painted fingers. Let's not have her turn out to be that kind of woman, okay? As soon as our munchkin is old enough to legally work—which is somewhere between twelve and fourteen years old, I think—she's going to be employed at your office. And when she's out of school for the summer, she can come on the road and assist me."

"I was twelve when I started working for my dad, so I'm not against that plan."

"Good."

"But let's get through this year before we start considering her teenage years. I want to enjoy every second of this stage while we're in it." I turned at the light. "When she's twelve or thirteen, she's probably going to hate us." I looked at Daisy through my rearview mirror. Her arms were in the air, her ponytail bopping, her pink nails flashing in the sunlight. "And the thought of that makes me one pissed-off dad."

"Ugh. No kidding. There won't be enough wine in this world to get me through that phase or her high school years. The thought alone makes me fucking shiver."

"A-fucking-men."

She turned down the music and looked over her shoulder as I began to slow toward the entrance of the school.

"Mommy, I was listening to Taylor!"

"We're almost there, so I want to talk to you for a second."

"*Okaaay.*"

"Are you ready for today?" Jana asked her.

"Yep! I love Miss Lark! She has the prettiest curly hair I've ever seen in my whole life, Mommy. I can't wait to see her again today. She's going to be the best teacher ever."

"I heard the meet-the-teacher night went quite well," I said to Jana.

Jana had had a booking last night that tied her up for several hours—something I'd known about—so I planned on taking Daisy to the school so she could meet her teacher and get comfortable in the classroom. But a last-minute meeting with the Westons popped up that I couldn't miss, so my mom took Daisy instead.

Jana had been disappointed that at least one of us couldn't be present for Daisy, but according to my mom, there had been many grandparents at the event, so we weren't the only parents who couldn't be there.

Jana shook her head and then pointed at my chest and then her own. "Parent of the Year awards—that's what we're winning, by the way."

"It all worked out." I laughed. "But, yes, I agree. We've been recipients before, and I'm sure we will be again."

Jana turned toward Daisy. "You know, first grade is a huge deal.

It's not like kindergarten. You're a very big girl now, and big girls have to listen to their teachers, so whatever Miss Lark says, you must do."

"With no talking back," I added.

"And you have to pay attention and you can't speak out of turn," Jana continued. "If Miss Lark wants you to raise your hand to talk, that's what you have to do. Got it?"

"Yep!"

"Daddy and I are going to walk you in, and then I'll be back this afternoon to pick you up."

I pulled into a parking spot and shut the engine off.

Jana and I had discussed escorting Daisy into school versus dropping her off from the car line. For her first day, that felt like the right move. I wanted to scope out the situation and make sure she got in safely, my heart needing to watch her walk toward her classroom—and I was sure Jana's did too. After today, the car line would be more than appropriate.

"Are you ready for this?" Jana asked me as I unhooked my seat belt.

"Fuck no."

"Daddy! You can't say that word! You owe me money!"

I smiled at her from the rearview mirror. "I can't believe we have a first grader."

Jana banged the back of her head against the seat. "I can't fucking either."

"Mommy!"

Jana laughed and whispered to me, "At this rate, she'll have the concert tickets paid off within her first week of school."

"No shit."

She smiled at me. "Let's go."

I got out, opening the door for Daisy, and grabbed her backpack as she climbed outside. I held the straps open for her, waiting until she slipped her arms through before I set the bag on her back. Once it was balanced, she took off across the parking lot, Jana and me behind her, following her down the sidewalk toward the entrance of the school.

"I'm proud of you for being so excited about today." I caught up to her pace and put my hand on her head, tilting it until her eyes met mine. "You're going to do great, and I know you're going to get excellent grades—just like your mom did when I met her in college."

"Uncle 'Ett told me I have to get all A's because he got B's, and I *haaave* to beat him."

She'd been calling my brother that from the moment she started speaking and still did even though she could now say his name.

"You don't have to compete with Rhett, baby." I gave her a little squeeze. "I just want you to do the best you can."

"That's an A, Daddy. 'Cause I'm smart, like Mommy."

I laughed. "You sure are."

We approached the entrance, surrounded by a small crowd of kids and parents, and I held the door for Jana and Daisy, joining them inside. Jana led us to an area where there was enough room for the three of us to stand without bumping elbows with other families.

"I love you," Jana said to Daisy, crouching so they were at eye level. "Have the best time today, okay? And I'll see you in a little while."

"Okay, Mommy."

I wanted nothing more than to pick my little girl up in my arms and swing her around.

But I wouldn't do that here.

I needed to treat her like she was a big girl.

So, I lowered to the floor and looked up at her. "I love you so much. I'll talk to you as soon as Mommy picks you up, and I want to hear how amazing your first day was."

"Love you, Daddy."

I kissed her cheek, and she took off down the hall, where a sea of kids was headed. Her ashy-brown ponytail that sat on top of her head was the only way I could distinguish her from the others.

"Why does this feel like the hardest thing we've ever done?" Jana asked.

I slowly looked at her. "Because we just watched our heart disappear." My hand went to the back of her neck. "The alternative is homeschooling, and neither of us is equipped to tackle that."

"She needs this." Her voice was only slightly above a whisper.

"She does," I agreed.

"But I want to hold her and never let her go."

"I know." I massaged over her hair, feeling how tight the muscle was beneath my fingers. "The day will fly by. She'll be back in your arms before you know it."

She nodded. "Right."

I had my own tightness, but it was in my chest.

I reached into my pocket, grabbed the fob for the SUV, and handed it to her. "I'm going to use the restroom. I'll meet you at the car."

"Really?" Her brows rose. "Or are you going to her classroom to make sure she got there and didn't get lost?"

That was exactly what I planned to do, but I didn't have a visitor badge—something that was required if parents roamed too far into the hallways. Since I didn't have time to get a badge, I hoped the policies were a little more lenient on day one.

Because, fuck, I just needed to know our girl was all right.

"I had too much coffee—that's all." I nodded toward the door. "Go. I'll see you in a second."

Before she could argue, I started walking in the direction of where Daisy had been headed, knowing there was a restroom not far away—a detail I remembered from when we'd toured the school. But when I reached it, I kept going, turning the corner to where all the first-grade classrooms were located.

Some of the teachers were outside the doors, greeting the kids as they entered. Others were already in the classroom, positioned at the front, speaking to the students who had taken a seat.

Daisy's room was the last door on the right, her teacher absent from the entryway, so I moved in front of it, peeking into her classroom. Daisy was seated in the second row, the straps of her backpack hanging across the top of her chair, sitting tall while she held a pencil that had a pink puff instead of an eraser.

My baby.

She couldn't look any cuter or tinier in a room that felt far too large and mature for her.

How is she six already? And in first grade?

Damn.

I was relieved that she'd found her classroom, that she was in her chair and already paying attention.

Jana would be thrilled when I told her—and I would.

As I started to turn around to head back to the entrance, my gaze shifted to the front of the class, where it connected with the eyes of the woman standing in front of the whiteboard.

The woman who was my daughter's teacher.

Miss Lark.

I took in her eyes.

Her hair.

Those lips.

And as the realization came over me, my fucking jaw dropped.

Chapter Eight

ADDISON

What in the hell is Ridge doing here? How did he know where I worked?

Did he follow me home from the club after my shift and put a tracking device on my car?

Did he somehow get my last name and research my employment?

Is he really going to this extent just to talk to me?

Is that flattering, or am I completely freaked out?

I didn't know.

I just knew I was staring at him in the doorway when he said, "Addy…" And I continued to look at him, completely stunned, when he added, "I need to talk to you."

I turned toward my class of students, my entire body shaking as I took inventory of what they were all doing. Some were in their seats, waiting for me to introduce myself. Some were still trickling in through the door in the back of the classroom. Some were clustered in groups, talking.

The clock on the wall showed that the bell wouldn't be ringing for another three minutes. But without my supervision and no other adult in the classroom, the kids had the potential of getting rowdy.

I didn't want to risk that.

I can't, I mouthed to him.

"Please," he said loud enough for me to hear. "I only need a minute."

I was gripping the lip at the bottom of the whiteboard where the eraser sat, my fingers squeezing so tightly that the metal was piercing my skin.

Why did I feel like even though I was fully dressed, he was staring at my naked body? That "Closer" by Nine Inch Nails was playing through the speakers and I was swinging around the pole as the band sang the lyrics about fucking like animals.

"Addy…"

Would he leave without speaking to me?

Am I pushing off the inevitable?

Is this even really happening?

"Ridge—"

"Give me one minute," he semi-repeated. "You *owe* me that."

I owe him?

A feeling came out of nowhere, bolting into my chest. It was strong enough that my hands released the small metal shelf, and I said to the students who were listening, "Excuse me for just a moment," before I made my way to the hallway.

Despite the spiciness in the air that was building with each step, my breath hitched as soon as I was close enough to really smell him. But that wasn't the only reaction happening inside my body. There were tingles too. Ones far too strong for my liking.

"What are you doing here?" I kept my voice as low as possible, but I couldn't hide the urgency and accusation in my tone.

"What am I doing here?" He cleared his throat and touched the knot at the top of his tie, sending me another wave of his scent.

This morning, it was a combination of all three—earthy, salty, and extra sassy.

"What do you think I'm doing here?" he asked.

This was my first day at this school. I certainly didn't want any administration to be walking the halls and see me talking to an uninvited guest who wasn't even wearing a visitor pass. This was a place for learning, not putting out personal fires—or whatever this was about to turn into.

"I think you're upset I didn't reach out, and you somehow found your way here, and you want to talk about it."

His hair was slicked and spiked, his beard brushed and trimmed, his lips parted, his blue and navy-flecked eyes gazing right at me. God, I wished he weren't so hot. I wished he didn't smell so good. And I wished I weren't this attracted to him.

"This isn't the place to have this conversation, Ridge. We can talk about it—"

"That's what you think?" He huffed and shook his head. "Do you see the little girl in the second row of your classroom? Ponytail, pink pencil, missing front tooth?"

I looked inside, scanning the children until I came across the one who fit his description. "Yes."

"That's Daisy. My daughter."

His…*daughter*?

What?

That's why he's here?

The little girl he'd spoken about when I met him was now one of my students?

I felt all the blood drain from my face. "Oh…"

I studied him—the details that I already knew—and then I glanced at Daisy. A name I'd written multiple times over the last couple of days as I got my classroom ready. The eyes, the chin, the same color hair.

My throat was on fire when I looked back at Ridge. "Daisy Cole, and you're—"

"Ridge Cole." He let that sink in. "When I dropped her off this morning, I was worried she wouldn't find her classroom or wouldn't feel settled. First grade is a big fucking deal—much bigger than kindergarten. So, I came here to check on her. What I didn't expect to find was you."

I was trying to process this.

For my brain to catch up to the reality of his daughter being in my class for the entire school year.

That I'd slept with Daisy's father only a few evenings ago.

His arms crossed, his jacket tightening around them, showing the size of his muscles. "We need to talk."

"Not here—"

"Certainly not here." His gaze was intensifying, to the point where I not only felt naked, but I felt like he could see the wetness inside me. "I'd tell you to call me, but you don't exactly have a track record of following through with that."

That was a whole other thing I needed to discuss with him.

Why was the list of topics so suddenly long?

"I—"

"Why don't you give me your number, and I'll call you?" he said, cutting me off.

Fuck.

Fuck. Fuck. Fuck.

That would give me time to get my thoughts straight, to calm my racing heart. I needed to feel less seen because here, at this very second, I felt like a spotlight was over me, and I was breaking out into a sweat.

His phone was already in his hand, so I rattled off my number and added, "I'll text you during my next break. I promise."

"I've heard that promise before." He smiled and took another peek inside the class. "Be good to my baby," he said before he walked away.

I took only a few seconds to stare at the back of him. He wore a suit in cobalt, the same color as his eyes. Brown leather shoes. A hand still holding his phone, the other at his side, fingers dangling. Fingers that I remembered so well—long, thin, extremely experienced, and well versed in the anatomy of a woman's body. A stature that was tall, broad, and incredibly sexy from this angle.

Oh God.

This would only be my luck, I thought as I walked back and positioned myself in front of the whiteboard, the bell going off as soon as I stilled.

I waited for the chatter to calm and for all the students to take their seats and for my throat to loosen and cool before I spoke. "Hello, everyone. I'm Miss Lark"—I pointed to where I'd already written my name on the board—"and I'm your first-grade teacher. I'm so, so excited to have you in my class and to teach you all the different things we're going to cover this year. Let's start by going around the room, and each of you will say your name and one of your favorite things you did over the summer. Who wants to go first? Raise your hand."

Almost every hand shot up in the air.

But the one that captured my attention was the little girl in the second row with a missing tooth in front and a puffy-topped pink pencil in her hand. She was adorable—her smile, her outfit, her enthusiasm as she wiggled in her seat.

I aimed my finger at her and said, "Why don't you start?"

"My name is Daisy Cole," she said in a mousy voice, appropriate for her age, which only made her cuter. "I'm six years old and in first grade"—she giggled as though she realized she'd given more information than was asked—"and my favorite memory from this summer is when my daddy took me to Disneyland. It was *sooo* fun. We rode all the rides together, and I got a bellyache 'cause I ate so much ice cream."

Chapter Nine

Ridge

"You're fucking kidding me," Rhett said from the other side of my desk after I finished telling the story about my run-in with Addy this morning.

I stared at the mouth of my coffee cup, the caramel-colored caffeine halfway up the ceramic. I pounded back the rest, wishing it were an endless supply of a filthy vodka martini.

I needed vodka a hell of a lot more than I needed coffee.

"I'm not going to lie. I'm a little floored right now," Rowan added.

She stared at me with wide eyes and a shaking head and a lip that was being gnawed on.

I didn't make it a habit of always discussing my sex life with my sister, but she'd walked into my office at the same time as my brother, and I had seen no reason to keep it from her. There was a chance she could even offer a perspective that I hadn't thought of.

And, shit, all I'd done since I'd gotten to the office several hours ago was think about Addy.

"Does Jana know about any of this?" Rhett asked.

"No," I replied. "I told her I was going to the restroom, and she waited for me in the car. She didn't know until after that I had gone to check on our daughter, and I left the Addy part out." I exhaled. "I don't know how she'd react, and I don't want to handle the weight of that right now."

"Which part would cause weight?" Rowan asked. "That she's also a stripper? Or that you've slept with her?"

I rubbed my hand over the top of my desk. "That I've slept with her teacher. I don't think the stripper part would bother Jana. She understands hustle and wouldn't knock another woman for that. But this is Daisy's first real class—it's the start of everything—and that affects our daughter."

The room turned quiet.

"All you've said is that you slept with her," Rowan voiced, her hand going to the edge of my desk. "What you haven't said is if you want to date her or if it was just a one-night stand…because, in a roundabout way, that also affects your daughter."

I gripped the back of my neck as I focused on my sister. "I gave her my number before she left my house—she didn't stay the night even though I wanted her to—and she never reached out. I had no way of getting in touch with her, but if I did, I would have."

"You haven't answered my question." She smiled.

"I liked her."

"Liked?" Rhett asked.

I hissed out a mouthful of air. "I'm pissed she didn't text or call. What the fuck, man? I thought things had gone well between us. We'd left the strip club, gone and grabbed some food. Then, I invited her over—something she didn't have to agree to—and things happened once we got back to my place. It wasn't one-sided, it was two-sided." I massaged my neck a bit harder, trying to make sense of it all. "She wanted me as badly as I wanted her. So, why the hell didn't I hear from her?"

"Maybe she thought, given the circumstances, you were only

after one thing," Rowan offered.

"I'd made it clear that wasn't the case." I released the mug, unsure why I was still holding it. "We talked about that actually. I couldn't have been more reassuring. Had I slept around? Of course. But I told her I was one of the good guys—and I meant every word of it."

Rhett shrugged. "Maybe she has a boyfriend?"

"Jesus, I hope that's not true." I stretched my arms up over my head. "Whatever is holding her back, I'm going to get to the bottom of it. We're meeting up tonight."

"Where?" Rowan asked.

"My house." I bent my arms, resting my hands behind my head. "Daisy's with Jana, and my place will give us some privacy since everyone in LA is a fucking spy."

"True that," Rhett muttered.

"Let's get back to our girl," Rowan said, leaning forward to rest her arms on her knees. "Are you going to switch Daisy out of her classroom?"

My brows rose. "Are you suggesting I should?"

She tapped her hand on my desk. "Well, the school is top-notch with an impeccable reputation. They wouldn't employ her unless she was exceptional at what she did."

When I had gotten to the office this morning, I'd checked out the school's website where her bio was listed. I was relieved Addison Lark hadn't given me a fake name, assuming her friends and family called her Addy for short. I'd also plugged her name into the social media sites and checked out the little information that was public, which was nothing more than a handful of photos.

It didn't matter what angle the picture was taken or what she was wearing in them.

She was one gorgeous woman.

"She has an undergraduate degree in elementary education and a master's degree as well. She student-taught at multiple well-known schools throughout LA. She tutors adults who can't read, and she also offers English SAT prep."

"Damn," Rhett whistled. "She's certainly qualified."

Rowan nodded.

"Now, you're the one who's not answering *my* question," I said to my sister.

She took several deep breaths. "Would I switch my daughter out of her classroom?" she repeated, staring at me, her face making no indication of which way she was leaning. "My main concern—and Jana's too—would be whether Daisy was getting the best education. That's one. Two, if something happened between you and Addy—whether that something was positive or negative—would Addy be able to set that aside and teach your daughter the way she deserved?" She sat up straight. "If the answer to both of those questions is yes, then I don't think you need to switch her out of Addy's classroom." She paused. "But I want you to remember something: if you two got together and things went south for some reason, Daisy is the one who would suffer."

I leaned both arms on my desk. "What do you mean?"

"If Addy started spending time at your house but then you two broke up," Rowan continued, "why would she suddenly not be there? Yet Daisy would still see her in the classroom every day, and that could be hard for our little one to process."

I couldn't even get Addy to call me. Progressing to the point where she started spending time at my house? That was a massive jump.

But a jump I wanted.

And if I got my way—which I normally did—she would be spending some time at my house.

"There's also the school aspect," Rowan said. "Why is Daisy getting called on more than the other students? Why is the teacher being harder on her? Remember, other kids can be tough nowadays.

You don't want Daisy getting any type of privilege when they're not."
She crossed her arms over her chest. "I almost think if you end up
dating her, you need to keep that part of your life separate from Daisy.
There should be no crossover at all. And at the end of the school year,
if you guys are still together, then it would be appropriate to introduce
her as your girlfriend."

"Don't you think you're getting a little ahead of yourself?" Rhett
said to her. "You're setting rules before there's even a foundation. Let
the motherfucker breathe for a second."

She eyed up Rhett. "Do you know our brother? Women are
obsessed with him. I would be very, very surprised if Addy is the
opposite. And if she is, Ridge is going to charm the hell out of her and
get what he wants in the end." She looked at me. "Tell me I'm wrong."

I chuckled.

She smiled. "Exactly." She then gloated.

"Still, there are a lot of ifs that are making this situation much
more difficult than normal," I said. "The most important part is
Daisy. And first and foremost, I need to protect my daughter."

Chapter Ten

ADDISON

I didn't know why I was so jittery and shaky as I shut my car door and walked up to Ridge's house. I'd had most of the day to prepare for this conversation; it wasn't like it had been thrown on me moments ago. But I still felt so lost in my thoughts, and that only got worse when he opened the door.

My eyes did a quick sweep—I couldn't stop them.

Gray sweatpants. A baseball hat. A white T-shirt that clung to his arm muscles and chest with just the right amount of bagginess in the waist.

Is he serious? Of all the things he could have put on, he chose the sexiest outfit ever?

Sigh.

"Addison, come in."

The sound of my full name was almost startling.

He held the door wide enough that I could slip inside. But not too wide because my shoulder swished against his chest, and with that, I got a tease of his hard pecs and a hint of his scent.

God, that scent. I swore I'd smelled it all day in my classroom and even when I'd gone home to change and eat dinner before coming here.

I waited in the foyer, frozen as I glanced up at the second floor. "Daisy isn't here, is she?"

"She's with her mom." He shut the door and moved beside me. "Can I get you anything to drink? Some rosé perhaps?"

I followed him into the kitchen, where he picked up a short, stemless martini glass and took a sip from it.

"I don't know," I said softly.

Because I really didn't.

Was drinking really the best decision tonight? Ridge was dangerous enough to be around sober; my attraction to him was so intense, and I didn't want to lose my senses by adding a buzz into the mix.

But one glass? I could certainly handle that.

"You have rosé?" I asked.

"It's what you drink, so I picked some up after work."

"That's so thoughtful of you." And it was that thoughtfulness that added to this breathless feeling that wouldn't, no matter what, go away. "Thank you. I would love some."

He went to the wine fridge and grabbed the bottle, which he opened and poured into a glass. Once it was in my hand, he said, "Why don't we talk in here?" and he took his martini into the living room.

I sat on the opposite side of the couch, putting plenty of space between us, squeezing the glass with both hands. "Let me start."

I'd been focused on my lap, and I slowly looked up at him. Even his gaze was lethal. The kind of stare that could probably earn him whatever he wanted with anyone he wanted.

"I'm sorry I didn't reach out to you. To just be totally honest with you—"

"The truth is all I want to hear, Addy. Let's cut any bullshit and just lay it all out there."

I nodded. I wanted that, too, but that admission didn't make the words come out any faster. "The truth is, I set up my classroom on Saturday, worked at the club on Saturday night; worked from home on Sunday, getting the rest of my lesson plans done, and Monday—today—was school, where I saw you."

He lowered his hat, giving me even less of his gaze—I felt it; I just couldn't see it.

"But did you want to talk to me? That's the real question."

I let that inquiry simmer. I let it build. And then I said, "I thought about it. A lot."

"And you decided against it?"

I shook my head. "I just wasn't ready."

"Because?"

"I'm working at a strip club, Ridge. It's not something I'm ashamed of; it's also not something I'm proud of. But it wouldn't feel right going on a date with you while I'm dancing for other men, putting my boobs in their faces, straddling their laps, pretending to ride them for money." My stomach started to turn. Not from my responsibilities—I'd accepted those—but at the thought of going out with Ridge while doing all of that at work.

"I don't have a problem with it." He rested his hand over the visor of his hat. "Not at this moment anyway."

"I've heard stories from the girls at the club. Dating nightmares. They told me that once a stripper gets into a relationship, they end up quitting because their boyfriend doesn't like them dancing. I can't be in a situation like that—I need the money."

"Who said I'd give you that ultimatum?"

"I just assumed—"

"Exactly." He took a drink and then set the empty martini glass on the table beside the couch. "Once you have the money, what does life look like then?"

I shook my head. "I don't know. Different, I hope."

Everything would be different once I sent my sister the remainder of what I'd promised. I could then just focus on the balance of my student loans and outstanding bills, which I'd probably be paying off for the rest of my life.

"But there's a whole other angle of this that we haven't discussed, and that's Daisy." I folded my legs, holding the glass in front of my feet. "I'm her teacher."

"I know."

"And I take that job more seriously than anything." I felt my head drop, my eyes close. "I'm in a situation where I don't know what to do. Technically, I should probably go to the principal and discuss this with her because it puts—"

"No."

I looked up. "No?"

"Your credentials are incredible, Addy. You're more than qualified to teach my little girl." His legs widened, and he pulled up one of his pant legs, showing his ankle and sock. "I want to believe that regardless of what happened or what happens between us, you'll always put Daisy first. That I can count on you to give her the best education possible."

"Oh my God," I whispered, the words coming out like a sigh. "Absolutely. Always. That goes without saying."

"Then, there's no reason to tell the principal or to switch her out of your classroom—something I had to consider, but I wanted to hear your take on things first."

I took my first sip. "I promise I'll give everything to your daughter—in the fairest, most equal manner."

"Good."

"But, Ridge..." My throat was burning. My hands and body were still shaking. My emotions were raging against each other, and I didn't know why. What I had to say should be so easy. It should come with no hesitation whatsoever. That just wasn't the case. "I think that what went down between us the other night"—I swallowed, waiting for the tightness to leave my throat, but it didn't—"it shouldn't happen again."

"Because my daughter is your student?"

I went to nod, but my head felt so heavy, so I had to say, "Yes."

He extended his legs over the ottoman, one of his arms going behind his head. Slowly, a smile crept across his face, like a facial hard-on—it was that hot. "All right, Addison."

There was my name again.

I took another drink, hoping the feeling in my chest would subside, and it still didn't.

It didn't matter what I wanted. What I could see potentially happening between us. What I felt.

I couldn't date a man while I was stripping. That would be wrong of me on every single level.

And I couldn't date a student's father.

What would Daisy's mom think? She'd probably have me reported to the school board and have Daisy yanked from my class, and the entire school would be talking about me.

I couldn't risk that.

My job meant far too much to me.

"I want to focus on Daisy," I told him. "I want both of us focused on her."

His head was moving, but it was more of a bop than a nod. "She's my daughter. I'm always focused on her."

I drained a little more of my wine. "Then, you understand where I'm coming from?"

For the second time today, I felt like I was naked.

But this time, there was no spotlight above me or song playing through the speakers. I was just sitting here, nude, and dripping from his stare.

"I appreciate that you're concerned about her," he said. "That's something I want in a teacher."

He hadn't really answered my question. But I wasn't going to push for more.

I wasn't sure I could even handle his answer.

"Thank you." I finished the rest of the wine. "I think I'd better get going."

He slowly stood and held out his hand, which I stared at, unsure what it was for, but part of me wanted to grab it and hold it and use it to pull me closer to him.

What the hell am I even thinking?

"Your glass," he said when I hadn't uttered a word or moved.

"Oh...right." I cleared my throat and handed it off to him and walked toward the back of the living room to turn toward the front entrance. But first, I looked over my shoulder to say, "I'm sure I'll be seeing you around the school, Ridge."

Another smile came over his mouth. This one was even sexier than before. "You sure will."

Chapter Eleven

Ridge

From: Addison Lark
Bcc: Ridge Cole
Subject: First week update!

To the parents and guardians of my first-grade class:

Since we're nearing the end of the first week, I wanted to send a quick update to let you all know that your children have done a wonderful job of adjusting to my classroom. For the first five days, I've focused on the transition. I've paid particularly close attention to behavior—in the classroom and hallways, during lunch and recess. I've also gone over the materials we're going to use this year and their locations, so the students feel comfortable and know where everything is. They've learned about the importance of a community, how they can help others and set boundaries—both personal and educational. Each student has also set a goal they would like to achieve and placed that goal on the star board, so they can work throughout the year on achieving it. They were very enthusiastic about setting their own goal and to hear they'll be able to take home their star if their goal is achieved. My goal, as their teacher, is to make sure each of their goals is met.

I hope, throughout the school year, to continue sending you weekly emails to keep you abreast of what they're learning, studying, and accomplishing.

Please let me know if you have any questions. I'm happy to discuss things in further detail or set up a parent-teacher conference if any concerns arise.

Sincerely,
Addison Lark
First-Grade Teacher

• • •

From: Ridge Cole
To: Addison Lark
Subject: Re: First week update!

Addison,

Daisy comes home from school every day with the biggest smile on her face. You've made me one happy father.

—Ridge

• • •

From: Addison Lark
To: Ridge Cole
Subject: Re: First week update!

Ridge,

Thank you for letting me know. I'm happy to hear she's enjoying herself so much.

Next week, we'll be starting homework assignments, so I'll be asking parents to monitor their child's progress and ensure the homework is completed before the next school day. I hope you're able to enforce a policy at home that would encourage Daisy to complete these tasks.

Sincerely,
Addison
First-Grade Teacher

• • •

From: Ridge Cole
To: Addison Lark
Subject: Re: First week update!

Whatever you need...I've got you.

—Ridge

• • •

As the call connected through the speakers of my car, I responded to Rhett's greeting with, "How's my girl?"

"Are you really checking up on us?" he asked quietly.

"Checking up? No. If that were the case, I would have called a lot earlier than nine at night." I turned at the light, speeding up after I passed through the intersection. "But am I inquiring? Yes. I fucking miss her, all right? Jana had her all week, and you have her tonight. I feel like I haven't seen my baby in months."

"We had a hell of a good time today. She kicked my ass in Putt-Putt and *somehow* convinced me to go for pedicures because she simply couldn't survive another minute unless her toes were pink and sparkly—"

"Hold on. *You* got a pedicure?"

"Do you honestly think she gave me a choice?"

I laughed. "Man, she has you whipped. Keep going."

"Dinnertime hit, and the princess demanded tacos, so that was what we had, followed by a movie. She made it a solid ten minutes before she fell asleep in my theater room, and that's where she currently is, passed out on my chest."

That would explain why he was whispering.

Not that he needed to. My girl could sleep through a goddamn tornado.

"Don't tell me you made the tacos?" I asked.

"Fuck no. You know me better than that."

I could envision Daisy asleep on my brother, her curls in his face, her tiny snores getting drowned out by the surround sound in his theater room. A sight I was sure was beyond adorable. What I couldn't envision was Rhett using his kitchen for anything other than grabbing Daisy a drink, so I wasn't at all surprised that he'd taken her out to eat.

"Wait until she asks for an egg burrito for breakfast—that's been her favorite lately. Or French toast—her second choice with warmed-up syrup and cinnamon butter."

"Jesus," he groaned. "Tell me you're fucking kidding."

"The kid likes good food. What can I say? She has my palate."

"It's a good thing our chef will be here in the morning. That's a project he can tackle, not me."

I slowed down as I approached the building and pulled into the parking lot, finding a spot in the back, and shifted into park. "What time do you want me to pick her up?"

"I can drop her off. I'll text you in the morning and figure out a time. It won't be early. Daisy and I will be sleeping in."

"If you can get her to sleep past seven, it'll be a miracle." I unbuckled my seat belt.

"You don't know the power of Uncle 'Ett."

I laughed.

"Where are you?" he asked. "I can tell you've been driving somewhere."

I rested my elbow on the window ledge and stared at the dark building in the distance. "A place I probably shouldn't be."

He was silent for a moment. "Are you at the fucking strip club?"

"I'll see you tomorrow," I said and ended the call.

I didn't want to talk about my decision or what I hoped to happen this evening. Nor did I need to be reminded that Addy was Daisy's teacher—something he might or might not have brought up.

In my mind, a line had been drawn down the middle of her two jobs.

And right now, I was standing on one side, not in the center.

I got out of my car and locked the doors and headed for the entrance of the club, paying the necessary cover to get access to both the VIP and main sections. Once I was in, I walked straight to the bar and scoped out the scene. I'd come early on purpose, unsure what time Addy got here and was assigned to a stage. I just hoped to catch her before she disappeared into a private room—another reason coming early had been part of my plan. The busier the club got, the more likely she'd be hired. And there was enough money in this town that the dude could request to have her all night, just like I had.

But from the looks of it, my timing was perfect. The VIP room, which I could see from here, was only about half full, the main room the same. She wasn't on any of the three stages, so I ordered a filthy martini from the bartender.

As I was handing her my credit card, I said, "Has Addy been on yet?"

She eyed me up and down. "The redhead?"

I nodded.

"And you are?" she asked.

I remembered Addy had told me that the women who worked here often quit once they got boyfriends. We weren't even close to a title like that, but I also didn't want to allude to the fact that I liked her in case it set off any alarms.

So, I replied, "A fan. Nothing more."

"The girls come and go so frequently, it's hard to keep track of all their names." She held a bottle of Tito's over a metal shaker, the vodka pouring out in a thin stream. "She was on not too long ago. I'm sure she'll be back in the rotation within the next couple of songs." She nodded toward the closest stage. "You should check out the blonde that's up there now. She's the most skilled we've got."

"I prefer redheads." I winked at her.

She finished adding the olive juice and began to rattle the shaker in the air. "We don't have too many of those. Addy might be our only one at the moment."

"I guess that makes her in high demand."

She poured the mixture into a glass and set it on the bar top, swiping my card and handing it to me, along with the receipt. "She's a newbie. Once she comes out of her shell a little more, she has the potential of being the most popular woman here."

"Then, I'm sure it'll be a fight for the private rooms. Sounds like a good problem to have."

"It's no fight." She smiled. "She goes with the man who pays the highest. That's how this business works." She immediately moved on to the next customer.

I gave her a generous tip and signed my name at the bottom and took the glass to a seat that was in the center of the room, giving me a view of all three stages.

This wasn't a contest among the men here; I would always be the highest bidder.

But as the song played and the blonde made her way around the pole, I couldn't stop thinking about what the bartender had said.

I'd told Addy that working here didn't bother me, but those words were starting to eat away at me.

So did the thought of her being the most popular woman here. That men, like myself, would come just to see her. To spend time with her. To shower her with their money. To get her alone and try to put their hands all over her fucking body.

That was what I didn't like at all.

Shit.

I took a long drink of the vodka, glancing between each of the stages as the song came to an end. A line of women was making their way out from the back—some were headed for the main area to try to score private dances, others went to the VIP room, the rest went toward the stages. I tried to look at their faces, but there were just too many of them.

Fortunately, the DJ made it easy, announcing the dancers who were entering the stage, and Addy was the first to be called, her name coming through the speakers as her heels hit the steps. They had to be at least five inches—shiny black spikes. And the lingerie set that covered her stunning body was a dark emerald lace bra and a pleated skirt that was short enough to show the matching thong beneath—a color that looked incredible with her red hair.

It had been too long since I'd seen those beautiful, perky tits and those juicy curves and that gorgeous face.

My dick was already hard.

She walked to the middle of the stage and gave the crowd a curtsy.

The crowd fucking roared, and the cash was already flying toward the stage before she even made her way to the pole. But once she was there, she pressed her back against the metal, slowly lowering until she was squatting. She gave several more smiles, teasing with the briefest sway of her hips, her legs then shooting out from each side, landing in a split.

That got the men to fucking scream.

A few were on their feet, hovering on the side of the stage, throwing bill after bill in her direction.

Addy didn't get up. She didn't move closer to them. She bounced in that position, holding the pole behind her, showing the men just how she would ride their cock if she were straddling them.

Another thought I didn't fucking like at all.

After a few more beats of Rihanna's "Don't Stop the Music," she pulled herself onto her knees, unhooking the skirt, and she left it by the pole as she got on all fours and crawled toward the men who were standing for her. She kept her distance, but due to the narrow stage, she was still within reach. With her ass planted down, her legs spread, the thong covering as much as it could, she gave those men a taste of my dinner.

A hint of what I'd gotten to devour and what I planned on eating again tonight.

My fingers clenched around the stem of the glass as I glared at the crowd that was forming, at the money that was being flung at her, at the thought that each of these men was going to go home and beat off to this memory of her.

I was one of them. I'd jerked off to her pussy every fucking night this week.

Addy unlatched her bra, tossing the lace toward her skirt, giving her breasts a heavy, hearty shake.

There was another eruption among the men—cheers and hollers. But their attention on her was no longer my focus.

Because Addy had slowly lifted her gaze and connected it with mine.

A redness passed across every inch of her as she took in my eyes, a flush that ended at the hard, pebbled peaks of her nipples...which she was now squeezing.

Making my hard-on fucking throb.

Chapter Twelve

ADDISON

What is Ridge doing here?

That thought repeated in my head as I stood in the middle of the stage, wearing only a thong, my hands circling my breasts, my fingers sliding toward my nipples—a move that I knew would make the men in the audience go wild.

And it did.

There were moans and shouts, and for every second I held them, squeezing the peaks, acting as though it was the most satisfying sensation in the world, more money was thrown onto the stage.

It wasn't like I was counting the seconds, stalled in this position to see how much I could make. The reason I didn't move was because I was frozen, unable to drag my eyes away from Ridge's stare—a stare that was making me feel completely lost and filling me with even more questions.

Why did he come back to see me? Hadn't I made myself clear?

But, really, was I surprised he was here?

Did I secretly want him to be?

I turned my back to him, slowly bending over to give the crowd a view of my ass, the way I could shake it—first with each cheek individually and then both cheeks together.

The move, one I'd perfected over my last couple of shifts, caused an uproar in the audience. So, I gave them several more sways while balancing on heels that were equivalent to standing on needles.

Was Ridge looking?

Did it matter?

I glanced over my shoulder, bypassing the eyes of the first couple of rows to focus on the middle, where he was sitting. He didn't have to lift his gaze, dragging it from my ass to my face. Because, like he'd told me, he was one of the good guys, and the good guy's eyes were already locked with mine.

Since my chin was still resting over my shoulder, I left him and scanned the audience, giving them a wink before I walked to the pole. The song—something I'd chosen at the beginning of the night—had only about two minutes left. I needed to earn at least a few hundred, and the way to do that was to straddle the metal and climb to the top before slowly swinging all the way to the bottom.

Never had I thought, during all the years Leah and I had been taking biweekly pole workout classes, it would give me the experience I needed for this job. But here I was, looking like an expert to these men.

Once I reached the highest part of the pole, I held on with my legs and bent backward until my head was pointed at the ground, using gravity to bring me to the floor.

But not quickly.

I kept my legs intertwined, allowing the music to guide my moves, and I gradually lowered. Once I reached the ground, I stayed on my back, and I held my lower body high. I swivel-kicked the air, clapping my heels together, followed by my thighs, before I rolled over, pointing my butt upward to straddle the pole from behind.

I could sense what every man in this room was thinking as they watched me.

It was as though I were inside each of their heads.

And I used those thoughts as fuel while I bucked my hips and bit my lip, forcing the fake pleasure to spread across my face. The pole slapped my ass with each thrust, as though it were a man positioned in doggy style.

That was the fantasy I wanted to create.

Because the more I satisfied these men, the more cash they tossed onto the stage.

Stripping, I had learned, was a cat-and-mouse chase, except the cat never caught the mouse.

But as I crawled toward the middle of the stage, eyeing Ridge, I realized how that wasn't true.

He had caught me.

He just couldn't keep me.

And now, we were here again, his eyes devouring me, his tongue circling his mouth as though he were between my legs, one hand gripping his cocktail and the other the armrest of his chair, like they were somewhere on my body.

With a stare that made me feel as if we were the only people in this room.

A gaze so strong and overwhelming that I almost didn't hear the song end, or hear the DJ saying my name, or see the security guard moving around the edge of the stage to collect my money. When the security guard finished, he stood at the bottom of the stairs, his hand out, waiting for me to clasp it to escort me down the steps.

As soon as I finished, I got onto my feet and slipped my arms through the straps of my bra, hooking it in the back. I accepted the security guard's fingers and walked down the short flight, taking the cash he handed to me once I reached the floor. I tucked the thick wad into my bra and weaved my way through the main area, a sultry grin on my face to entice this hungry audience. I wasn't more than a few paces past the stage when I felt a gentle swipe across my thigh.

It was so light that it could have been a feather.

But I knew it wasn't because the feeling was so achingly familiar. So was the texture of his skin and the level of his heat—two things I could never forget.

Two things I had thought about since I'd left his house.

His touch impacted me in a way that made me stop and glance down, meeting Ridge's seductive stare.

I'd been so far inside my head that I didn't realize I'd reached the center of the main lounge, where he was stationed, his hand still raised from the armrest, his pointer finger triggered, showing me that was the one he'd used to touch me.

Those fingers. My God. They are…magic.

"Going somewhere important?" he asked.

"No." My smile faded, my eyes narrowing at him. "I'm just… going."

Except I didn't move.

I couldn't.

"If you're going, as in leaving, it'd better be with me."

I laughed—a reaction that was easier, that came with less pressure, than saying words.

"Is that a yes?" He cocked his head.

I crossed my arms. "No."

"Then, what will it take to get some of your time?" He reached into his pocket, took out his wallet, and gave me a fold of bills as large as the one in my bra. "That amount should do it."

There were so many layers to this. His money was burning the skin of my palm. My brain couldn't keep up with all the noes that were accumulating each second in my head.

I shouldn't take his cash.

I shouldn't go into a private room with him.

I shouldn't even be talking to him here.

But what I found myself saying was, "You want me to finally dance for you?"

"You know that's not what I want."

I swallowed, the tightness, the quivers both making it so difficult. "I know nothing, Ridge."

He shook his head as though he were the teacher. "That isn't true. You know just what I want. And if you didn't know that the night I took you home, which would shock me, then I'm positive you can feel it right now by the way I'm looking at you." He nodded toward me. "What are my unspoken words saying to you, Addison?"

I glanced to my right and left, checking to see if anyone was close enough to hear him. Even though they weren't, I still said, "Addy."

"I respect that you don't want that side of you to surface while you're in here. But you need to know I've seen straight past Addy and I'm looking directly at Addison. It doesn't matter what you have on or what stage you just walked off. What I see is the gorgeous woman beneath."

Why was that one of the hottest things anyone had ever said to me?

Why were there goose bumps on every inch of my body?

Why was air coming out of my lungs in fast, breathless pants?

"What do you want from me, Ridge?"

"Tonight?" He smiled. "Your time."

"That's it?"

He stalled in seconds, but what was showing in his eyes was louder than anything he could ever possibly say. "We can start there."

I laughed again. "And you think us spending time together is safe, given our situation?"

"Safe?" His stare lowered down my body, and he let out a deep, gritty chuckle. "The thoughts in my head aren't safe at all." He locked eyes with me again. "But you can trust me."

"What does trust have anything to do with this?"

"It has everything to do with it." He moved his finger in a circle. "If you took any of these men into the back, you'd be filled with worry and what-ifs over what they were going to do. You don't have the same fear with me." His teeth briefly grazed his lip. "But you do have a fear…"

"And that is?"

"How are you going to stop yourself from sleeping with me tonight?"

Chapter Thirteen

RIDGE

"What are you thinking about?" I asked Addison as she sat in the chair next to mine.

The room was dark, except for two spotlights—one in the front, close to the door, and another in the back. The glow from both was just enough to light up her face and bare skin.

This wasn't the same private room as last time. This one was even smaller. And there was a salty odor lingering throughout the small space, like the poor bastard who had been in here before me had sweat himself to death.

"I can't say it's just one thing," she replied. "It's…all the things."

"Start with something."

Her chest rose even though most of it was covered by her arms. "The reason you're here."

"You know that answer."

"No, I don't. I mean, I have theories. And each one is *a lot* to take in."

This woman got more interesting by the second.

"Why don't you tell me what they are?" I leaned back in my seat and rested my foot over the opposite thigh.

Where I was getting relaxed, she was more upright, her back fully erect. "Theory one: you like the challenge of trying to get someone you can't have since I made it extremely clear the last time we were alone that we could never do this again."

I laughed.

She was so fucking cute when she was trying to prove a point.

"What exactly is *this*, Addison?"

"Huh?"

"You just said we can't do this. What is this?" I waited. "Because all we're doing is talking. So, is that what you meant? Or were you referring to something else?"

"I'm half naked, Ridge. I wouldn't call this a normal conversation."

I waved my hand across the air. "I didn't notice."

There was just enough light to see her brows lift. "You're telling me you don't see the bra I have on right now?"

"If I looked down, sure, I'd see it. But your arms are covering most of your chest, and it's dark in here, and if I'm being honest, I'm not interested in looking at your bra. I'm far more interested in hearing your next theory."

"*Hmm.*" She stalled. "Before we get to that, are you really going to tell me you didn't see me braless onstage?"

I smiled. "You were on a stage?"

"Ridge…"

"Yes, I saw you. Yes, I watched you. Yes, it turned me on. But not in the way you're thinking. You could have been fully dressed—it wouldn't have mattered to me." I leaned forward to get closer to her. "Remember this, Addison: I've already seen what's under that bra and those panties. I got to see because you came back to my house and I got to peel the lace off your body. If I'm going to see your tits and pussy again, I prefer it to happen under my control and not because you're on a stage, stripping off your undergarments for eyes that aren't mine."

I could almost hear her breathing.

"You and my real name—it's becoming a thing, isn't it?"

"Any motherfucker in this building can call you Addy. I'm the only one who can call you Addison—I assume. I like that."

She went quiet for a moment. "You haven't answered my question."

"Which is?"

"You want me because you can't have me."

I leaned back, giving her the space she needed while she stewed in the silence.

I had quite a few years on her, and what that gave me was experience with people. What I'd learned was that an environment that wasn't filled with words made most people uncomfortable. So, they did things or they said things to fill the quiet gap.

"Tell me I'm wrong," she voiced.

Point proven.

This was too fun.

"Do I want you? Hell yes. Do I want you because I can't have you? Fuck no." I traced my fingers down the side of the chair. "You're the one saying I can't have you. What I'm saying is that it's just a matter of time before it happens."

She sucked in a breath. "You think I'm going to give in?"

"Yes."

"What makes you think that?"

"Instinct."

"*Instinct?*"

The range in which her voice changed was as cute as the way she was staring at me.

"Your biggest hang-up is that you're Daisy's teacher. I appreciate that it's a concern. I want my daughter to be your top priority. But I don't want her to be the only one who has you. I want an equal share."

I rubbed my hands together. "You can spend the days with her and your nights with me—while Daisy is asleep or with her mother, of course."

"She's not my biggest hang-up, Ridge. She's one of my many hang-ups."

"Same thing."

She laughed. "Not even close."

"Minor details that can easily be worked out."

"Why?" Her voice was now a whisper. "Why do you want me?"

"Why?" I repeated, a word that had haunted me since we'd met. "A very wise man told me—in a way that wasn't quite as raw as this—that I needed to open my fucking eyes and see what was right in front of me. And when I did that, when I really looked, my stare landed on you."

She twirled a piece of hair around her finger. "And I just happened to be practically naked at the time."

I got up and walked to the darkest part of the room, leaning my back against the wall. "From over here, all I can see is a faint outline and shadow of your body. I can't see your hair color. I can't see your face. I can't tell if you're curvy or tiny. I'm telling you, if we'd met this way—just like this—I would feel the same way I do right now. You know why?"

"No."

"Even in the dark, it's the way you make me feel when you look at me. What I hear in your voice when you speak to me. There's a kindness. A gentleness. A maturity. A loyalty that runs thick and deep." I returned to my seat. "But there's more—so much more. There's everything Daisy has said about you, and that's only confirmed what I already knew." I put my hand on her armrest. "I don't care that you're my daughter's teacher or that you have an issue with us meeting here or that the timing in your life is weird—or fucked up or however you put it—or any other hang-up that's making you unsettled. I just want to spend more time with you, Addison. I want to see where things can go." I lifted my hand from her armrest and rubbed my thumb across her lips. "I want to see how hard I can make you smile."

"You're wild—you know that?"

"What I am is determined. When I want something, I feel there's no reason to hold back. And you, Addison Lark, are what I want. Damn it, I can still taste you on my fucking tongue."

As soon as the last word left my mouth, she shifted in her seat. Crossing her legs and then recrossing them as though the feeling inside her body was too much to bear.

"So, if that takes me coming here to spend time with you, then I guess I'm going to become a regular."

"What if I don't want you to come here?" She sounded out of breath.

"You didn't say that to me when you left my house." I paused. "Is that what you're saying to me now?"

Her hand was suddenly on my arm. "I need this job, Ridge."

"I'm not telling you to quit." Even though I wanted to—*fuck*. But I certainly wasn't in a position to tell her to give up this job. "If anything, I'm supporting you. I'm willing to come back as many times as I can to see you. I'm paying an obscene amount of money to cover the remainder of your shift. What I'm not doing is giving you a hard time about working here."

"But—"

"Are you going to tell me that I haven't crossed your mind once today? Or when you were onstage, scanning the audience, there wasn't a tiny inkling of hope that I was in one of the seats? Because the second we connected eyes, I didn't see shock on your face. What I saw was satisfaction."

"I—"

"Don't lie to me, Addison. I'll be able to hear it."

"I thought about you," she whispered.

I chuckled. "I know."

I used her armrests to pull her chair closer, our knees now aligned. "Let me tell you what I've thought about today." I stopped to breathe her in. "I woke up this morning, wishing the lips I was licking weren't mine, but yours. That I could start with your mouth and slowly work my way down to your pussy. When I was in the shower—the hot water blasting against my skin, my hand stroking my dick—I wanted the wetness I was feeling to be from your cunt." I let that hit her. "And when my phone rang as soon as I got out, I wanted your name to be on the screen. That was only the first twenty minutes of my day, but the thoughts didn't stop there. They kept going."

"Ridge…"

"Tell me what you've thought about."

Her chest rose as she took a breath.

"The funny thing is, you don't even have to tell me. I already know. Your eyes have been giving it away since they locked with mine tonight." I held the side of her face. She didn't pull away; she pushed against my palm instead. "You're filling your head with reasons why we shouldn't when the only thing you should be focused on is why we should."

"Why we should…" she whispered.

"Yes. Why we should," I repeated. "You know these fingers"—I gently tapped them against her cheek—"are going to feel incredible when they're in your pussy. When my tongue is on your clit. When my cock is thrusting inside you, making you fucking scream."

"Never…" Her voice trailed off, and she slowly shook her head. "Never have I ever met anyone like you."

"And you won't again. That's why you shouldn't let me go, Addison. That's why you should get up from that chair and come over here."

"And do what? Dance for you?"

I let out a huff of air.

It didn't matter what I said; she would never accept that I wasn't here for that.

"No dancing," I told her. "What I want is for you to sit on my face."

"Here? No." I could hear the hesitation in her voice. "There are cameras. My manager could walk in on us. Plus, I don't want to do anything like that in this room." She swallowed, taking a second before she added, "There's you, and there's this club, and I want to keep those things separate."

"Then, leave with me. Now. Because I don't know how much longer I can wait to taste you again."

Chapter Fourteen

Addison

As Ridge kissed his way up my stomach, his lips still wet from what he'd just done between my legs, I grasped the top of his hair and waited for him to open his eyes and look at me. The shivers hadn't stopped running through me, my body so sensitive from the shuddering orgasm he'd just given me.

"You've got a serious superpower—you know that?"

The smirk that spread across his face wasn't just sexy; it was scandalous. "I have many. Which one are you referring to?"

"I told myself I was one and done, that this wasn't going to happen. No matter what you did, no matter what you said, I wouldn't change my mind. Yet I'm here, at your house, still dripping from the shower and that naughty tongue of yours, and I'm spread across your bed, knowing in a matter of minutes, I'm going to be screaming again."

He chuckled as he hovered over me, reaching for the condom he'd already placed on the nightstand and tearing off the foil corner. "I can't deny that I'm irresistible. It was a trait I was born with. But that's not why you're here."

His lips were on mine, moving them apart, his tongue filling the open space. I found myself moaning from the taste of it, from the feel of it, from the way it caused the tingles to peak.

"You're here because you want me as badly as I want you and you couldn't fight it a second more."

A swish moved from the top of my body to my toes.

It wasn't only from his touch.

But also from the truth behind his words and the way they felt as he spoke them against my mouth.

"Put this on me, Addison." He held the condom in front of me, and when I went to grab it, he added, "But use your lips."

"Is that your way of asking for a blow job without actually asking for one?"

He smiled. "I'm far from shy. If I wanted you to suck my dick, I would ask. Which is something I'd never turn down, but at this second, if I don't find myself inside of you, I might explode."

"Is that so?"

As he rolled onto his back, I placed the condom on his lower stomach and moved down his body, taking in each ripple and cord of muscle that I passed along the way. My God, this man was perfection. The scent of his earthy and salty skin, the way he tasted like warmth, the masculinity I felt every time I kissed him.

Why did it feel like I couldn't get enough?

I continued to lower, getting closer to his hard-on, but I didn't go straight there. I kissed around the entire area—the base of his stomach, the inside of his thighs. I skimmed across his sac, giving each side a gentle lick.

"Fuck me," he exhaled, his hand shooting into my hair, squeezing my locks.

He wasn't guiding me. He was simply holding on.

When my lips landed again, they were on his tip, spreading to take him in, my tongue swirling around his crown.

The truth was, giving head wasn't something I'd ever desired. I'd done it in the past. It just wasn't something I craved.

But while I lowered down Ridge's shaft and glanced up his body, I couldn't believe how beautiful he was. How turned on I was just by looking at him. How there was this pulsing need inside me to make him feel as good as his mouth had just made me feel.

I didn't know where that need came from, but as I took in as many inches as I could handle without gagging, drawing back and bobbing again, I had the strongest desire to hear him moan.

Once I achieved that sound, as it vibrated through my ears, my next goal was to watch him squirm.

So, I picked up my speed and covered the bottom of his dick with my hand—the section I wasn't able to reach with my mouth—and I worked the two together.

"Fuck," he hissed. He was holding my head with both hands, his knees now bent and his back slightly arched. "That feels so fucking good."

I suctioned my cheeks inward, using my tongue, tightening my fingers around him.

That was when he began to move with me, arching every time I took him in, moaning as I pulled away.

He was giving me everything I wanted.

Everything except his cum.

I wanted to feel it hit the back of my throat, the warmth of it as it traveled down to my stomach.

Something told me it wouldn't take much more before that happened, not if I kept up this pace.

So, I didn't let up. I kept the same pattern, taking in as much as I could hold, releasing him, repeating until I heard, "If you don't slow down, I'm going to come."

I placed my lips on his tip. "That's what I want."

He gave me a deep chuckle. "Because you don't want me to fuck you?"

"No, I want that. Trust me, I do." I licked down to his balls. "But I want this too."

"You can't have it all—at least not right now. You have to choose, Addison."

Choose?

How could I even do that?

"Sounds like I need to choose for you." He slid his dick out of my grasp, grabbed the condom off his stomach, and rolled it over his cock as he got onto his knees, positioning me at the end of the bed.

His movements were fast, like a rehearsed routine with confidence in each step.

The moment my butt was positioned near the edge, he stood in front of me, my legs surrounding him, his fingers on my pussy.

"I thought you might need my mouth again, but you're still so fucking wet." He aimed himself at my entrance. "You've been thinking about this, haven't you? The way I'm going to fuck you, the way I know just how you like to be fucked."

My teeth were on my lip. I didn't remember putting them there; they'd just gone there.

Out of need.

Or out of necessity.

"Yes."

"You haven't been able to get me out of your mind." He gently stroked in, his thumb on my clit, rubbing that spot as he dipped in further. "And the more you think about me, the wetter you get."

An overwhelming surge was shooting through me, causing the back of my head to push into the mattress, my stare no longer on him. "I haven't stopped thinking about you."

"I know." He reared back and thrust in. "Do you think about me when you go to bed, Addison?"

An image of myself was in my head. I was tucked under the covers of my bed with a vibrator in my hand, holding back my screams so

Leah couldn't hear me. I'd masturbated every single night since I'd slept with him. And during every one of those sessions, the only thing I had thought about was Ridge. So, when he'd admitted to me earlier that he touched himself in the shower, thinking of me, I'd almost died from the similarities.

"Yes," I said, dragging the word out to multiple syllables.

"Do you fantasize about what I'm doing right now—how fast I fuck you, how deep I thrust into your pussy, how hard I stroke you"— he turned his hips, hitting an upper angle—"and how I know what you want without having to ask me?" His thumb was still on my clit, but he was rubbing it in circles.

He knew me. He knew what I wanted. There was no doubt about that.

And with each bit of movement, he was causing me to build around him.

"Yes," I admitted. "But what I also think about is the way you look at me."

"You're telling me you can feel the power of my stare?"

His words were added foreplay. The combination doing something to me that I couldn't come back from.

"I can feel your eyes inside of me, Ridge." My legs bent. My hands clenched the blanket. "I can't even describe it. But that's how I knew you were at the club tonight. I felt you before I even saw you."

"Look at me, Addison." He was pumping into me even harder. "I want you to feel my stare and take it in while you're coming."

He knew every time without me even having to tell him.

I lifted my head off the mattress, and the second we connected eyes, I was screaming, "Ridge!" A blast catapulted through me, and with it brought a surge of sensations. I couldn't define them in my head; I couldn't make out their differences. It was a cocktail of pleasure, and it was all rushing through me. "Ah!" I gasped in a breath. "Fuck!"

"Hell yes, that's the sound I want to hear." The smirk returned to his lips, but this time, it ended with his teeth, where he gave his bottom lip the sexiest graze. "You just got so fucking wet." His mouth stayed parted, his eyes feral as they focused on me and, at the same time, looked right through me. "And tight—fuck—you're tight."

My shouting hadn't died down. I could barely breathe.

This feeling was just so much.

The intensity.

The way it lingered, the longer he pounded me.

And as it peaked, hanging there for several seconds, my legs caved inward, my fingers too numb to grip the comforter, so I released it, and the shudders took over.

When I began to come down, I shouted, "Ridge!" Not because I'd reached that point, but because it felt just as incredible as everything else.

"That feels good, doesn't it, baby?"

The jitters were like waves crashing against each other, slamming in the middle of the ocean without washing ashore to fizzle out. And they were everywhere—in my chest, sinking around my nipples, in my navel, on my clit, inside my pussy.

"My God," I groaned. "Are you even human?" My thighs opened around him, my hands unfolded from the fists, and I tried to find my bearings.

He chuckled. "We're going to do that again."

"Of course we are." I took a breath even though it felt impossible. "Because it's you."

"No." His voice almost sounded like a growl. "Because it's you."

His hands were suddenly underneath my lower back, lifting me off the mattress. He brought me up against his chest, and with my legs already around him, my arms circled his neck.

"You like carrying me," I whispered, remembering he'd done this last time, but this time, I had no clue where he was taking me.

"I like you."

I let out a small laugh. "I can tell."

I suddenly found myself against a wall, so he no longer had to hold my back, his hands going to my hips, where he positioned me in such a way that he could sink into me.

I cried out from my pussy still being so sensitive, but also from how good he felt.

"If you can tell I like you, then"—he rocked back and forward, my wetness making it so easy for him—"what does this tell you?"

His strokes were turning sharp, each one making me moan louder.

"That you want me," I said.

"What else?"

I was holding him so tightly with our bodies pressed together. His skin was the only thing I could smell, the heat that radiated off him enveloping me.

"That you want to come inside me."

He let out a deep, sexy exhale. "Fuck yes."

He bucked up, and I gently hit the wall.

But it didn't bother me. In fact, I loved it.

"What else, Addison?"

With each drive, I rode higher against the drywall, and as he pulled back, I lowered. The pattern caused my skin to burn from the constant rubbing and impact.

Still, I wouldn't change it.

If anything, I wanted more.

"Answer me," he demanded.

I couldn't even think at this point. "That you can't get enough of me."

"Right again."

I gripped the back of his head and connected our lips.

Because I had to.

Because I couldn't go another second without kissing him.

Because the need inside me was so strong that I found myself holding our faces together so I could get more than just a peck.

"Do you know what that just earned you?" he asked when he pulled away.

My eyes slowly opened, and I searched his face, trying to make sense of what he'd just said. "Earn me?"

There was a shift in the way he was holding me. An adjustment that sent me even harder against the wall. But it was during that minor slam that I realized what he'd meant.

The thumb he'd given to me earlier was back in my favorite spot— at the very top of my clit, grinding it in a way that had me panting, "Ridge!"

"You're going to come."

"Yes, I'm—"

"You don't have to confirm, I can already feel it."

"I want you to come with me."

"But I was going to give you a fourth orgasm. And a fifth—"

"Please," I begged. "I want to feel it. I want to see it on you." I kissed him again. "I want to taste it on you."

I didn't know where this need was coming from. Maybe it was because he'd made the choice for me earlier and he wouldn't come in my mouth. Maybe it was because seeing the vulnerability on his face the last time we'd been together was as sexy as his expression when he'd surfaced from between my legs.

But I wanted it.

And I wanted it now.

"You sound like me, Addison."

"You're a bad influence."

His laugh came from a dark, guttural place.

He gave me several more strokes, grunting after each one, his beat increasing, his power maximizing. "You're sure this is what you want?"

"Yes! Because I'm seconds—"

"I know you are, you're fucking milking me."

The moment he stopped speaking, I completely lost control.

There was nothing to hold back.

I was already gone.

The pleasure was driving straight through me, reaching every part of my body, causing the shudders to take over. "Oh! My! Fuck! Ing! God!"

"Tell me you want it." He was gripping me so tight, pounding into me so hard; I couldn't even take a breath.

And he wanted me to talk?

While shuddering?

When my entire body was on fire?

"I want it!"

A sound released from him, like a rage of emotion, mixed with ecstasy, and once it hit my ears, his thrusts began to shorten. His strength didn't lighten at all; he was still deliciously rough and perfect, only his speed lowered.

"Addison, fuck."

"*Mmm*, yes. You're giving me just what I want." I boosted myself up to his ear. "Fill me, Ridge."

I took in his face, the way his eyes and lips, even his cheeks, turned feral from my words, from his orgasm. Hunger and satisfaction began to take over his expression.

But there was something else too.

Something I couldn't quite detect, but it sent another wave of tingles through me, causing my nails to dig into his shoulders and my legs to squeeze around him. My lips to form an oval, and "Ridge," came yelling out of them.

I didn't know when we'd stilled.

I couldn't recall the details of transitioning from screaming to quiet—I was far too worked up to distinguish time.

I just knew that every pore on my body was lit, like a bolt of electricity was moving through the tiny holes, the current staying fresh and alive.

My muscles felt like they were waking up again.

The numbness was working its way out of my skin.

My eyes were open, taking in his face and the handsome cobalt gaze that was staring back at me.

I didn't know how long we had been there, focused on each other in silence.

I only knew that at some point, he asked, "Do you know how fucking good you feel?" His lips were against mine, his breath filling my mouth. "How I want to spend all night right here, inside of you, and never move?"

"Technically, you can."

He'd insisted on driving, so I'd left my car at the club. I was here until he agreed to take me back there or I called a rideshare to come and get me.

Last time, I never would have been okay with not having my car.

This time, I hadn't even put up a fight.

Which went against every promise I'd made myself, considering I wasn't even going to allow myself to kiss him.

"Does that mean you're spending the night?" he asked.

I repeated the question in my mind. I hadn't even thought of the possibility until now. But there was something I needed to know first. "When does Daisy get back?"

"My brother is dropping her off in the morning. It won't be early. He told me the two of them would be sleeping in."

I laughed. "Either your kid is a unicorn and is one of the few who actually sleeps in or your brother is going to be extremely disappointed in the morning."

"She's no unicorn—I can tell you that." He grazed my cheek, smelling it, kissing it. "Rhett knows she'll be up before dawn. He just wants to spend as much time with her as possible."

"I love that."

He continued to look at me, waiting for an answer.

"I mean," I started, "I don't have anywhere I need to be, so—"

My voice cut off when he pulled me from the wall and carried me toward his bed. It was only a few paces away, and he set me on one of the sides, pulling the comforter back and tucking me beneath it. When he was satisfied with my placement, he went into the bathroom, where I assumed he was flushing the condom. Once he returned to the bedroom, he got in on the other side of the bed and moved toward the middle, his arms circling me, pulling me against him.

My head found his chest, my hand on his lower stomach, my fingers pressing the hardness of his abs and the short, dark hairs that covered his muscles.

"This doesn't suck."

I laughed at his statement and glanced up, meeting the most beautiful smile. "No," I said, "it doesn't."

Chapter Fifteen

Ridge

Me: *Good morning, gorgeous. I missed having you in my bed last night.*

Addison: *Oh, yeah? How much did you miss me?*

Me: *You want the details? Because I can get really specific…*

Addison: *Ha! Your daughter is sitting less than 10 feet away from me. Maybe you can share those details when she's not in my line of sight.*

Me: *Deal.*

Addison: *Cute story for you: we talked about our weekends at the beginning of class, and Daisy spoke about her time with Uncle 'Ett.*

Me: *Man, I love that kid.*

Addison: *You've got a good one.*

Me: *When can I see you again?*

"Do you have a second?"

I lifted my head, looking at the doorway of my office, where Jenner Dalton, the attorney for the Cole and Spade Hotels brand, was standing with Brady.

I set my phone down, the screen facing the desk so I wouldn't be tempted to stare at it, and replied, "Yeah, come in."

They closed the door, and before the gentlemen took a seat in front of my desk, Jenner handed me a folder.

I opened it while Jenner said, "It's the permit for the Beverly Hills remodel. I just picked it up from the county."

I scanned the multiple sheets of paperwork, which confirmed everything he'd just said, and I closed the lid and set the folder on my desk. "So, all of our alterations have been approved?"

"Yes," Jenner replied. "The remodel can start immediately."

"Hold on a second," I stammered. "I thought we weren't doing the remodel of Beverly Hills until all the construction was finished at our property in Malibu?" I waited for one of them to respond, and when they didn't, I added, "You're telling me you want both properties to be under construction at the same exact time?"

"The sooner it's done, the sooner we can offer even more amenities, the sooner we can bump the rates up even higher," Brady said. "I see no reason to wait."

I pulled at my tie, loosening the knot at my throat. "We need an executive meeting. I need to see if everyone else agrees."

"You think they wouldn't?" Brady pressed. "Because I think everyone in this room knows they'll agree with me." He nodded toward me. "Including you."

I pushed back in my chair, glancing at the phone, fucking dying to know if there was a message from Addison waiting for me on the screen. If I looked at it and there was, I wouldn't be able to stop myself from responding, and the guys would lose my full attention.

"Do you know how much work that's going to be?" I barked. "As it is, I'm already spending three-quarters of each workday in Malibu. How in the hell am I going to divide my time between both properties and fight the traffic going back and forth between them?"

"Easy solution," Brady said. "Buy a helicopter."

"You're fucking kidding," I shot back.

"Hell, I bought a plane." He laughed. "Shit, I bought two for the company. Why not add a helicopter while we're at it?"

Jenner crossed his legs, his foot shaking in the air. "Now, that might not be agreed upon among the executives, but I can't lie, I'm all for it."

"Listen, man, at least you're home every night for Daisy," Brady continued. "The rest of us are traveling across the globe to be on location at our hotels. Lily and I went from Scotland to Bangkok, and we're still only half done. We've got at least a few more months in Thailand before we can move back home."

Brady and I'd had a rocky start when the Coles and Spades merged. There were many things about him I didn't like. He said what was on his mind, he gave no fucks, he found the most negative part of any conversation and highlighted it. But as I'd spent more time with him, I'd realized the good outweighed the bad.

But in this instance, I'd like to kick his ass out of my office.

"You're saying I have it easier because I'm home," I voiced a little louder than I needed to. "Is that what you're telling me?"

Brady's brows shot up. "Would you rather be away from Daisy? Because those are your two options. Stay home and deal with a remodel—or two. Or hit the road and homeschool your daughter." He leaned onto the edge of my desk. "We signed up for this. We knew precisely what we were being dealt when we began working for our families." He pounded the edge of the wood before he moved back. "You'll figure it out. I know you will. You've got it in you."

"Asshole."

Brady nodded. "I know I am."

I looked at Jenner before I dismissed them from my office. "Any other news to share, or are you only dropping one bomb on me today?"

"More news? No." Jenner crossed his arms over his chest.

"We do have a question," Brady said.

My gaze shifted between the men. "Yeah?"

"Where the hell did you disappear to the night of my bachelor and Lily's bachelorette party?" Brady inquired. "I'm assuming you met someone. That's why you took off and never came back." He smirked. "Who is she?"

"You're fucking kidding me." I sighed.

"I didn't want to ask during our last executive meeting. You know, in case you didn't want to say something in front of his wife." Brady nodded at Jenner, referring to Jo, who was one of our partners. "And since the outing, I haven't had a chance to get you alone to ask." He strummed the armrest of his chair. "So, I'm asking now."

"You think you deserve an answer?"

"Deserve? No." Brady shrugged. "Want? Yes."

"Asshole—again."

"So, are you going to tell us?" Brady asked.

I was silent for a few moments, staring at each of their grins. Damn, these motherfuckers thought they had earned themselves the world. "You're right, I did meet someone." And I couldn't think of a single reason to keep her a secret. I just wished I had more to tell.

"Nice," Jenner replied. "Who is she?"

I could see right through them, my head shaking as I said, "Don't act like you don't know."

Brady chuckled. "She was one of the strippers, wasn't she?"

"And she also happens to be Daisy's first-grade teacher," I told them.

Jenner balled his fist and put it up to his mouth. "Fuck." He paused. "I'm assuming you discovered that after the bachelor party?"

I nodded.

"Are things good?" Brady asked. "Or is that connection making things a bit messy?"

My head dropped, my stare once again falling on the back of my phone case. "A little of both, I guess. The connection doesn't bother me, but it does her. She's having a hard time separating the two gigs and where I fit in, and then there's the whole Daisy layer, and that complicates things even more."

Jenner pointed at his chest. "We've all been there, my man. In some way or another, my brothers and I have rocked every forbidden boat, and in each situation, it's worked out. Things will work out for you too."

Was that true?

I picked up my phone, unable to wait a second longer, and read the message Addison had just texted.

Addison: *Don't kill me for saying this, but how about when I finish out my job at the club? The guilt of spending time with you and spending time there—with them—is literally eating me alive, Ridge. I can't do both. I hope you can understand that.*

I put the phone down, squeezing the case in my palm, and said, "I don't know about that. Things seem to be getting more difficult by the second."

"Why is she stripping?" Brady asked.

I shook my head. "She hasn't said. I just know that when she saves the amount she needs, it'll come to an end, and that'll make things much easier on us."

"You're telling me you're going to wait that long?" Jenner asked.

"Fuck no," I replied. "But I can't force her to see me."

"You can't?" Brady tapped his hand on my desk before he stood. "Given that she's Daisy's teacher, I'd think you could put yourself in front of her anytime you fucking want."

Jenner got on his feet, and they walked to the door.

"How much are we talking?" Jenner asked with his hand on the doorknob. "Five grand? Twenty? A hundred?"

"I don't have that answer either," I told them.

"Dude, you need to start asking some goddamn questions," Brady voiced.

Jenner shifted his weight. "You know, the easiest way to fix this problem is with money. You have it. So, fix it."

Jenner's idea was something I'd thought of many times and something I wasn't opposed to. In fact, I'd tried to come up with ways to give the money to her without Addison knowing it was from me. But her pride was the only thing holding me back. She wanted to do this on her own.

Could I be patient enough to let her?

Fuck, I didn't know.

Instead of explaining that to them, I chuckled and said, "Fellas, I hear you, but I've got to take things slow. I know what I'm doing. You don't have to worry about me."

Brady looked at Jenner and then smiled at me. "We know."

They left my office, and I picked up my phone and reread Addison's last message.

Me: *Is the club off-limits too? I was thinking about going there this weekend…*

Addison: *I can't stomach how much you're spending on me.*

Me: *I can afford it. You don't have to worry about that.*

Addison: *I know… I Googled you. Let's just say, my jaw is still on the floor. Cole and Spade Hotels, Ridge? You said nothing about it to me. Why?*

Me: *You don't really talk about your time at the club. I don't discuss the inner workings of my job. It's that simple.*

Addison: *But you don't exactly have a job. You have an empire.*

Me: *I share an empire with several other people, but, yes, it is quite the undertaking.*

Addison: *Which explains why you're spending so much time in Malibu. I read that you're doing construction at that hotel, almost a full remodel, and that you're the man in charge. That's amazing— truly.*

Me: *Do you want to see it?*

Addison: *Do I want to go to the beach, my favorite place in the* *world? What kind of question is that? LOL.*

Me: *Don't tease me, Addison. I'll pick you up right now…*

Addison: *And leave your daughter with a substitute teacher? I would never. ;)*

Addison: *Hear me out. I have about two months left. Maybe less if things continue to go well. I care about you, Ridge, and what I'm doing feels so wrong. I want it to feel right. You deserve that.*

Me: *We deserve that.*

Addison: *Best answer ever.*

Chapter Sixteen

Addison

The first thing I saw when I opened my eyes wasn't the sun that was just starting to peek through the bottom of the blinds. It was the light from my phone as it vibrated on my nightstand.

Sigh.

I'd fallen asleep last night with my laptop next to me, my mail beside it. A calculator. A printed spreadsheet that was helping me keep track of everything. I traced my finger over the trackpad to check the time on my home screen and saw it was a few minutes past six. My alarm would be going off in a few minutes anyway, so rather than try to force myself back to sleep, I rubbed my eyelids, stretched my arms over my head, and reached for my cell.

Morgan: *Hi! I miss you!*

Morgan: *I can't even remember the last time I slept. Why did I decide to become a doctor again? I swear I've been at the hospital for the last 4 days straight. Or maybe it's been 5. Actually, I think it's been 6.*

Morgan: *Good Lord.*

Morgan: *I'd call you, but it's way too early. I think. Or are you* *up? I'm delirious…clearly, LOL.*

Me: *I'm up, but I need coffee before you call, or I'll literally turn into a bear.*

Me: *But hi! I miss you too! LOL!*

Morgan: *I wish we were going for coffee right now.*

Me: *You need sleep, LOL. The last thing you need right now is caffeine.*

Morgan: *Truth.*

Morgan: *So, the second payment is due next week. Just wanted to give you a heads-up in case you forgot.*

Me: *I'll have the money. I'll be sending it over, don't worry.*

Morgan: *Full-time teacher, bartending at nights. I don't know how you're making it all happen and not sleepwalking from being so tired all the time.*

Morgan: *I'm so proud of you, Addy.*

My stomach ached as I read her messages. It killed me that I couldn't tell her the truth about my second job. But if I told her what I was really doing, she'd beg me to quit. She would never ever want me to take my clothes off for money. And that would result in her not accepting a single dollar from me.

So, I kept my mouth shut and continued to lie.

Even though it hurt.

And even though I hated liars and I was going against everything I believed in.

Me: *Love you. Talk soon.*

Morgan: *XO*

I sat up a little higher, puffing the pillow behind my back, picking up the spreadsheet that I'd been going over before I fell asleep.

The numbers just weren't mathing.

All I'd wanted to do since I had been a kid was teach. I absolutely loved children. I wanted to be a part of molding their future.

But when I had been working toward that dream, I hadn't

anticipated how I was going to financially survive.

Because when I looked at the columns and rows of my expenses—the amount I needed to live on every month, plus how much it cost to put a roof over my head and have a car to drive and what I owed in bills and to my sister, I was in the negative.

Not just by a little, but by a lot.

The money I needed to send to Morgan was far more than I could afford. Without stripping, there was no way I'd be able to make the payments to her. And what I was looking at right now, how far behind I was, I would more than likely have to keep the job at the strip club for longer than I'd planned, or I'd never be able to get caught up.

Unless I hit the lottery—something I didn't even play since I didn't want to waste money on a ticket.

It was the most defeating feeling.

That even though I sacrificed, that I worked instead of partied, that I raided Leah's closet instead of buying new clothes, that I saved instead of spent, it still wasn't enough.

• • •

Ridge: *My morning view. The only thing that would make it better is if you were looking at it with me.*

I stared at the photo Ridge had sent. It showed the most breathtaking waves and the deepest, bluest water and the sandy shore that sparkled from the sun. If I closed my eyes, I'd be able to feel it. Smell it. Taste the salty sea on my tongue.

But I couldn't.

I had a class of first graders who were silently completing a reading comprehension worksheet. If they looked up and saw my eyes closed, all hell would break loose.

Me: *You're so sweet. :)*

Me: *BTW, I'm extremely jealous. Kiss the ocean for me. Tell it I miss it.*

Ridge: *You should go to the beach this weekend.*

Me: *I'm working at the club. I suppose I could go late morning, but I just have so much to do at home.*

Ridge: *You need to start making time for you, Addison.*

Me: *Are you Dad-ing me right now?*

Me: *LOL.*

Ridge: *Yes—because you need it. The beach, I mean. ;)*

Me: *You're right, I do.*

· · ·

Ridge: *Good morning. Tell me…how's my baby doing today?*

Me: *She came in full of smiles with the most adorable ponytail that I'm assuming you did, and that pink checkered skirt she has on is so freaking cute. She told me her daddy picked it out. I melted—in case you were wondering.*

Ridge: *I was asking about you.*

A rush moved through me, bringing a tightening to my chest and a grin across my lips. I couldn't even sit still in my chair, my skin tingling to the point where it felt like there was electricity zapping it.

How could a sentence that was really so simple make me feel this way?

Why was it repeating in my head, spoken in Ridge's sexy voice?

Me: *I would be a lot better if I were in that photo that you sent yesterday. My toes in the sand, my face looking up at the sun. Yes… that's what I want.*

Ridge: *And that's what I want.*

· · ·

Me: *So, there was a little accident with the pink checkered skirt. Don't murder the teacher when you see it, K?*

Ridge: *Just tell me she's okay. That's all I need to hear.*

Me: *She's absolutely fine, I promise. We were doing an art*

project with some paint, and the entire container of yellow spilled on
her lap. I scrubbed her skirt and her legs, but she's kind of a mess.

Ridge: *Sounds like she needs a spa night in Dad's jetted tub.*

Me: *With extra bubbles—do it right, Dad. ;)*

Me: *Which is only fitting, considering you have the best bathroom*
I've ever seen in my life.

Ridge: *You haven't tried out my tub yet...*

Me: *Oh, but I eyed up that big, beautiful beast, LOL.*

Ridge: *I built it for two.*

Me: *Is that so?*

Ridge: *Are you looking for an invite?*

Me: *Don't send one... I won't be able to say no.*

• • •

Car line would be the bane of my existence.

The teachers were on a rotation, so every couple of weeks throughout the school year, I would ensure the kids got into the right vehicle. It was the most exhausting part of my day. Everyone was a little more on edge at this hour—the parents rushing through the line; the kids hungry and tired, unafraid to get into any car even if it was the wrong one.

Fortunately, I only had a handful of students left. Daisy ended up being the last one, her tiny fingers tugging on my pant leg, her arm pointing at the black Range Rover that was a few cars back in line.

"That's my daddy."

Of course, I knew Ridge was approaching before Daisy even said a word. Not because of the SUV, but because of the way my body reacted when I sensed his stare on me.

A man whose eyes could make me wet.

Whose breath could make me break out in goose bumps.

Whose fingers I could feel even though they hadn't touched me in days.

Daisy's fingers clasped mine, startling me out of my thoughts, and she walked me to the edge of the sidewalk where Ridge was pulling up. The passenger window rolled down, and he looked at us through the open space from the driver's seat.

I instantly got a whiff of his cologne, my heart pounding as the scent swished inside me. But that wasn't the only thing that made me throb. He was dressed in a charcoal-colored suit with a silver tie, the knot loosened at his throat, and the first button of his starched white shirt was undone, showing a hint of his chest. An outfit that was straight-up scorching. And then there was his hair, a tad messy, like my fingers had run through it and tugged the strands, a look that was far sexier than freshly gelled hair.

My God, he was handsome.

A heat was moving across my cheeks. I couldn't stop it. I couldn't even attempt to calm it. I was suddenly sweating even though it wasn't hot outside.

There was just something so vulnerable about standing here with his daughter. It didn't feel like I was swinging naked around a pole; this felt like I was walking across a stage to get a diploma.

A side of me I was most proud of, and he was seeing it—really seeing it. Unlike when he'd come to my classroom on the first day of school and I was too shocked to appreciate he was there.

But here, with his daughter's hand clasped in mine, it was completely different.

"Daisy, are you going to properly introduce me to your teacher?" he asked.

His voice had just the right amount of grittiness to it, his smile charming and seductive, his eyes slowly dipping down my body before they met mine again, holding my stare steady.

"Miss Lark, this is Daddy. Daddy, this is Miss Lark." She giggled.

I squeezed her fingers. "Thank you for the wonderful introduction, Daisy."

He chuckled. "Miss Lark, I don't think you want to call me Daddy…" He winked. "My real name is Ridge Cole."

If my skin was flushed before, it was burning red now. "Addison." My voice wasn't much more than a whisper. "It's nice to meet you."

"And you," he said. He glanced at his daughter. "Daze, climb in. We've got work to do, kiddo. We need to get your homework done before we meet Uncle 'Ett and Aunt Rowan and Uncle Cooper and Rayner for dinner."

"Yay!" She released my hand and rushed toward the backseat, pulling at the handle to open the door, which I helped her with. "I wanna feed Rayner like Auntie Row let me do last time. The little noises she makes when she swallows is so cute, Daddy!"

I waited until Daisy was in her seat and shut the door. "You guys have fun tonight."

"Hey, Miss Lark," I heard as I began to walk away.

I glanced over my shoulder, and Ridge's gaze was not only hitting my face, but reaching beneath it and lowering to my chest. It felt as though he were wrapping his long, talented fingers around my heart, making the little breath I was holding stay frozen in my lungs.

"I loved getting the chance to see you."

• • •

Ridge: *And I fucking loved how red your cheeks just got.*
Ridge: *By the way, Addison, you look gorgeous today.*
Me: *You knew exactly what you were doing with that Daddy comment.*
Ridge: *Didn't seem like you hated it.*
Me: *You're playing with fire, Mr. Cole.*
Ridge: *Are you telling me to stop?*
Me: *No.*
Ridge: *I didn't think so.*

• • •

Ridge: *Good morning, beautiful. I'd thought I'd share my view—and, yes, I kissed the ocean for you.*

Me: *Here's my view…and, yes, that's peanut butter on Daisy's shirt. She missed her mouth when she was eating her snack, LOL.*

Me: *That beach, Ridge. I would kill to be there right now.*

Ridge: *Come to Malibu with me.*

Me: *Now? I'm working, as you know. Sigh.*

Ridge: *Not now. I'm working too. You're at the club this weekend?*

Me: *Yes.*

Ridge: *One night this week then.*

Me: *What about Daisy?*

Ridge: *If Daisy's your only concern, don't let her be. That's an easy solution.*

Me: *You know I have other concerns.*

Ridge: *And you know none of them bother me.*

Ridge: *We're just going to the beach, nothing more. Don't get inside your head about it.*

Me: *Because you know I am. LOL.*

Ridge: *Say yes, Addison.*

Ridge: *You need this. We need this.*

Me: *Okay…*

Me: *Yes.*

Chapter Seventeen

RIDGE

Addison had said yes to going on a date. Getting her to agree had been the hardest part, an obstacle I'd subtly worked on during our text exchanges over the last several days. Once I had gotten her confirmation, I had been sure everything else would fall into place.

And I was right.

While we sat on a blanket on the beach, she tucked her legs up to her chest, wrapped her arms around them, and gazed at the water. Unafraid by its vastness, unfazed by any of the surfers or people walking by. And that smile—I'd never seen anything like it.

Pure happiness.

Like nothing or no one could fuck up this moment.

Every time she took a breath, I could see the stress leaving her body. I could see the relaxation taking over. Unlike when she'd gotten in my car to drive here, there was no anxiety in her voice, no strain in her shoulders, and no tension in her inhales and exhales.

Was it the beach that had taken it all away?

Or me?

Which prompted the question, "When did you fall in love with water?"

She slowly looked at me. The sun was warming her freckles, and her hair was flying into her face from the breeze. I didn't tuck it away. Instead, I took out my phone and pulled up the camera and snapped a photo, tilting the screen toward her.

"So you can see what I see."

As she looked at the picture of herself, her smile grew—something I hadn't thought was possible.

"When?" she asked as I slipped my phone back into my pocket.

"As far back as I can remember. We didn't take a ton of vacations when I was growing up. Mostly just places we could drive to. But each of those instances revolved around water." She tucked a chunk of her hair away, and it immediately returned. "I remember my parents turning into totally different people when they were near an ocean. They'd build sandcastles with us and take us swimming. There was so much laughter and fun." She paused. "It wasn't that way at home. They both worked nonstop, and when they weren't, they were stressing about work."

"Like you were on the way over here…"

She released a long breath. "You noticed."

I put my hand on her lower back. "You might think I don't know you at all, and it's true that we just recently met, but I'm learning you, Addison. What I saw during the drive was nothing but stress."

She faced the water again, balling her body up even tighter. "You really are learning me."

"Talk to me. Tell me what's bothering you."

Her eyes closed.

While I waited for her answer, I took a drink of the rosé I'd packed for us in the cooler.

"I wish this world didn't revolve around money," she finally said, her voice soft and full of emotion. "That's what got me in this situation."

"What situation?"

She gradually turned her head to look at me. "Having to work at the strip club."

"But it's temporary." I lifted my hand to her face, moving the hair that was now clinging to her lips. "You said yourself that after a month or two, you'll be done."

"I don't know if that's true anymore."

I searched her eyes. "What changed?"

"Nothing." She mashed her lips together. "I just took a hard look at what I owe, and it's worse than I thought."

"How much are we talking, Addison?"

Her throat bobbed as she swallowed. "Do you really want to discuss this?"

"Of course I do. I wouldn't have asked if I didn't."

She rocked over the blanket, reaching for her wine and taking a long drink. "I owe my sister twenty thousand. In addition to that, I owe about one hundred twenty-five thousand in student loans, and I need no less than thirty-five hundred a month to live—and that's living modestly with little to no extras. The math doesn't math on my teaching salary." She went quiet, rubbing her hands over her knees. "The club has helped a lot, especially with the payments to my sister. I've paid her almost half. But I need to put a dent in my student loans, or I'll just continue to drown." She placed her forehead on her knees. "That's why I'm going to have to work there past the two-month mark. If I can whittle away at the one hundred twenty-five grand, I'll be in a much better situation."

My life had gone so differently. My father had paid my college tuition—I never even had to think about taking out a loan or making a payment. And as soon as I graduated, I'd walked into an executive role with a salary in the high six figures. That was nine years ago. Since then, my earnings had quadrupled—an increase I knew wasn't normal by any stretch.

That didn't mean I didn't sympathize. That I didn't fucking ache for her. That my heart didn't break to hear what she had to sacrifice just to make things work—and it sounded like they were barely working.

Not only was she someone I cared about, but she was my daughter's teacher. Her role in my life held so much meaning.

But this went deeper than only being Daisy's first-grade teacher and having debt.

"This affects us, doesn't it?" I asked.

She lifted her forehead to look at me, eventually nodding. "I can't, out of good conscience, be with you while I'm still there. That doesn't mean I want things to end. I'm not saying that at all." Her hand found mine and held on. "I just want us to go slow. Like turtle slow. And once I can kick the club to the curb, things will be a lot different for me. For us." She squeezed my fingers. "But I understand if you don't want to wait—I know I'm asking a lot. I know I'm putting restraints on something that should be growing, and that isn't fair, and it's extremely selfish, and I feel like shit about it—about all of it."

"Addison—"

"No, I have to get this out. I want you to understand." She was gazing at the ocean again. "The last time I felt this overwhelmed was when I went to my best friend, Leah, and told her about the twenty thousand and how I needed to find a way to make money quickly." She shook her head. "We literally tried to come up with every option. OnlyFans"—she laughed—"influencing, bartending, being a shot girl—Ridge, we played out every scenario. None of them could earn me what stripping would. So, I walked into that club, on the complete opposite side of town from where I taught, hoping to never run into any of my students' parents, and did what I had to do." Her teeth grazed her top lip and then her bottom one. "What I never expected—what wasn't on my bingo card—was you."

"And you wanted nothing to do with me."

She smiled, huffing out some air. "That's not true!"

"It's somewhat true."

"I was just fighting it—that's all. In my head, I still fight it. I can't help it. The whole situation just upsets me. I wish I hadn't met you there. I wish—"

"I don't wish that at all."

She scanned my eyes. "Why?"

"Because it's shown me what you're willing to do to survive." I cupped her face. "Most people wouldn't have done what you did. That takes courage and guts and balls."

Her chest rose, and she seemed to hold in the air she'd inhaled. "I'm just grateful—that's all. Grateful my parents paid for my freshman year of college and that they were even able to do that. Grateful that they worked their asses off to give my sister and me everything we needed. And still, they never missed a game I cheered in or a meet Morgan swam in. They were there, always, through everything."

She turned her body toward me, and my hand fell from her cheek.

"Is that why you're paying your sister?" I asked, trying to piece this all together since it was a detail she'd left out. "Are you doing something for your parents?"

"Their thirtieth wedding anniversary is this Christmas. When I asked them what they were doing to celebrate, my father said they were going out to dinner and buying a new couch. A couch, Ridge. Because they've had the same one since we were kids." She untucked her legs and crossed them in front of her.

"I told Morgan, and she said she was going to book them a vacation. She started sending me options to get my opinion on where I thought they'd enjoy going, and we decided a cruise would be the best thing for them. That way, they could see multiple places, and all the food and drinks would be included—something I know they wouldn't splurge on, and they'd probably skip meals just to save money." She took another drink.

"I couldn't stomach the thought of Morgan picking up the entire bill. It's not right, not when my parents have done so much for me, so I'm splitting the cost with her."

I wrapped my hand around the back of her neck. "The twenty thousand is your half?"

"Yes, half of the airfare and the twenty-one-day cruise through the Mediterranean. A trip they would never take because they wouldn't spend that kind of money. And, yes, I'm stripping off my clothes and showing my boobs so my parents can have the most monumental anniversary celebration that they'll remember for the rest of their lives. Being able to do this for them means everything to me, and, damn it, they deserve it."

Whatever I had previously thought about Addison didn't even compare to the feelings I had now.

She was doing all of this for her parents, just to show her appreciation, giving them something they would never do for themselves. She wasn't just stripping. She was working two jobs, she was putting herself in even more debt, she was pausing a relationship—all for them.

She was the most selfless, thoughtful woman I'd ever met in my life.

I didn't care what I had to do, how long I had to wait; she was going to be mine.

"Come here..."

Her brows rose. "What?"

I held out my arms. "Come here right now."

Emotion instantly filled her eyes before she collapsed against my chest. I locked her within my arms, breathing into the top of her head, pressing my lips on her hair.

"You're incredible—I hope you know that. I hope you feel that in your heart. Not just as a daughter, but as a person. For what you're doing, for what you're sacrificing—"

"I'd do anything for them." She gripped my waist with both arms. "Shit, I was even going to show my feet on OnlyFans. It's just too bad that didn't work out, it would have been a lot easier than doing weekends at the club."

I chuckled. "You wouldn't have met me."

She unraveled to connect eyes with me. "Feet aren't your thing, huh?" She smiled.

"Yours are beautiful—but, no, they're certainly not my thing." I rubbed my nose against hers. "Do you know what is?"

"I have many guesses."

"Like?"

Her arms lifted to my shoulders. "My chest."

I pecked her cheek. "Solid guess, and, yes, that's my thing, but it wasn't what I was thinking."

"My ass?"

"*Mmm*," I moaned against her neck. "Yes, that too. But guess again."

"My legs?"

I hovered my lips over hers and whispered, "Your lips," before I kissed her.

Chapter Eighteen

ADDISON

As soon as Ridge pulled back from our kiss, my hands immediately went to my mouth, touching different spots on my lips.

Why did that embrace feel so unlike all the others we'd had before?

I hadn't expected him to kiss me. Not after I told him I needed to extend my time at the club. I was positive that was only going to upset him, and he was going to tell me this wasn't going to work or that I was unwilling to commit or I was just prolonging the inevitable for reasons he didn't care about.

That hadn't been the case at all.

He'd opened his arms and hugged me.

Which was what I needed more than anything. Because there were moments—and they happened nonstop—where I doubted my ability to keep going despite how badly I wanted to do this for my parents. And now that I'd given my sister around ten thousand and I was halfway there, my student loans felt like an endless mountain that I would never be able to dent.

But as Ridge's hand went to my face, stroking my cheek, I didn't feel that way. For the first time in a long time, I felt hope.

"Thank you," I whispered.

"For what?"

I stole a quick glance at the sky as though my heart had spilled out on the clouds. "For not running. For understanding. For accepting my decisions and not judging me for them."

"Addison, I haven't been in your shoes. I have no idea what it feels like to tackle what you've taken on. I admire you for it. And I commend you for doing it all on your own and not asking for help or quitting, which many others would have done too." He fanned his hand over my cheek and handed me my wine.

"Quitting isn't in my blood." I gave him a small smile. "I'll get there. We'll get there. It's just going to take a little time."

I took a long drink and popped a piece of cheese into my mouth. He'd brought an entire charcuterie board, and this was the first thing I'd eaten since we'd sat down.

When we'd arrived at the beach, my stomach couldn't handle even the thought of food, and I barely tasted the wine. The stress had been that thick. I didn't know where all that tension and anxiety had gone. It couldn't have just been the view that made it leave my body. Because it didn't matter what environment I was in; I couldn't forget that I still had an endless amount of responsibility on my plate and my schedule wouldn't be lightening anytime soon.

If tonight had shown me anything, it was that I'd never felt more accepted in my life.

Ridge was the man for me.

And suddenly, everything felt different.

Yet not a single thing between us had changed.

I clasped the back of his hand, pushing it harder against my face, nuzzling his palm. "You know, it's funny. I find myself looking at Daisy while she's in my class, comparing all the characteristics she's inherited from you." My thumb went to his eyebrows and the corners of his eyes, where little lines were permanently etched. "She has your eyes." My gaze lowered. "And your lips and your smile." My fingers went to his chest. "And your heart."

"And my nose—poor thing. She got cursed with the Cole beak." He laughed.

"You have a great nose—don't say that." I ran my finger down the slope of it.

"Narrow, but long, unlike her mother's button nose, which would have been much more fitting on my daughter."

"I haven't met Mom yet. I'm sure she's gorgeous."

I didn't want to admit that I'd looked her up, and she was, in fact, extremely gorgeous. She also couldn't have been more opposite than me. She had long black hair and a boho style with a full sleeve of tattoos. Her account showed her on location, doing makeup for celebrities, their faces once she was done with them, and pictures of her and Daisy weaved in between.

The way Daisy looked at her mom in those photos, I could tell how much love was between them.

"She's an incredible mother," he replied.

I let out a small laugh. "I see what you did there."

He grinned. "I'm not going to comment on my ex's looks—any man would know that wouldn't be a smart move."

"She's not just your ex, Ridge. She's Daisy's mom. That makes her more important than anyone. I want you to know I get that." I switched up my position and got on my knees. "I've taught lots of kids who come from broken families, and I've had to navigate those dynamics. I think that's prepped me to put any kind of jealousy aside." I wasn't sure that had come out right, so I added, "What I'm trying to say is that if you tell me things are over between you and Jana, then I believe you. Saying your daughter's mother is beautiful isn't going to make me go wild on you...if that's what you're afraid of."

He scanned my eyes several times. "You're the oldest twenty-four-year-old I've ever met. I certainly didn't have your maturity at your age." He rolled up a piece of prosciutto and fed it to me before taking a slice for himself. "Hell, Jana was almost pregnant then, and I didn't know what the hell I was doing. We were both going so fast, personally and professionally, it's all a blur. But I remember being a cocky punk who was positive he knew everything."

"I can't even envision that side of you." I swallowed the meat he'd given me. "Can I ask you a weird question?"

"Sure."

"Was Daisy planned?"

"No." He shook his head. "She was the surprise of a lifetime. An amazing surprise, but a surprise I was not ready for." He took a drink. "Jana was in the beginning stages of her career, traveling the world, and she was reckless about taking her birth control. Not on purpose, just, you know, being young and dumb." He took another bite of the meat. "We knew the risk, we just didn't think it would happen—at least I didn't." He smiled. "And then it did, and, fuck, it rocked everything."

"Look what you ended up with." I could feel my eyes sparkling as I thought about her. "She's so perfect. And not just the cutest kid ever, but she's kind. Patient. She's thoughtful and considerate, and she's so sweet to the other kids in class."

He traced his thumb over my lips. "Can I tell you how hot it is that you love my daughter?"

"I think I have a bit of an advantage because I get to spend so much time with her. I probably know her better than I know you." I winked.

"We're going to change that."

"Yeah? When we're going at turtle speed?" I tapped his chest. "Because that'll be very impressive."

"Trust me."

He gave me a slow kiss that was more breath than tongue.

It was like he wanted to fill me with his air, and he wanted me to hold it in.

So, I did.

"Come on," he said when he pulled away. "Let's go for a walk."

He helped me to my feet, and I glanced down at the setup he'd made for us—the cooler that sat on the corner of the blanket, the bottle of wine and glasses.

"What about all of this?"

"It'll be fine. We won't be gone long."

He clasped my hand, and we headed toward the water. When we reached the wet sand, the muddy substance sticking between my bare toes—a feeling I loved—we continued in a straight path, hugging the ocean's edge.

"I need to spend more time here," I admitted. "I don't know why I don't make it as often as I'd like—if it's fighting the traffic that stops me from coming or unsuccessfully squeezing in the time. But whenever I'm here, I say to myself, I'm coming back in a few days."

"And then you don't." He released my hand and put his arm over my shoulders.

"Nope. I don't."

He pointed at a crane that was diving into the water for a fish. "Daisy loves it here, too, and I always have these plans to take her, and they fall through, and she ends up in the pool instead. If I didn't work here, I think I'd forget how pretty it is."

"Speaking of work, are you going to show me the hotel?"

"Not tonight." He kissed the side of my head—a gesture so sweet that I couldn't hide my smile. "We'll save that for another visit."

"Because?" I glanced up at him, clasping the fingers that hung over my shoulder. "I'm just curious—that's all."

"I don't want to take you away from the sand." He pulled our bodies closer together. "The hotel isn't going anywhere. We need this far more than we need that."

"But I do want to see it."

"You will. I promise." He tightened his fingers around mine. "I want to admit something to you."

"Okay…" I said with hesitation.

"I told my family about you." His smile was growing. "And my partners."

I didn't know why that admission made me giddy. I'd just talked to him about the pace of our relationship, and if we were going as slow as I'd said, it seemed that conversation with his family and partners was a bit premature.

I needed to tell that to my stomach because it was exploding with bursts of excitement.

"What did you say?" I asked.

"Well, they all noticed that I'd disappeared from the bachelor and bachelorette party, so that was where the questions started, and it led me to tell them about you." He moved his lips to my ear after he kissed my lobe. "And how once I convince you that your hang-ups aren't really a thing—that they bother you, but they don't bother me— then I'm going to convince you to date me."

I wasn't sure I was ready for this answer, but I still had to ask, "Was your family bothered that I'm a stripper?"

"Not at all. You have nothing to worry about there."

I stopped walking, putting my back to the water as I looked at him.

"And you're really unbothered by the club?" I waited. "You've said that to me before, but I want to know if it's still true." I paused again. "Be honest, Ridge."

His arm had fallen from my shoulders, his hands now holding my waist. "The truth is…until you're mine, I don't think it matters what my opinion is."

I tried to see through his eyes, like he was able to do to mine. "What does that mean?"

"It means I'm not going to weigh in. I know how badly you need this job."

"You just gave me your answer without giving me your answer."

"Addison…" he whispered. He cupped my face, tilting it up toward him. "The last time I was at the club, the bartender told me that, soon, you'll be the most popular woman there." His gaze intensified. "That made me think that men would come just to see you and spend time with you and shower you with their money."

"You mean…like you?" I was teasing, but it probably wasn't the right time for a comment like that.

"They want to get you alone so they can put their hands all over your body." His fingers turned stronger, and he moved his face closer. "Do I like the thought of that? No. Not even a little bit. Can I tolerate it?" He took a deep breath. "Yes." He exhaled the air he'd just inhaled. "At this moment, I can—because I know why you're there and what you need from that club and that there's an end in sight. But if you want me to be completely honest, it's not what I want. I don't want to share you—visually, financially—nor do I want you to give your time to someone other than me. I want those hours, Addison. I want you to spend them with me." He stretched out his fingers, some going beneath my chin, others reaching toward my ears.

"But what I won't do is make you choose. I'll never put you in that position. I wouldn't want an ultimatum, and I won't give you one. So, I'll deal with this until it's over, and that's when I'll get everything I want." He gave me a light kiss. "I get you."

"I don't deserve you."

"I don't deserve you." He kissed the middle of my forehead and the bridge of my nose. "When you're ready, I'll be here." He glanced down at my lips. "And it'll just be us and Daisy, and the club will be a long, distant memory."

Chapter Nineteen

RIDGE

Addison: *I can't believe we stayed at the beach until midnight. I hope you know I had the best time. In fact, I haven't had a moment like that—one as special as you made it—in a long time.*

Me: *That means we need to do it again.*

Me: *Next week, same time, same place?*

Addison: *YES.*

Addison: *But will your mom be okay with watching Daisy again? I feel bad…*

Me: *My mom begs me every day to give my nanny a day off so she can watch my daughter until I get home from work. She asks for her every weekend, and Rhett does too. Don't feel bad. She has the best time at Grandma's house and her uncle's place. She'd probably rather be there than home because neither of them ever tells her no.*

Me: *Besides, Daddy needs some time for himself…*

Addison: *DADDY!*

Addison: *OMG, I'm dying.*

Me: *LOL. Jana is back in town next week, so she'll have Daisy when we go to the beach. Grandma or Uncle Rhett won't even be needed.*

Addison: *Does that mean Jana will be coming to the parent-teacher conference?*

Me: *Yes, she rearranged her schedule so she could make it.*

Addison: *Does she know? About us, I mean.*

Addison: *I'm only asking because I need to prepare myself for what I could possibly be walking into.*

Me: *I didn't think I should tell her until things between us turned more serious. I'm just trying to respect your timeframe and speed. I don't want you to take any of that the wrong way, Addison. I should have called you and explained this over the phone instead of texting it.*

Addison: *It wasn't a trap, Ridge, don't worry. ;) I get it, and I fully support your decision.*

Me: *You sure? I'm not trying to hide it—or hide you. Trust me, that's not the case at all. But given that you're Daisy's teacher, I want to tread a little lightly with Jana. I just don't know how she's going to react.*

Addison: *I know how this works, remember? I've seen a lot of it, minus the me-involved part—that's definitely new. Jana is going to want to protect Daisy at all costs. She's Mama Bear—at least, that's the case in most situations. Let's go super slow and gentle with her.*

Addison: *I'm just throwing this out there, but if we have to wait until the end of the school year to tell her, I'm okay with that. I swear. I don't want Jana to be an obstacle or for her to have to worry about anything at all. We have enough obstacles as it is, ya know? But I also don't want to lie to her. She deserves the truth.*

Addison: *Man, this is wicked hard.*

Me: *I wish you were in front of me right now.*

Addison: *Why?*

Me: *So I could tell you how amazing you are and then fucking devour you.*

Addison: *<3*

. . .

Me: *We're not waiting until the end of the school year. I'll figure out the Jana part when the time is right.*

Addison: *If the right time doesn't come until summer break, I'm just saying I understand.*

Me: *I love that about you.*

. . .

Addison: *Do you know what I love about you?*

Me: *Tell me.*

Addison: *I've been thinking about this since the beach. Because you shared a bottle of rosé with me there, and that wasn't the first time you'd done that.*

Me: *That's what you love about me? That I'll drink your wine?*

Addison: *That it's not the kind of wine you'd probably choose and it's not even close to your fave drink. But you sacrifice to make me happy, and that's beyond sweet of you. So, yes, I love that. It's an extremely sexy trait.*

Me: *Keep going…*

Addison: *I also love the picnic you made for us. The blanket, the food. It was perfect. You didn't just bring me there. You thought it all out, you planned. You made it special.*

Me: *When time is limited, every second counts.*

Addison: *Not everyone understands that. I LOVE that you do.*

. . .

Me: *For some reason, I'm looking at the beach a little differently this morning.*

Addison: *Are you standing on the back patio of the hotel?*

Me: *Yes.*

Addison: *Look to your right, about fifteen feet, halfway between the lounge chairs and the water.*

Me: *All right, I'm standing here now. Tell me why this spot is so special.*

Addison: *We stopped there on the way back to the blanket, and you kissed me. I'd never been kissed like that before.*

Me: *Addison…for real?*

Addison: *It's true. You've kissed me a ton of times, obviously, but never like that.*

Me: *What made it so different?*

Addison: *The way you held me, the way you positioned my lips. The only air I was taking in was yours. You were all I could feel. On me. In me. My body was on fire, Ridge.*

Me: *Do I have to wait until next week to do it again?*

Addison: *I mean, I get thirty minutes for lunch every day. That's about the only free time I have until the weekend—where you know I'm working at the club both nights.*

Me: *What time is your lunch?*

Addison: *11:45*

Me: *I'll be there.*

Addison: *You're kidding?*

Me: *Do you really think I'd kid about something like that?*

Addison: *Ha! No…*

Me: *I'll text you when I arrive.*

Addison: *You'd really come all the way here from Malibu just for a kiss?*

Me: *I'd go anywhere to be able to kiss you.*

• • •

Me: *I'm here.*

Addison: *Head around to the back of the building to the teachers' parking lot. We have less of a chance of being seen there. I'll be waiting outside.*

. . .

"Hi," Addison said as she climbed into my front seat. Her skin was already flushed, her teeth taking hold of her bottom lip and not letting it go.

Strands of her auburn hair hung close to the sides of her face, several of the curls threatening the corners of her eyes and lips. Her neckline was open, a gold necklace hanging in the center with an *A* charm. A jean jacket covered her arms, and the rest of her body was hidden beneath a dress that didn't hug her curves, but didn't mask them either.

"You look so fucking gorgeous right now." My eyes took their time rising to hers.

"Well, I'm kinda speechless over what you have on."

"Work attire. That's all it is."

"If I worked with you and I got to look at that all day"—she shook her head, her teeth back on her lip—"I'd get nothing done."

I chuckled. "You like the red?" I fingered the bottom of my tie.

"It's your color. More so than the navy, which I originally thought was the best color on you and nothing could look better. Until I saw this." She nodded toward my chest. "Red it is—and it's hot as fuck."

"When I put it on this morning, it reminded me of your hair." I reached toward a chunk of her strands hanging over her shoulder and gently ran my fingers through them. "I guess I was missing you."

She turned her face, giving an angle that was more of her profile. "What were you thinking about?"

"How I wished I had woken up next to you. Taken a shower with you. I wanted you in my closet, so I could watch you get dressed." I clasped the back of her neck, her hair falling over the sleeve of my suit jacket. "I wanted to bring you your first cup of coffee and see you take a sip."

"Your words are like porn."

I laughed. "I'm verbally romantic, huh?"

"But here's what I've learned about you: You're not just talking to hear yourself speak. You mean every one of those words."

I nodded. "I do." I smiled. "And you thought you knew more about my daughter than me."

"I'm getting more. Piece by piece."

"I need you to tell me something…"

She took a deep breath. "Okay."

"When I do this"—I leaned in until only about an inch separated us and aligned our mouths—"what does it mean to you."

"The closeness… I'm assuming it's because you want to smell me."

I slid my hand to her cheek, holding her steady. "I did that the second you got into my car."

"You want to feel me."

"Go deeper, Addison."

"Taste me."

"And when I do this"—I ran my thumb across both lips—"what am I doing it for?"

"You're memorizing me."

"I know the feel of you. Try again."

"You're prepping me."

I huffed. "I'm prepping *me*. Touching you is as powerful as foreplay."

She let out a small moan. "Every second you make me wait is torture."

"I know."

"Ridge…" She was gazing from my right eye to my left. "Kiss me. Please."

I tilted her face back, pressing my thumb against the side of her mouth, inventorying every crevice of her lips, the soft skin that was coated with a layer of gloss, the whiteness of her teeth hinting from behind.

"You have no idea what you do to me," I told her.

Her hand went to the back of mine. "If you think you're the only one feeling *this*...you're wrong."

I kissed the side of her face that I wasn't gripping, the edge of her ear, the middle of her cheek, the corner of her mouth, and when I centered myself in front of her, I didn't slam our lips together.

Even though the hunger was tearing through me.

Even though my hard-on was fucking raging.

I carefully locked us together, breathing her in as my tongue slipped through her parted lips, and when my lungs were filled with her, I exhaled.

I didn't pull away.

I didn't release her face to caress other parts of her body.

I did what I'd promised.

I gave her a kiss she'd never forget.

• • •

Addison: *WOW. Wow...*

Addison: *Ridge, I can still feel you. On my lips. On every inch of my body. What did your lips do to me?*

Me: *They just kissed you.*

Addison: *But that wasn't just a kiss. That was... I don't even know what that was.*

Me: *Should I warn you?*

Addison: *About what?*

Me: *That if you fall in love with me, it'll only get better.*

Addison: *I don't know how it can get better than that...*

• • •

Me: *Good morning…*

Addison: *Hi! I slept like the dead last night.*

Me: *I'm jealous. No one got any sleep over here last night. Heads-up, Little Miss is extra spicy today.*

Addison: *I turned her attitude right around, and she's all smiles now. Are you doing all right?*

Me: *Now that I'm talking to you…yes.*

Addison: *I dreamed about your lips.*

Me: *Where were they?*

Addison: *Everywhere.*

Me: *You'd better have been screaming when they left your body.*

Addison: *More word porn. Are you trying to kill me?*

Me: *I enjoy getting you wet. I can't help it.*

• • •

Me: *You're at the club tonight, aren't you?*

Addison: *Yep.*

Me: *I had all intentions of going. Rhett was going to take Daisy, but I just found out that she'd invited the neighbor's daughter over for a slumber party. My kid, the fucking neighborhood party planner.*

Me: *I'll be painting nails tonight…in case you need a visual.*

Addison: *I'm melting. Seriously.*

Addison: *You can come visit tomorrow night.*

Me: *We're headed to the hockey game to meet with some clients. One of them is on the team, and after the game, I'm positive they're going to want to go out.*

Addison: *I'm obsessed with your life. That sounds so fun!*

Me: *It would be better if I could come see you.*

Addison: *We have our beach date. That I'm literally counting down the seconds for.*

Me: *Will you text me when you get home tonight?*

Addison: *Is this a DADDY thing?*

Me: *LOL. No, it's a Ridge thing. I want to make sure my girl gets home safely because I'm not there to drive you.*

Addison: *Melting. Again.*

• • •

Addison: *Home. <3*

Me: *Was it a good night?*

Addison: *I missed you…*

Me: *Think about me in your dreams.*

Addison: *xo*

Chapter Twenty

Addison

For the briefest of moments, I looked down at the sandy beach, where my hand was linked with Ridge's. I felt the heat from his skin, the protectiveness from his grip. I saw the masculinity in the size of his palm and the length of his fingers and the dusting of hair by his wrist.

And while I stared at it—at us, bound—I found myself clenching him.

There wasn't a blanket beneath us this time. There had been earlier, but we'd moved locations since we'd arrived, and we now sat on the wet sand, where the water was lapping our bare feet.

But the water went further than just our toes. It covered our hands during each wave. Our forearms. It went past our butts, the coldness of the Pacific making us laugh as the salt fizzled behind us.

No words, just sounds and senses.

As I lifted my eyes to his face, every thought began to pour through my head.

How did I get this man?

How did I end up here?

Why is he so into me?

Will he wait?

My heart told me he would. Especially by the way it was slamming in a constant rhythm inside my chest.

By the look on his face, he seemed as content as I was.

As happy.

He was falling in love with Malibu.

The shore and ocean.

Because of me.

But there was something so evident in my thoughts, so pressing, and I wondered if he realized it too.

It was that it didn't matter where I was. It could be the beach, the club, Ridge's house. What mattered was that I was with him.

He was the link.

The bond.

Not the water or the shore or the sand or the salty smell.

Ridge…was everything.

He slowly turned his head and looked at me. His eyelids narrowed the longer the silence pulsed between us, his lips pulling wide.

That smile. *My God.* How could something trigger so many thoughts and emotions and tingles at once?

He nodded as though he could hear everything in my mind and then said, "I know, baby. I know…" He allowed a few seconds to pass—while my world rocked because he really did seem to understand what I was thinking—before he broke the quietness again. "Do you see it?"

I shook my head. I was far too focused on him, on the explosion within my brain to see anything else.

He unclasped our hands and put his arm around my shoulders, pulling me against his side. "Look." He used his free hand to point in the distance.

I followed his finger and immediately knew what he was referring to. While I'd been staring at him, the sky that was just above the water had begun to lighten from the sun, turning a deep copper and gold and bright yellow—colors that were almost ombré as they lifted toward the center sky, which was now baby blue. And in the middle, the rays were starting to shoot across the blue. Those rays moved gradually as the sun lifted from the horizon, the brightness casting sparkles across the indigo water and deepening each of the hues as it rose higher.

"It's so beautiful," I whispered.

"Our first sunrise."

It hadn't hit me until then.

That we'd watched the sunset many hours ago, and now, it was rising.

That we'd been here all this time.

That pretty soon, we'd have to go to work.

"I can't believe we've been here all night." My voice was still soft, as if I didn't want to disrupt the sky. "And we need to leave so we won't be late to work. It's going to be a long day without any sleep."

"But worth it."

When I glanced at him again, his eyes were on me, his fingers diving into my hair, his thumb stroking my cheek.

"Twelve hours," he said. "That's how long we've been here."

"It feels like we just arrived."

He smiled. "All of those hours of you getting more of me. You must almost be an expert at this point." He winked.

"You certainly are. You're in my head—and I don't know how you got in there or how to get you out."

"A place I'm enjoying very much." He pulled me closer, our faces almost touching. "And to think, I kept you clothed this whole time and never once did I get you naked."

I laughed. "Let's not downplay the naked times. I love those just as much." I leaned into his face and kissed him. "But tonight—this, us—was the most special."

Chapter Twenty-One

RIDGE

"I need a status update on each of the properties you're all working on," Jo said, glancing around the conference room table at the faces of our executive team. "Brady, why don't you start?"

Brady kicked back in his chair and crossed his arms behind his head. "Things are going well in Bangkok. Lily and I are only home for a couple more days before we return to Thailand. I'll be able to give you a more detailed analysis when we get back since I'm expecting the crew to have moved mountains while we've been gone." He smiled. "Wait until you see the hotel, you guys. It's fucking sick."

"Are you on track to hit the completion date?" Jo asked him.

Brady nodded. "We should be good."

Jo jotted some notes on her pad of paper and addressed Macon. "Now that Kauai is finished, are you scouting for another property?"

"I'm always on the hunt," Macon replied. "I've got a few locations brewing."

Jo looked at Cooper. "Tell me about Lake Louise and downtown Banff."

Cooper whistled out some air. "We're in the thick of it—aren't we, baby?" he said to Rowan.

"God, we are," Rowan sighed.

"We're about halfway there, maybe," Cooper continued. "Or *technically*, I guess you could say. But there's still a long way to go. I've been riding the hell out of the contractor to try to speed things up. We're behind, but hopefully, we'll get caught up."

"Jesus," I said, shaking my head. "That was a visual I did not want."

Cooper flipped me off. "I didn't mean it *that* way."

"Of course you didn't." I laughed at him and reached into my pocket, grabbing my phone, which was vibrating.

Addison: *Sitting in class, dreaming about YOU and the beach… but mostly you.*

Me: *What do those dreams look like? Are you naked in them?*

"Ridge?"

"Huh?" I glanced up, realizing Jo, along with everyone else, was looking at me. "Yeah?"

"Do you want to give us a status update on the Malibu and Beverly Hills hotels?"

Brady tapped his thumb on the table. "No, he'd rather fixate on his girl. I'm assuming that's who you were texting since you were looking like a dreamy-eyed chick the whole time."

I set my phone down with the screen facing the wood. "It's none of your business who I was texting."

"Which means that's exactly who he was texting," Macon teased.

"I think we need a status update on the teacher," Brady added. "Let's start there. We can get to Malibu and Beverly Hills after."

I shook my head, running my hand over the top of it. "You fools aren't getting anything out of me."

Cooper looked at Rowan and smiled, adjusting his tie before he said, "That's because things are getting serious between you two, aren't they?"

"Things aren't getting serious," I told them. "At least not in the way I want them to. But I'm working on it."

"You caved," Rhett said, slapping his hand on the table. "It only took you a fucking second, and you're already talking about her."

I laughed. "I barely said anything."

"But you said something," Rhett shot back. "And these fucking vultures will eat up even the smallest morsel, which you just gave them."

"Vultures? That's the best you've got?" Brady barked. "Because this group—minus Rowan and Jo—is far worse than a bird of prey, you motherfucker." He looked at me. "Why aren't things serious yet? I thought you would have locked her down by now."

I glanced at my brother, who was rolling his eyes at me. "We have some logistics we need to work out first," I voiced to the group, "and then we should be good."

"You're telling me she hasn't quit the strip club yet?" Cooper asked. "Is that still the issue?"

Nothing was a secret within this crew. Once a brother or sister or cousin found out something, shit spread like goddamn wildfire.

I shook my head. "She'll be quitting soon. In the meantime, we've been spending more time together, and things are certainly progressing in the right direction."

"Has Jana met her?" Macon asked.

"She will tonight." I gripped the edge of the table. "We have a parent-teacher conference at school."

"You mean, the two of you have a meeting with just Addison," Rhett clarified. "Am I right?"

"Yes," I replied. "It'll just be the three of us."

Rowan's back shot up straight. "Wait, you're not going to introduce Addison as your girlfriend during the meeting...are you?"

"Shit no," I huffed. "I'm not going to say a fucking word to Jana about what's happening between Addison and me. I'm just saying, the two women are going to meet. That's step one." I swiveled in the chair. "Addison suggested that maybe we should wait until the end of the school year to tell Jana or even during the summer—you know, so we don't rock the boat."

"Do you want to know what I think of that?" Rowan asked.

I laughed. "I'm sure I know, but go ahead." I nodded toward her. "Hit me with it."

"I hate that idea," my sister said.

"Me too," Jo agreed.

"Honestly, I do too," I said. "I'll have the conversation with Jana once things are sealed between Addison and me."

"Which means it'll be happening very soon," Rhett said.

"Probably," I voiced.

"Now, it's my turn to be honest with you," Brady said, leaning his arms on the table. "Hear me out. I'm glad it's you needing to have that conversation and not me." He smiled.

"Why?" I pressed.

"Because it's going to suck. And I don't envy you one bit."

• • •

Addison: *I wasn't naked in those dreams…but I can be in the future.*

Addison: *Shit, now, you've got my brain going a million miles per hour, thinking ALL the things.*

Me: *You're fantasizing about my tongue, aren't you?*

Addison: *Yes.*

Me: *And my fingers…*

Addison: *Staaaap. I'm staring at your daughter while she's finishing a worksheet, and I need to scrub my brain with bleach.*

Me: *LOL.*

Me: *Listen, about tonight.*

Addison: *Yeah, we need to talk about that.*

Addison: *I don't know why, but I'm nervous. Tell me not to be nervous.*

Me: *Don't be nervous. As far as Jana is concerned, we're just two parents coming in to discuss our daughter with her teacher.*

Addison: *I like that plan. My stomach also likes that plan. Not the time or place to address anything other than Daisy's progress.*

Me: *Agreed.*

Addison: *Then, I'll see you tonight?*

Me: *Do me a favor and don't look too sexy. I don't want to be tempted to reach under the table and finger you during our meeting.*

Addison: *RIDGE!*

Me: *I'm just warning you.*

• • •

Addison tucked a chunk of hair behind her ear, revealing a thick gold loop and a cuff around the top of her cartilage. An ear I was fucking dreaming about kissing as Jana and I sat on the other side of the table as her. Addison's hands were clasped on top of a folder that she'd opened several times during our meeting, showing us different sheets of paper that she'd specifically prepared on Daisy. Every time she spoke, I was more focused on her lips than the words coming out of them. She'd bitten off most of her gloss, her teeth repeatedly finding some part of her lip to chew during the fifteen or so minutes we'd been in here.

She was hiding her nerves well, but I could feel them.

Only because I could feel her.

"We've gone over Daisy's reading skills, her listening and comprehension," Addison said, her hands now beneath the table. "We've discussed the curriculum we've covered so far in math, social studies, and science. In addition to her overall behavior within the classroom, the hallway, lunchroom, and recess." She looked from Jana to me and back to Jana. "Now, it's time for you to ask me any questions. I'm happy to answer anything." Her teeth resumed their chewing, this time targeting the corner of her top lip.

Jana glanced at me and then said, "Admittedly, I've been working out of state since Daisy started school, but Ridge has mentioned to me that he's extremely impressed with what he's seen from her so far, along with the homework you've assigned and how much stronger she's gotten in reading in such a short time."

"I appreciate that." Addison smiled. "She's one of the most enjoyable students I have in my class."

Daisy's progress was something Jana and I discussed often. I had no doubt it was due to Addison being a rock-star teacher. And even though my attention had faded in and out during this conversation, one thing was certain: Addison's presentation had been impressive as hell.

"Not to get personal," Jana said to her, "and maybe Daisy has brought this up during class—I don't know—but Ridge and I are co-parenting our daughter in separate homes. With all the back and forth, I just want to make sure we're doing everything we can to further her education." Jana pushed down on the top of her floppy hat and then ran her hand down her bare arm as though she were trying to warm herself up.

At one point, I would have done that for her, the heat of my hands always changing the temperature of her skin.

I wasn't missing that role. I was acknowledging how much had changed because, now, it was Addison's skin that I craved.

"Are there any books you suggest we read?" Jana continued. "Ones that could guide us on how to navigate our situation? I would love some tips on how to successfully balance home life and education when a child is just starting school and bouncing between Mom's house and Dad's house."

"We don't want Daisy to feel affected in any way," I offered. "And so far, I think we've done a great job with the transition between our two homes. But school is an obstacle we don't know much about, and we just want to make sure she continues to excel."

"Of course." Addison nodded. "For what it's worth, there are other students in my class who are in a similar situation as Daisy—and I'm only saying that so you don't feel like you're the only ones. I'm happy to provide a list of books that I think could help. Books that I've read so I feel comfortable passing them along, given their gentle but effective approach. I'll be sure to email you that list by the morning." Addison moved her hands back up to the table, playing with one of the rings on her finger. "I do want to say, Daisy is one of the most grounded students I have. I can tell she had an extremely strong foundation coming in, and she's already performing in the top percentage of the class—socially and academically."

"She's been a social butterfly from the moment she could speak, hasn't she?" Jana said to me. "We certainly know who she got that from." She eyed me with a grin.

I chuckled. "It wasn't from me."

While I stared at Jana, I could feel Addison's eyes on me.

But despite her being tempting as hell, I made a conscious effort not to look at her.

Jana was worried about how to navigate between our homes, and at the moment, I was far more concerned with not giving Addison an amount of attention that would set off a Jana alarm.

"Is there anything else you'd like to discuss?" Addison asked.

"I think we've covered it all," I said to Jana.

Jana nodded. "Yes, I agree."

Jana and I stood, and she reached across the table to shake Addison's hand.

Addison immediately reacted, clasping Jana's fingers. "It was great to meet you. I'll be in touch with the book suggestions."

"Thank you," Jana said.

I took her hand as soon as she released Jana, and I said, "It was great talking with you, Addison."

"Likewise," Addison replied, her voice more formal than casual.

The moment her fingers dropped from mine, I held out my arm, signaling for Jana to walk out first, and as we made our way through the classroom, I took a peek at Addison from over my shoulder. She'd left the table we had sat at, and she was standing by her desk, holding a bottle of water that she hadn't sipped from yet.

Her eyes were locked with mine.

And even though I only got a few seconds to gaze at her, I could see the mask melting from her face, and I scored a smile before I turned the corner and joined Jana in the hallway.

"I feel good about that meeting," she said as we made our way toward the exit.

"I agree."

"Do you have any concerns about her age?"

"Her age?" I tried to keep my voice low and unemotional.

"She can't be more than, what, twenty-two, twenty-three, tops?"

Rather than comment on her age—since I knew the answer—I held the lobby door open for her and shifted things a little by saying, "Do you find that as a negative?"

"Someone with more experience couldn't hurt. But you've said you're pleased with Daisy's progress so far, right?"

When we reached the front of her car, I stopped and turned toward her. "Daisy's doing great. There's nothing to worry about as far as her education is concerned."

"I just wish Addison had a few more years under her belt—that's all." She shifted her weight, crossing her arms over her chest. "She did sound confident though, especially with the co-parenting part, and she was definitely reassuring."

"I think she's going to be good for our girl."

"Because she's gorgeous?" She rolled her eyes, letting out a small laugh. "Don't tell me you didn't notice."

It didn't matter if she was my ex or not; I wasn't a fucking idiot, and I knew better than to go there. "Because the school wouldn't have hired her if the administration didn't think she was qualified and up to par with today's standards." I needed Jana to know I was on her side when it came to our daughter. "We'll keep an eye on things, and if you don't think Daisy is making the kind of leaps that she should, we'll reevaluate." I paused. "Sound good?"

She nodded. "Let me know if you want to pop over sometime this weekend to see her. If not, I'll plan on dropping her off on Monday."

"How long is this trip for?"

She moved all her hair onto one shoulder and finger-combed the strands. "Just four days. I'll be back in time to pick her up from school on Friday." She pulled out her key fob with her other hand. "Hey, I meant to ask you. Did you buy the concert tickets?"

I chuckled. "Yeah, I did."

"And am I going to kill you over how much you spent?"

"I'm never going to tell you how much I spent, so no."

"Ridge…" She stood frozen in the doorway of her car, assessing my face. "You got VIP tickets, didn't you?"

I took a few steps toward my car. "Why would you think that?"

"Because I know you better than anyone and I can see right through you."

I just hoped that was all she could see.

I gave her a smile and turned around, waving to her over my shoulder as I headed to my car. Once I was in the driver's seat, I watched Jana pull out of the parking lot, and I took out my phone to send Addison a text.

Me: *God, you're amazing.*

• • •

Addison: *Not sure if you're still up?! It's been a long night…and I've had a few drinks with Leah.*

Me: *Are you all right?*

Addison: *Yeah, yeah. 20 meetings was a lot.*

Me: *Ours couldn't have gone better, I don't think. You're impressive—I hope you know that.*

Addison: *I didn't get the sense that Jana agrees with you.*

Addison: *I don't know, maybe I'm just too far inside my head.*

Addison: *But I was right about her, Ridge, she's gorgeous.*

Me: *You're too far inside your head. She loved you. It's all good. I promise.*

Addison: *Good night. <3*

Me: *Sweet dreams, baby.*

• • •

Me: *I'm just checking on you this morning and making sure you're all right.*

Addison: *I'm all right. Thank you. <3*

Me: *Tell me you're not still inside your head.*

Addison: *I'm working my way out.*

Addison: *I just worry about everything. Jana seems amazing, and I don't want to step on any toes, nor do I want this to be messy in any way. Ya know?*

Me: *It won't be. We're going to figure it out together.*

Me: *I'll see you at the club tonight?*

Addison: *You know I'll be there.*

Chapter Twenty-Two

Addison

Two more weeks, which was four more shifts, counting tonight. That was my estimate of how much longer it would take until I paid off my sister. Of course, that didn't mean I could stop working here. If I could just get twenty or thirty thousand paid down on my student loans and get caught up on my bills, I could quit.

At least, that was what I kept telling myself every time I walked through the doors at the start of my shift. And every time I got onto the stage. And every time I gave a lap dance.

And every time I was hired to go into a private room.

I could do this for my parents.

And then I could do this for myself.

It was just a minor bump in the long, arduous ride of life.

But it was getting hard.

Harder actually.

Especially during the moments when I was completely alone with a guest. When I was solely responsible for entertaining his eyes. When I became the object of his desire and I had to navigate those thoughts and not let them consume me.

The private dances—aside from when Ridge hired me—lasted for one or two songs, three max.

All I had to do was act.

Pretend.

Zone out and remind myself that I was doing this for the money.

I made sure to keep eye contact and constantly part and bite my wet lips and make the kind of sounds he would want to hear.

But during every instance, the set of eyes that gazed back wasn't Ridge's. Neither was the hair or the scruff or the sexy jawline or the Cole nose that I found so hot.

So, to get through it, to survive, I replaced his features with Ridge's.

That was what kept me going. What made each second of the song more tolerable.

Until it suddenly wasn't.

My back bolted straight, and my muscles tightened, and every piece of hair on my body stood up.

I grabbed his wrist to pull his hand off my breast and warned, "You can't touch me there."

The rules were explained to every guest who hired me privately the second they sat in this chair.

My waist was allowed; anything higher or lower wasn't.

He'd agreed.

They all agreed.

With his hand now returned to his lap, I backed away from the chair and adjusted my skirt, trying to catch my breath in the process. I was halfway through the song, so my bra was already off and on the floor. There was nothing left to remove from my body. My skirt was so short that I was basically in only a thong.

To waste some seconds, I turned around and gave him my backside, lowering my arms to the floor, and tucked my face into my knees. I slapped my thighs together, shaking my ass, and glanced at him through the space between my calves.

He was leaning forward, his face far too close to my butt...like the asshole was trying to smell me.

I quickly rose and faced him, guiding him away by gently pushing on his chest, and stood on either side of his legs. A position I dreaded whenever someone was in this chair, but a position that was necessary for the job.

The outside of his thighs was barely touching the inside of mine when his hand returned to my breast.

Had he not listened to what I just said?

Who the hell did he think he was?

I grabbed the back side of his palm. "You're breaking the rules again."

"Fuck the rules." His voice was like acid, burning through my skin.

And the moment those vile words left his mouth, his fingers tightened.

He wasn't just holding it.

He was squeezing.

His hand was like a vise, taking every bit of breath out of my body and worsening when I attempted to loosen his grip.

"Let go of me!"

"No." I got a strong whiff of beer and cigarette from his breath. "I paid for you. I'm getting my money's worth." His other hand was on my inner thigh, rising at an uncomfortable speed. "While you're in this room, these are my fucking titties. That's going to be my pussy. And I'll touch you whenever and wherever I damn well please."

"Let go of me!" I repeated, hoping the pitch of my voice would alert the staff and a security guard would come running in.

But I couldn't wait for that to happen.

He was hurting me.

He was touching something that wasn't his.

He was breaking my rules.

I tore at his fingers, stabbing the backs with my nails.

He didn't budge.

The only thing that changed was his expression, the passion building in his eyes, the desire bleeding from his lips.

This sick fuck was enjoying this. Something told me that the more I thrashed and yelled, the more turned on he was.

He was after the fight, and he wanted me to give it to him.

I shouted a final attempt. "Let go of me right fucking now!"

And when he didn't move, when his hand was getting dangerously close to my thong, I lifted my leg and aimed my heel at his balls, and I kicked as hard as I could. When that didn't feel like enough, I stomped a second time, and my ears were instantly filled with his groans, but my body was free from him.

"Take that, asshole!"

"You fucking whore!"

I left my bra where it was on the floor, not even bothering to reach for it, and I ran from the room, holding my chest as I rushed down the hallway—the walls, the strobe lights, the voices all a blur—and went past the cashier, which dumped me into the main lounge.

Unlike the private room, it was full of light.

Was that why there were tears, why my eyes felt like they were on fire?

And my breath—it was gone.

I scanned the room, looking for something, anything—mostly just familiarity.

But nothing seemed right.

It was all so far away and yet insufferably close.

The music was too loud.

The smell was thick and sickly.

My feet wouldn't move. It felt as though they were glued to the ground. But my head wasn't, and I looked from side to side to see where I needed to go.

Where I should go.

Where it was safe.

Where no one would touch me.

Why couldn't I move?

"Addison."

The sound of my name hit my skin and bounced right off.

"Addison, look at me."

I felt something on my face, like hands.

And that voice—it was achingly familiar.

A stare I could feel even though I couldn't feel anything at all.

"Addison, baby, look at me."

I didn't know what I was gazing at since it seemed like I wasn't looking at anything at all, but something began to come into focus.

A chest. Neck. A sexy jawline that I remembered so well.

Lips, a Cole nose, and cobalt eyes.

Ridge.

"There you are," he said.

He was holding my face.

He was locking his stare with mine.

But…

I didn't believe it was him.

I made everyone in this club look like Ridge.

I changed their eyes to his. Their hair. Their cheeks. Their nose.

"No." I shook my head, feeling hands on my cheeks. "No, it's not you."

"What do you mean, it's not me? Addison, I'm calling you by your real name. You go by Addy in here. How would I know that?" He paused. "Listen to my voice. Doesn't it sound like me?"

I blinked several times. His face didn't change.

Neither did the feel of his hands.

Or the smell of his cologne that my nose was just now picking up on.

"What happened to you? Where's your bra?" His fingers were at the bottoms of my eyelids. "Why are you crying?"

I swallowed, searching for my voice, my throat feeling so heavy and tight. "He touched me."

"Who touched you?"

"A guest."

"What do you mean, he touched you, Addison?"

Even though it was Ridge, it wasn't. Because everything about him was different.

His voice.

It was stern. Dominant.

His eyes.

They were angry and revengeful.

"He was hurting me. He wouldn't let go. I asked him to again and again, and he wouldn't." If Ridge wasn't holding me so tightly, I would have looked behind me at the mouth of the hallway to see if the guest had come out. "I kicked him. And then I ran."

"Are you okay?"

I nodded.

"Where are your clothes?"

I didn't know.

But I did.

"In the back room—" My voice was cut off when his hands left my face, and his arms surrounded me, and he lifted me into the air and held me against his chest. As he carried me, we passed the main lounge, then a short hallway, and finally the cashier, who was stationed by the entrance.

"Where the hell do you think you're going with her?"

Ridge halted and turned us around.

I blinked, staring at the man in front of us, realizing it was my manager.

"I'm taking her home," Ridge shot back.

"You can't do that." He took a step forward. "She's an employee. She's working. She's—"

"Watch me," Ridge barked.

My manager's neck craned back. "Watch you?"

A security guard had joined him, and they were both getting closer to us.

"Her shift is over," Ridge said. "She's no longer one of your employees. Once I put her in the car, I'll be back to deal with you. Don't fucking move."

Ridge kicked open the door to the club, the gap now wide enough that we could fit through, and he brought me to his car. He maneuvered me in a way that he could open the passenger door, and he carefully set me on the seat. Once he was happy with my placement, he reached behind me and returned with a blanket that he placed over me.

"Daisy gets cold, so I always have one in my car." He knelt; his face lined up with mine. "I'm going to lock you in. I don't want you to be alarmed. I just don't want anyone to be able to get into my car." He moved some hair off my face and adjusted the blanket, and he reclined the seat several inches. "I'll be back in a couple of minutes. Will you be all right here?"

I nodded.

"Addison, I need you to speak. I need to hear your voice."

"Yes." I didn't know where his hand was, but I somehow found it and held it. "Where are you going?"

"First, I'm going to deal with your manager. Then, I'm going to find the motherfucker who touched you, and I'm going to kill him."

Chapter Twenty-Three

Ridge

"Where's your office?" I said to Addison's manager once I walked back through the entrance of the club, the motherfucker still standing there with a bodyguard.

The manager crossed his arms over his chest. "Why?"

"Unless you want me to out you in front of your employee"—I nodded toward the young woman who was standing at the register—"and your patrons"—I nodded toward the group of men who had just come in—"then I suggest we go somewhere private."

The manager looked me over like I was scum. "Who the fuck do you think you are?"

I smiled.

I didn't get this question a lot. But when I did, the gratification felt so good.

"Ridge Cole, an owner of Cole and Spade Hotels. That's who I am."

The manager and bodyguard looked at one another.

I didn't need to mention that my name came with power, that my pockets were deep enough to buy this strip club, the building, and to pay the salary of every employee here for the rest of their lives.

They knew.

Which was only confirmed by their expressions.

"Follow me," the manager said.

He led me to the section of the club where the private rooms were located. Rather than go to the right—a hallway I'd walked down enough times since Addison brought me into one of those rooms during each of my visits—he took me to the left, past the cashier, and into a tiny office.

There were two folding chairs. The bodyguard took one, and I took the other. The manager sat behind his cheap, small desk.

"I'm assuming Addy is your girlfriend—"

"Addison," I corrected. "If you're going to talk about her, you need to address her properly."

"Addison," he said.

Before he could utter another word, I voiced, "What Addison and I are is none of your business and irrelevant to this conversation." I leaned closer to the desk. "When I found her this evening, she had just run out of a private room, where one of your customers had sexually assaulted her. What's the purpose of having cameras in those rooms if no one is watching the footage to ensure *your* employees are kept safe?"

"We have a security guard stationed—"

I pounded my fist on the fake wood. "I don't give a fuck where he's stationed. He clearly wasn't close enough to intervene or do anything to help her."

"Mr. Cole, I think you're getting confused by what our employees do here and what these private rooms are for."

"Confused"—my brows rose—"is the last thing I am. Addison sets boundaries in those rooms. I know because I've been in there with her multiple times. If those lines weren't defined, that would be one thing. But they are, and one of your customers crossed that boundary."

"Define 'crossed,' " the manager said, using air quotes.

"He forcefully grabbed her chest and wouldn't let her go. To the point where she had to take matters into her own hands and protect herself."

"He touched her tits," the bodyguard said. "That's it?"

I didn't like his tone.

I also didn't like how he was downplaying the incident as though her tits were open to the fucking public.

My neck swiveled so I could take in the sorry excuse of a man. "It's a boundary. He crossed it." My stare returned to the manager, and I pointed at his computer. "Why don't you pull up the feed so we can see exactly what he did?"

"Not an option," the manager said.

My anger fueled me to chuckle. "Why?"

"Because you're not an employee."

"Don't bullshit me," I growled. "We both know a place like this doesn't have a rule like that."

The manager rocked back in his chair. "I don't have access to the feed."

Fucking liar.

I set my arms on the edge of his desk. "Don't make my legal team come in here and bury this club. The second they get ahold of the footage—and they will—the PR damage alone will put you out of a job, and the doors of this establishment will be locked forever." My eyes narrowed. "Or you can play nice and give me what I'm asking for." I pulled out my phone, entered my password, and found Jenner Dalton's contact information, my thumb hovering over the Phone button. "Do I make the phone call? The choice is yours."

His stare hardened. "You're a son of a bitch—you know that?" He typed something on the keyboard, moved the mouse around on its pad, and turned the screen toward me. "Just so you know, I haven't seen any of this."

"Do you think, at this point, I'm holding *you* liable?" I spit. "I already know you're underqualified for this position, and whatever idiot hired you clearly didn't know what the fuck they were doing." I ground my teeth together. "Pull up the camera feed. I'm losing my patience."

What was showing on his monitor was feed from the hallway that led to the private rooms.

He rewound the footage until I spotted her and said, "Stop."

The footage began to play in real time. He noted which number door she had taken the customer to, and he pulled up the individual feed for only that room.

As I watched the screen, seeing the bastard take a seat and spread his legs and cup his hard-on, my jaw clenched.

My hands balled into fists.

I hadn't anticipated what it would feel like to see this on the screen. To witness a man be this close to Addison, to put his hands on her, to look at her in a way that should only be reserved for me.

I didn't care what we were or what pace we were moving at or whether we had titles or not. In my mind, that woman was mine.

And seeing that he was touching her, that his grip was aggressive and attacking, was sending me so far over the fucking edge.

But it didn't just end there.

He put his face in her ass when she was bent over, and his hand skimmed the inside of her thigh as well.

There was no volume. I couldn't hear the exchange of words. I could only see her lips moving, my mind filling in the words that she was shouting at him.

"Look at what that motherfucker is doing to her." I stared at the manager, demanding a response. "You can't tell me he's not crossing a line." When he said nothing, I slapped my hand on the desk. "Answer me!"

"I think it's best that I say nothing."

That response made me want to reach across the desk, pick him up, and slam him on top of it. But that wouldn't get me what I ultimately needed from him.

So, I hissed instead, "And I'm the son of a bitch." When Addison kicked the man in the balls and took off from the room, the customer falling off his chair and shriveling up in a ball on the ground, I seethed. "Where is he?"

"Who?" the manager asked. "The customer?"

I nodded.

"Why don't you go see if he's still here?" the manager said to the bodyguard.

The bodyguard left and shut the door behind him.

The second the handle clicked in the lock, the manager turned the monitor so I could no longer see it, folding his arms on top of the desk. "Don't ask me for a copy of that feed. I won't give it to you."

I said nothing. I just continued to stare at him, letting him simmer in silence, guessing my next move.

I could take this in many different directions.

But only one worked to Addison's benefit, even if the others would self-satisfy me.

"I don't want the feed." I crossed my legs and my arms and felt the smile slowly creep across my face. "There's something else I want instead."

• • •

"How's the temperature?" I asked Addison, dipping my fingers into the bath I'd drawn for her to ensure the water wasn't scalding. "Do I need to add in some cold water?"

Even though she'd asked for it to be extra hot, I didn't want her burning herself.

"It's perfect." She spread some of the bubbles up to her neck. "Just what I needed. Thank you." She reached over the lip of the tub to put her fingers on mine. "Are you sure you don't want to join me?"

I wanted nothing more.

But she'd had herself a hell of a night, so I wanted to give her some space at the same time.

I grabbed a washcloth from the tray beside the tub and dipped it into the water, getting it wet enough so that while I was massaging it across the top of her shoulders, I was cleaning her at the same time. "This one's just for you."

She continued to hold me, locking our stares. "I'm okay, Ridge."

"I know."

"You're worried. I can feel it. You don't have to be." She adjusted her position, sending a wave of bubbles to her feet. "Kicking him in the balls was the most liberating feeling in the world. And I got to do it twice because the first kick hadn't felt like enough." She went quiet, but I could tell she wasn't done. "I'm just glad that when the adrenaline took over, it turned me into a badass. If I hadn't done what I did… I don't know what would have happened."

I ran my thumb over her forehead, down her cheek, palming the side of her face. "After you left the room, he fell to the ground."

Her eyes widened as she silently stared at me. "How do you know?" She sat up a little higher. "Wait, you saw the camera feed?"

During the drive to my house, we hadn't discussed what had happened when I went back inside the club. She didn't ask a single question, and I said nothing about it. I asked her if she wanted to go to the police, and when she said that was the last thing she wanted, I had taken her here, the conversation minimal until she got in the bath.

"I saw all of it," I admitted.

"And my manager did too…"

"He's no longer your manager, Addison."

"He fired me?" Her voice was barely above a whisper. "I just need to understand what I'm facing here. Just because I can't go back—or I shouldn't go back—doesn't mean my bills go away."

"You're telling me you'd return?"

She tilted her head, elongating her neck, her eyes then closing. "I don't want to. I never wanted to even work there in the first place. But I'm so close to paying off my sister. Like, two weeks away. And then I was going to pay down a huge chunk on my student loans." She looked at me again. "That's the first time anything like that ever happened to me there. Maybe if the manager promised to beef up security or..." Her voice drifted off. "Why am I even letting myself go there?" She paused again. "I've lost it...haven't I?"

"You haven't lost it."

"But I'm focused on the finances when I should be thinking about my safety. And in regard to my safety, why would I even consider putting myself in that situation?"

I dropped the washcloth and held her chin. "Because what happened there could technically happen anywhere. Who's to say a teacher couldn't pull you into a closet at school and do the same thing? Or when you're out and someone yanks you into an alley? I get where your head is at. This isn't easy—at all."

She nodded, resting her hand on top of the water. "Except in those situations, I'm not half naked."

I slid my hand into her hair. "You don't have to even think about it anymore. You never need to step foot in that hellhole ever again." I reached into the pocket of my jeans and pulled out the folded envelope. "For you."

"What is it?"

"You can call it a severance. A payoff. Or what's keeping that motherfucker from getting sued."

She searched my eyes. "Ridge...what are you saying?"

I set down the envelope and held her face with both hands. The words I was about to say had been in my head since I'd joined her in the car. They had pulsed through me while I carried her from my garage to my en suite. I wanted to wait for the right moment to have this conversation. It seemed like this was it.

"I didn't want to be that guy, Addison. But, shit, from the moment I first tasted you, I wanted to tell you to quit. I wanted to write you a check and take away every worry you had. But the more I learned about your situation, the more I saw how prideful you were."

Her light-brown eyes were gazing back at me, the emotion beginning to fill them.

"You wanted to do this on your own, it was important to you. I didn't want to take that away from you. I thought it would be the last thing you'd want from me."

"You read the room right." She gave me a soft smile. "Besides, I wouldn't have cashed your check."

"I know." I traced my thumb over her lips. "But the thought of you going to the club every weekend"—I shook my head—"was getting harder to stomach. Every goddamn day, I was feeling worse about it. I didn't want you on that stage. I didn't want those men giving you money. I didn't want them fantasizing about you. It even got to the point where I didn't want their eyes on you—something I hadn't felt at the beginning, but I feel that way now."

I took a long, deep breath.

"When I saw you rush into the lounge, braless, looking terrified and defeated and in the middle of a panic attack—" I cut myself off, needing a second before I continued, running my hand over my head to try to calm myself down. "I'll never forget that moment. I'll also never forgive myself for not writing you a check and getting you out of that fucking nightmare of a place."

"It wouldn't have mattered. Like I said, I wouldn't have cashed it."

On my way back into the club, the plan had started to formulate in my head. By the time I got to the manager's office, I already knew what I wanted and what I was going to ask for.

And the bastard had made it so easy for me.

"Instead, you're going to accept a check from him." I opened the envelope, unfolded the wide paper inside, and held it up for her to see. "If I'd gotten my legal team involved, you would have gotten a lot more. Hundreds of thousands, I'm sure—"

"Oh my God, Ridge." Her hand went over her mouth as she looked at the amount on the check. "Fifty thousand? That's what he gave me?" Her hand then returned to my arm. "It's plenty. I don't need a cent more. I shouldn't even take it because it's from him."

"But you're going to take it."

She hesitated and finally said, "Yes, I will."

"It's enough to pay off your sister and to make a large dent in your student loans."

"It is." I could tell she wasn't done speaking, and I could also tell she was still upset. "I just feel bad that I didn't work for that money."

"Addison, don't say that. You worked your ass off for that money. Not to mention, that asshole put you in an environment that wasn't safe. In a place like that, protocols need to be established to ensure what happened to you doesn't happen to anyone else. The fact of the matter is, he just doesn't give a fuck. So, look at this money like a future advance on dancing you no longer have to do."

She slowly nodded. "You're right." When I set the check down, her hand moved to my knuckles, rubbing the cuts across my skin and the blood that had dried, which I hadn't yet washed off, and the dark purple bruises that were starting to form. "Tell me what caused this."

"You weren't the only one who felt liberated tonight."

Her brows rose. "You punched my manager?"

I smiled. "Let's just say, the motherfucker not only has broken balls, courtesy of you, but he now has a broken nose too."

"Ridge"—she let out a tiny laugh—"you're kidding?"

"The only good thing that fucking security guard did this evening was find the man who had assaulted you. The dumbass hadn't left the club, so I was able to give him a little piece of my mind."

Her head tilted as she gazed at me. "You came to my rescue. In ways I can't even process yet."

"Baby," I whispered, "you don't need to. You just need to know that I'm here."

"About that…" She turned quiet for several seconds. "You know, working at the club was the major thing that was holding me back from you. There's still the teaching layer, but it was the club that ate at me the most."

"I know."

"And because of you, that's no longer an issue." She sat up even higher and put her arms around my shoulders, hugging me against her wet body. "Ridge, I'll never be able to thank you for tonight."

"No thanks needed. I would do it all over again in a heartbeat." I held her tightly, and when I sensed she needed more, I squeezed her harder. "I care about you, Addison. There isn't anything I wouldn't do for you."

"Ridge…"

"Yeah?"

"Fuck turtle speed."

I let out a deep chuckle. "You've never said anything sexier."

Chapter Twenty-Four

ADDISON

Ridge wasn't like the men from my past—the boys who only thought of themselves in every scenario and constantly put me last, who were more bad than good. Ridge was a dream. A man who had proven he'd do anything for me, who would protect me, who would punch an asshole and break his nose for my honor.

And even though I was squeezing him within my wet, naked arms while the rest of my body was still in his big, beautiful tub, I had a hard time believing that he was real.

That someone like him truly existed.

That he'd carried me out of the club and to his car and brought me to his house.

That tonight had even happened.

That he'd made sure this was the last time I would ever step foot in the club because he didn't even want the customers' eyes on me.

Because I was his.

And I wanted to be his.

"If you're not going to join me," I said into the side of his neck, "I think it's time for me to get out."

His arms loosened from around me, and he went to the other side of the bathroom to grab a towel, which he unfolded and held open for me to step into. Once I climbed out of the tub, he wrapped it around me, clasping it in the back.

"Let's get you to bed."

His shirt was soaked from our hug. The water from the bath was dripping off me, along with the bubbles, hitting spots on the floor that were well past the rug I was standing on.

But Ridge didn't even attempt to dry himself off or remove his shirt or wipe up the floor.

All that mattered in this moment was me.

Since he was still holding the towel behind my back, I assumed he was waiting for me to walk into the bedroom.

But I didn't move.

I undid the top three buttons of his shirt, and pulling from the bottom, I lifted it over his head. "You have too many clothes on to go to bed." I took in his gorgeous smile as I unhooked his belt and the button and zipper of his jeans and let them fall, along with his boxer briefs, to the wet floor.

He slid out of his shoes and his clothes.

And even though his hand hadn't left the towel, I pulled it off my chest and encouraged him to let it drop, the two of us now standing naked.

Ridge had every opportunity to let his stare fall down my body, and he didn't.

His eyes stayed on mine.

And while they did, he gazed at me like I was the most beautiful woman he'd ever seen—something he'd done since the first time we'd met. But what was also in that riveting stare was a feeling that went beyond my appearance and what he thought of it.

Ridge looked at me with love.

An emotion that didn't just hit, but it penetrated my soul.

"Mine."

As that one word resonated, my eyes fluttered closed, and I filled my lungs by taking the longest, deepest breath.

Mine.

Something I wanted, but didn't feel right about having.

Until now.

Now, everything felt right.

"Yes." I smiled. "I'm yours."

I circled my arms around his neck and leaned up on my toes, hovering my lips in front of his. With that discussion out of the way, there was one thing left to do that would make this night leave my mind.

"Make me forget him."

The only thing that could remove those images from my head was if Ridge replaced them. If he put his hands all over me, his lips, if he had me screaming so loud that I couldn't recall a single moment from the club.

From that request, Ridge could have touched me anywhere.

But he chose my face, palms on my cheeks, thumbs on the sides of my lips.

I gave him a slow, gentle kiss. "Don't try to talk me out of it either. I've never wanted something so badly in my life."

"Addison—"

"I know you're about to ask me if I'm sure. And I am. I'm positive." I smiled, holding him even tighter. "The other thing I'm sure of is that you don't have to wear a condom." I ran my fingers through the back of his hair. "Don't worry; I'm fully protected." I tried to read his eyes, and when I couldn't, I added, "Unless you're uncomfortable with the idea and then—"

I was suddenly in the air, and while his arms held my weight, my legs circled his waist, and my forearms rested on his shoulders.

Even though our positions were different, he didn't move; he stayed standing in the same spot.

"You're mine."

He wasn't asking.

He was telling me.

And even though we'd already confirmed that, I could understand his need to hear it again.

Because part of me needed to say it again.

"Yes," I voiced softly, giving him a kiss.

"Then, yes, I'm comfortable with not wearing a condom. But I need to confirm you really know what you're asking for, Addison." He studied my eyes. "That you really want me to ravish you the only way I know how." He continued to scan my eyes. "Because I'm not sure that's what you need right now. This evening wasn't easy on you, baby. When I saw the footage"—his jaw clenched, and his teeth ground together—"when I witnessed the way he grabbed you—"

"And I don't want you to be easy on me either." I let that process before I added, "I want you to just love me tonight, Ridge. Please."

"Addison"—he shook his head as though he was registering what I'd just said to him—"what the hell am I going to do with you?"

I held my lips against his and whispered, "You're going to make love to me."

"A demand I don't know that I can refuse."

"Then, don't."

There was movement, but we didn't go far, just to the large counter in his bathroom, the section between the double sinks, and that was where he set me down. Even though I was settled on the hard stone, my legs stayed around him, and my shoulders leaned back until they hit the mirror behind me.

The second the cold glass touched my skin, he sank into me, giving me every inch of his hardness that I'd asked for.

"Oh, Ridge!"

"Fuck," he moaned.

But it was more than a moan.

It was a noise that set the whole mood.

The sound vibrated through my chest, making my nipples even harder than they already had been.

"You have no idea how tight you are." His forehead pressed against mine. "How wet." He wrapped his fingers around my breast and grazed my nipple. "How fucking perfect." The rubbing turned to a pinch, followed by a pull.

I left his shoulders and held on to his upper arms; the muscles felt like rocks beneath my nails.

"Ridge!" I gasped in some air as he reared his hips back, making me instantly miss the fullness until he thrust back in. "Yes!"

Since he no longer had to hold me, he had the use of both hands, and one went to my face, his thumb tracing my lips before it dipped into my mouth.

I sucked on it—the tip, the base, the length—like it was his dick.

And then I moaned even louder than he just had, his thumb popping out in time for me to shout, "Harder!"

"Do you know what you're asking for?"

His movements were steady, and there was nothing soft about them.

But I wanted more.

I wanted his power.

I wanted to feel it through my entire body.

"Yes," I said, drawing out the word. "And I want it faster."

"You're a naughty fucking girl, Addison."

When his hand disappeared from my face, I anticipated where I would feel it next, especially as his speed began to pick up. When his grunts were filling the room, when the wetness and bubbles from the bath were starting to mix with the sweat on his body.

What I didn't anticipate was how it would feel when it landed on my clit.

"Fuck!" The back of my head hit the mirror. Not hard enough for it to break, just enough for it to make a sound. "Yes!"

"You want more?"

"Always."

"Bend your knees, Addison. Wrap your toes around the counter."

I followed his order, quickly realizing this new position gave me everything I'd been begging him for. Because now that my legs weren't around him and they were spread a bit more, there was nothing holding him back; he could reach the farthest part of me.

A spot beyond what he had hit before.

But he didn't just tap it, like his crown was the beak of a woodpecker, knocking endlessly. Instead, he stroked his tip across it, like there was a knot that he was massaging out, and when he drew back, he rotated his hips, caressing my walls, adding even more friction.

Nothing I was feeling was normal.

This was something on a whole new level.

"Oh! My!" I screamed, eventually following that with, "God!"

"You're going to come."

I didn't know how he knew, but there hadn't been a time when he was wrong.

This was no exception.

He gave my clit another flick, and within a few plunges, I was yelling, "Ridge," at the top of my lungs.

Shuddering.

Losing all control of my body.

The tingles were coming in that fast and hard.

"Ridge!" I shouted again.

If there was somewhere to fall, I would have since I was positive I could no longer bear my own weight. But the mirror held me, keeping me in place while he thrust his strength into me, filling me, making the electricity swirling in my stomach rise as high as my neck and as low as my toes.

"Ridge," I shouted one final time.

Because it was the only word in my head.

Because I couldn't even imagine trying to form something that had more than one syllable. My brain couldn't handle it, not when I was this wound up.

"Fuck, baby, it feels so good when you come."

Even though my orgasm had passed, he was still sliding in and out, but his pace had slowed, and so did the amount of pressure he gave me. My breath hadn't yet returned, nor had the numbness left my body; I was still in that sensitive place where every shift caused a spark.

"You get so wet. So tight." His lips were against mine. "Your pussy becomes so needy for me." He moved his mouth to my ear. "I want you to fucking need me, Addison."

His words were making me moan.

The rawness.

The grittiness of his tone, like he'd just woken up but without the sleepy sound.

My toes released the lip of the counter, and my legs wrapped around him.

"Tell me you need me again," he demanded.

"I need you." My palms gripped the sides of his face. "God, I need you, Ridge."

"Tell me you're going to come so fucking hard that you're going to milk the cum out of me."

If I'd considered this less than a minute ago, I was sure I couldn't get off a second time.

But that was how quickly things had changed.

That was what this slow, steady, relentless rhythm had already done to me.

"We both know you're going to get me there quickly, so, yes, my pussy is going to milk you."

"Quickly, huh?" His chuckle was as deep as his voice was. "I like a challenge I know I'm going to win."

I dragged my teeth over my bottom lip. "Show me, then."

I was off the counter in seconds and back in his arms. He carried me out of the bathroom and into his bedroom. Since my back was to the room, I couldn't see his destination. I could only feel him lowering me and the softness beneath me when he set me down.

I wasn't on the bed.

I was on the bench in front of it. A wide, oversize rectangle, decorated in black velvet-like fabric.

"Get on your knees."

My chest released the longest exhale as his command simmered through me.

When I didn't instantly move, he held my chin, aiming my face up at him while he pumped his dick with his other hand. "Hurry."

Between his order and the sight in front of my eyes, the amount of hotness was explosive.

I lifted myself from a seated position and flipped around onto my knees, spreading my legs just enough that would grant him the access he'd had on the bathroom counter. I balanced on my palms, my fingers bending around the edge of the bench.

While I waited, I glanced over my shoulder. Ridge was still stroking his cock, but while he did it, he was taking in my body, covering every inch of me with his stare.

"Fucking look at you," he said, dragging out each word, his gaze finally meeting mine. "I can't believe I get to fuck you." He licked his lip. "Or that you're mine."

"All yours." I gave him a playful smile. "Now, hurry."

The height of the bench was just the right alignment, so all he had to do was step forward, and his tip was already at my entrance. Both of us were so wet that he slid right in.

"Fuck yes," he rumbled.

The fullness was what I experienced first.

Even though I'd already felt it tonight, the new position was entirely different from the last one. I didn't know how it was even possible, but it felt like he was reaching an even deeper spot.

And when he dived into me, fully burying himself, he stayed there for a pulse. Part of it felt like a tease; he was making me miss the friction. But the other part didn't need the pressure because my body was building without it, using the stillness to ramp up my orgasm.

"Ah!" I panted. "This feels"—I took in more air—"so good."

What never stopped moving was his hands. They were everywhere, constantly wandering my body, squeezing my nipples, slapping my ass, gripping my hips.

"Addison," he hissed. "You'd better stop pumping your ass like that, or you're going to make me come."

I was meeting him in the middle. But beyond that, I was bucking my hips upward, forcing him to hit my walls, and with that came a whole new sensation.

One that was sucking all the wind out of me.

"I want you to come," I pleaded.

Because I was on the verge.

And I knew I wouldn't be able to hold it back for much longer, not with how quickly my body was returning to that place. And especially not if he kept up this pace, the slamming, the arching, the twisting—a combination I couldn't come back from.

I locked my arms and tightened my grip and looked at him over my shoulder. The hunger in his eyes was feral. The tug of his lips made him look unhinged.

This wasn't just the sexiest man alive.

He was a man giving me everything he had.

And the both of us were on the verge of screaming.

Not only could I feel it inside of me, but I could sense it in his strokes. How they had turned into short, sharp thrusts, each one ending in a long, loud grunt.

"Ridge," I cried, the tingles moving higher in my body, "I want you to come right now."

The last word had barely left my mouth when he reached around my side and grazed my clit.

"Oh!" I searched for air, for words—for anything. "Yes!"

He gave my clit that tiny motion again and again, sending my whole body into overdrive.

Waves of pleasure were spreading through me at a rate I couldn't even fathom, and what made the moment even more intense was getting to watch when the same thing happened to him. When his eyes narrowed, when his lips drew wide, when his teeth bared. When the sensations were flushing through his body so strongly that he shouted, "Fuck! Yeah!" And, "Goddamn it, Addison, yes," came next.

By the time he reached his peak, his momentum starting to die out, I was already shuddering, exhaling, "Ridge," every time I was able to take in a breath and release it.

My knees were weakening.

My arms were no longer locked, my hands threatening to give out.

"I'm filling you with my fucking cum."

Why was that image so incredibly sexy?

I could feel it—the extra wetness. Especially as he began to slow, both of our bodies needing a point of stillness.

And when he finally gave it to us, I was still looking at him.

Gazing.

Taking in that face, those eyes, the Cole nose, and his scruff that I just couldn't get enough of.

He'd done everything I'd asked of him.

And now, tonight wasn't even a bad memory. Tonight, aside from this, hadn't even existed, as far as I was concerned.

He gently pulled out, wrapped an arm around my stomach and another behind my knees, and flipped me around after he lifted me into the air, carrying me back into the bathroom, where he stepped into the shower. He set me in the corner while he turned on the water, adjusting the temperature to the heat he preferred before he pulled me in to join him, guiding me under the stream.

"You awakened a fucking beast inside me." He squirted some soap in his hand and gently washed between my legs, rinsing me off, along with his fingers, before he cupped my cheeks and pointed my face up at him. "You know that, don't you?"

"Because you don't have to wear a condom?"

"You would think that." A smile moved across his face. "But, no." He rubbed his nose against mine, and then his lips brushed my pout. Somewhere during one of the passes, he kissed me. "It's because you gave yourself to me."

I'd just found my breath, and yet it was still so hard to breathe.

So hard to think.

So hard to believe that this was the man who wanted me. Who had waited for me. Who had done everything in his power to protect me tonight.

"What's going to happen when I tell you I love you?" I didn't know where the question had come from; it just fell out of me.

"Why don't you say it and find out?"

Chapter Twenty-Five

Ridge

"Do you know what I love?" I said to Addison as I walked with her on the beach in Malibu. The sun was just starting to dip as the ocean lapped our feet, the sound of the waves and birds a harmony that I would have paid top dollar for if the water wasn't so close to LA.

As she looked at me, the wind was blowing her auburn hair into her face, and she did nothing to move it away. It was almost as though she enjoyed it. "Tell me."

"That no matter how many times I bring you here, you look at the beach like you've never seen it before."

Her smile tonight was warmer than normal. Enticing. And addictive as hell.

I swore her eyes were lighter brown than they typically were, and they almost matched the beige sweater that hung low on her shoulders, baring most of her upper back, which wasn't covered by her dress.

"This is going to sound funny," she said, "but in a way, every time I come here, I see it so differently. That's because of you, Ridge."

"What do you mean?"

With our fingers linked, she swung our arms. "My emotions affect the way I see things. The sky, for example. In the past, when I was having a hell of a day, I'd see the clouds that were about to turn into a storm. But given that I'm the happiest I've ever been, I only notice the big, billowy white ones or the thin, wispy streaks of fluff. And every time we're here, I see something new that I've never seen before, and it shocks me—in a breathless kind of way." She pointed toward the water. "Like that break over there, about a football field away, where the waves move in opposite directions as if the tides are changing in that exact spot. Do you see it?"

I'd stopped listening after she admitted her feelings. I could focus on nothing else, not even what she was referencing with her finger.

So, I pulled her hand up to my lips and got back to the main point by saying, "You're the happiest you've ever been…"

"Yes." Her smile softened in a way where it was still there, but she was hiding her beautiful teeth. "Now that we're *together*, together, so much has changed. Ridge, I've never felt like this in my whole life."

Since that *together*, together moment had happened, the night of the incident at the club, I'd been bringing her here every Saturday. This was our fourth one in a row. And each date was nothing like the one prior. I'd rented us a boat with a captain for the first Saturday, a catered picnic on the sand for the second, and some paddleboarding for the third. As for tonight, Addison had no idea what I'd planned.

Surprising her was something I loved more than anything.

And because my staff needed some time to set up, I'd walked with her about a half a mile in the opposite direction of the hotel, waiting for the text from my team that told me to head back.

Once I felt the vibration in my pocket, assuming it was them, I turned us around and asked, "What do you see when you look at the sky tonight?"

"Is that a trick question?"

I laughed at her grin and the cuteness of her question. "Not at all." I nodded toward the water. "The sun is getting ready to set, so I imagine billowy and wispy aren't the way you'd describe it."

"You're right." She was on the inside, closest to the ocean, her bare feet kicking up drips of the salty water every time she took a step. With her face pointed at the horizon, she said, "Gold and orange. Those are the colors filling my vision. I don't even notice the clouds."

"Why?"

"Because the sun is dominating my line of sight." She turned her head toward me. "Just like you do whenever I'm around you. All I see is you." Her eyes narrowed while she took me in, but her smile didn't dim at all. If anything, it grew. "I think that makes you my sun, Ridge."

"I'll take that title." I winked.

"What do you see when you look at the sky?"

I released her hand and threw my arm around her shoulders, bringing her even closer. "I don't even see a sky."

"You're kidding, it's over there—"

"That would mean I'd have to take my eyes off you. I can't do that, nor do I want to."

She held my hand that hung near her tit. "How do you do that?" When I didn't immediately reply, she continued, "How do you make me feel like I'm the most important woman in the world and the only one you've ever wanted?" She raised her other hand in the air between us. "And I don't say that to take away your love of Daisy or Jana—I don't mean it that way at all. I just mean that when you look at me, when you say those kinds of things to me, I feel"—her eyes closed as though she were searching for the right word—"like you've placed a spotlight above me and you're the only person in the audience."

"I'm just telling you exactly how I feel. They're words that come from the sincerest place in me." I pointed at my chest. "Right here. My heart."

"I can tell."

I kissed the side of her head, breathing in her vanilla-latte scent. "I have one request though." I noticed we were getting closer to the hotel, and I could see all the preparation that I'd organized.

"Yeah?"

"Let's no longer use any references that involve a stage unless we're talking about a concert—*that* I can handle. The thought of you back at the club, I cannot."

"Deal." She laughed as she leaned back to look at me. "Those days are long over, thanks to you." She let out a long, deep sigh. "I know I already told you this a few weeks ago, but I can't express enough how good it felt to send the remaining balance to my sister and to pay off a massive chunk of my student loans. The weight on my chest is finally starting to lift, and I feel like I can breathe again."

What she didn't know was that the weight wasn't just lifting; it was disappearing. But she wouldn't know that until she received her next student loan statement, which would show a zero balance. It had taken a little maneuvering to make that happen and a lot of help from her best friend, Leah, who I'd met when I stayed the night at Addison's last week.

I couldn't live with the idea that she was going to make payments for the next twenty years, working multiple jobs to make that happen. That shit hadn't sat well with me at all—because I didn't want her to have to work multiple jobs, not when I could do this for her, and I wanted to do it for her, even though I knew it was important for her to work off that debt.

She could fight me all she wanted, and I suspected she would, given how prideful she was, but I also knew she was worth far more than what she was paid.

Hell, I would give her a million, and she would be worth every goddamn cent.

"But what made carrying all that weight worth it," she continued, "was seeing my parents' faces when Morgan and I gave them the gift.

You know, they're still texting me every day, telling me it was too much and they're having a hard time accepting it, but they've already packed their suitcases even though they don't leave for months." Her smile was achingly beautiful as she spoke. "God, they're adorable."

"You did it right, baby."

She nodded. "I know."

And because she knew that feeling, the pleasure that came when you gave something to someone so fucking deserving, she would understand how I'd felt when I paid off her student loans.

I held my lips against the side of her head. "Hungry?"

"Why? Did you just hear my stomach growl?"

I chuckled. "No, but mine is doing the same."

We were about twenty yards from the hotel, and I turned her toward the water, standing behind her with my arms crossed over her chest. The sun was lowering fast, and I wanted to make sure she saw the descent. But while she was focused on the beauty in the sky, I was gazing at the hints of her face that I could see from above.

The length of her eyelashes, the arch of her nose, the sides of her thick lips. The creaminess of her freckled skin, the gorgeous red hair that surrounded both sides.

"Stunning," I whispered.

"Isn't it?"

"Remember, if I was looking at the sky, that would mean I'd have to take my eyes off you. I can't do that, nor do I want to."

"Your compliments will forever make me swoon." She turned around and threw her arms around my neck and kissed me.

I gave her a quick flick of my tongue and pulled away, holding her face with both hands. "I know you think we're spending the night at my place tonight, but we're not."

Her brows rose, a sly grin reaching all the way to her eyes. "We're not?"

"I reserved us the penthouse suite at the hotel."

"The Malibu hotel I haven't yet seen?" She kissed me. "That I've been nonstop asking you for a tour of?"

"Yes, that one. And that"—I nodded toward the beachline, where a small tent had been set up, strung with twinkling lights, a table and two chairs beneath it, surrounded by candles that had been sunk into the sand—"is where we're having dinner."

Her mouth opened several seconds before she said, "You're kidding me."

"I would never do that."

When she looked at me again, there was so much emotion in her eyes. "Thank you—those words aren't strong enough, so I need to say them again and again and again."

I held her chin, rubbing the silky skin around it. "Before you thank me, you might want to have dinner first. Hell, you might hate it."

She let out a small giggle. "Impossible."

"I know. Because we're having ramen. Your favorite."

Chapter Twenty-Six

Addison

When my eyes opened, it took me a second to realize what I was looking at—the sheer curtains that were letting in hints of the morning light; the feathery, oversize white comforter that was comfier than anything I'd ever owned; decorations done in light blue and sand, off-white and gold—the colors of Malibu. And behind me—the source of the warmth, stronger than any sunrays, a tightness of arms more powerful than any shackle—was Ridge.

He'd planned a night that was dreamier than anything I could have ever conjured up. An incredible viewing of the sunset, followed by a four-course dinner of seaweed salad, steamed gyoza, ramen, and mochi. Each bite was accompanied by the flicking candles that surrounded us and the crashing waves on the beach.

A meal that was, hands down, one of the best I'd ever eaten.

By the time we got up from the table, we needed to walk off our fullness, so Ridge gave me a tour of the hotel—something I'd been begging for since the first time he'd taken me here. Even though I'd never been inside a Cole and Spade Hotel before—their room rates and restaurants were far above my budget—therefore I couldn't compare it to their other properties, I could say without any hesitation that it was the nicest, most beautiful resort I'd ever seen. He was only halfway through the renovations, but he was still able to show me photos of the before, so I could see all the changes and the intricate designs he'd implemented—some were structural, some decor—and all had made a major impact.

I'd never questioned Ridge's talent, immediately knowing the moment I had stepped foot in his house that he was successful, but getting to see his capabilities and hear the way he spoke about the business brought on a whole new level of admiration.

I had one sexy, skilled man on my hands.

And when we eventually made our way up to the suite, I saw that his planning hadn't ended at dinner. Inside, candles were lit on every surface, and there was champagne waiting for us on ice. Rose petals were sprinkled on the floor and the bed and floating on top of the bubbling Jacuzzi tub. This time, he joined me in the water for a long, sensual soak, and when he had carried me to the bed, we had been covered in bubbles and bits of flowers.

I wasn't sure how many hours ago that was or how much sleep I'd actually gotten, but as I glanced through the sheer blinds, taking in the variants of blue that shone through from the other side, every part of me felt satiated and rested.

"Are you awake?"

Ridge's voice was only a hint above a whisper, mixed with that morning roughness. If I had still been asleep, it wouldn't have woken me.

"*Mmm*." I loosened the grip he had on me and rolled over to look at him. "Good morning."

"Have you been up for long?"

I folded my arm under the pillow and puffed the down under my face to prop me up a little. "A couple of minutes. So, no, not long." I smiled. "I was just reminiscing over last night." I placed my hand on his cheek, the coarseness of his whiskers a welcome sensation. "Which was one of the best evenings ever."

He turned his face to kiss the inside of my hand. "There will be many more just like that one in the future."

Not only was he sexy and skilled, but he was also the king of word porn.

"I can't wait," I told him.

He pushed a piece of hair out of my eye—something he did often. "Are you hungry?"

"You're not serious? Because after that dinner, I don't think I can even look at food until lunchtime, and even that would be a stretch."

"That's too bad since there will be coffee and breakfast delivered in about"—he glanced over his shoulder at the clock on the nightstand—"thirty minutes."

I sighed. "Coffee does sound like heaven."

"So will breakfast when you see it."

I leaned up even more, bending my elbow to rest my face on my palm. "What are we talking? Pancakes? Waffles? French toast?"

His stare turned more intimate, and at the same time, it intensified. "I feel like this is a challenge."

I laughed. "Well, you nailed dinner. I'm so curious what you would choose for breakfast."

"Do you want me to tell you your favorite pancake flavor?"

"Oh, I'm dying to hear this."

He moved onto his back, placing his crossed arms between his head and the pillow. "If you were going to order pancakes—which you wouldn't—you'd go with blueberry. Plain pancakes would be too sweet for you. And since you gravitate toward fruit that's tart, I'd say blueberry would suffice. Maybe even raspberry."

He was describing me perfectly, things I couldn't believe he'd picked up on.

"Ridge, I'm speechless right now."

"You think I didn't notice what you picked out of the charcuterie board when I brought it for our first beach date?" He smiled. "And how cantaloupe and melon didn't make an appearance when I brought that salty prosciutto the last time we were here even though that fruit mixes amazingly well with the meat."

"Those fruits are just so"—I felt myself making a face—"bland and boring. And, yes, I noticed." My expression turned to a smile.

"But if given a choice, pancakes, waffles, or French toast wouldn't be your pick. Your choice would be more savory, like a breakfast burrito with a side of grilled avocado, which will be coming on the tray that gets delivered soon."

"Stop it."

"And crispy home fries."

I touched my stomach, surprised by how I suddenly no longer felt so full. "I honestly can't even with you right now."

He cupped the side of my neck. "How'd I do?"

"You couldn't have done any better." I grabbed the back of his hand and nuzzled into the front of it. "It's such a turn-on that you know me this well. That you pay attention. And that you remember even the finer details."

"You matter to me." His thumb stretched to my lips, pulling at the bottom one. "More than you probably even realize."

"Oh, no, Ridge. I realize. And those feelings are reciprocated—trust me." I finally released his fingers and ran mine over his bare chest. "What's your plan for after breakfast?"

"We'll pack up our things here, and I'll take you home. Then, I've got to go to Jana's and pick up Daisy. Jana flies out late this afternoon for a ten-day work trip."

"I want to ask you something…it's going to be a tough question." I sat up, folding my legs in front of me.

"Ask away."

I rubbed my hands together, linking my fingers, bending them back and forward. "I'm not trying to rush things—please know that. I'm all about taking our time and—"

"You don't have to sugarcoat the question, Addison. I know that's what you're doing. I want you to feel okay about asking me anything."

I nodded, stalling a few moments before I said, "When do you think it's time that I meet Daisy outside the classroom?"

"That's something I've been thinking about a lot. But the first step is Jana. I need to have a conversation with her before Daisy meets you in a personal setting. The last thing I want is my daughter to tell her mother that Miss Lark was hanging out at her dad's house—because Daisy will. The one thing my girl is excellent at is ratting someone out."

I laughed, knowing just what he was talking about since I'd experienced it in class. "I understand."

"But that doesn't mean I'm putting it off."

"I know." My voice was soft. "You're just waiting for a time that feels right."

"On Jana's end, meaning I need to feel her out and assess her mood and pick a time when it makes sense to tell her. It has nothing to do with me not being ready as far as you and I are concerned, and it has everything to do with making sure Jana is ready to handle your transition from teacher to girlfriend and hearing how all of that went down and how we met." He mashed his lips together. "As for timing, things have felt right between us for a while, baby. In my opinion anyway."

"Mine too—you know, minus the whole *turtle speed* thing that I'd insisted on because my morals were getting in the way." I winked, but the lightheartedness ended as soon as I added, "Telling her how we met. That's...mega heavy."

"But important."

"And just something else for me to worry about. What if it disgusts her? What if—"

"I'm going to stop you right there because you don't have to worry. Jana is open-minded about most things. The teacher part, I'm assuming, would bother her much more than the stripping."

When I swallowed, my throat was so tight. "How do you know that?"

"Because I know her and because I don't believe she'd ever knock another woman's hustle. Not when the motivation is family, like yours was."

I appreciated that—I did—but I still wanted to die, so I said, "That doesn't make me feel better."

"Listen to me…" As he stalled, he rubbed my skin in a way that was intended to make me feel better, and his expression softened. "If I didn't believe in us and think we were in it for the long haul, I wouldn't even be considering this. I want you to know that too. And I know we don't have years under our belt. Shit, we don't even have six months, but there's something different about us, Addison. I want Jana to know that, and I want her to understand."

"Are you saying I'm wifey material?" My grin was wide, my giggle as honest as I could be.

"That's exactly what I'm saying."

• • •

Ridge: *Not waking up to you this morning sucked.*

Me: *SAME.*

Me: *And I'm not kidding. I was just thinking that when my eyes opened and there weren't any arms around me or a rock-hard, sweltering body behind me. ;)*

Ridge: *That was a good night at the hotel, wasn't it?*

Me: *It'll be impossible to beat.*

Ridge: *One day, you're going to open your eyes to me every morning…*

Me: *You mean, you'd do that with Daisy home?*

Ridge: *Once she understands how I feel about you and she accepts that there's someone else in my life who I care for deeply,* *then, yeah, I would.*

Me: *I understand her mind more than anyone, and I want those mornings to be a reality—let's be real—but I don't want to rush it either. Hangouts and day/night dates with the three of us—for sure. Her crawling into bed with us every morning? We need to take that extra slow.*

Ridge: *You and your turtle speed, LOL.*

Me: *You said it, not me. Ha-ha!*

Ridge: *But you're right, and I love that you get it and you get her and what she needs.*

Me: *The last thing I would ever want is to come between you and your daughter. But if we go slow and get her used to the idea, it'll make it easier on everyone.*

Ridge: *Fuck, you're the best.*

• • •

Me: *We just finished a reading comprehension worksheet that pointed out the difference between nouns and verbs—I'm talking basic, recognizable words that revolve around food and animals and sports—and Daisy crushed it. 10 out of 10. Your daughter is a superstar!*

Ridge: *Proud dad moment.*

Me: *You've been working with her, haven't you?*

Ridge: *I picked up some reading workbooks that you'd suggested, and we do a couple of pages each evening. She doesn't get dessert until she finishes. That girl likes her M&M cookies, so she gets it done.*

Me: *You're ruthless.*

Ridge: *I believe you also called me that the other night…*

Me: *Who gives someone three orgasms in the shower? You're not even normal, Ridge Cole.*

Ridge: *I'm addicted to your pussy. I can't fucking help myself.*

• • •

Ridge: *I know I'm seeing you tonight, but I wanted to tell you this before I forget… Jana is helping Daisy with her homework right now, and she just texted me that she's blown away by the way Daisy is reading and how far she's come from the beginning of the school year. She's extremely impressed with you, Addison.*

Me: *What makes me the happiest is that Daisy is improving. But I can't take all the credit. You and Jana are working behind the scenes too.*

Me: *Still…yay! <3*

• • •

Me: *Are you at work?*

Ridge: *Yes.*

Me: *Would it be inappropriate if I swung by?*

Ridge: *My office, you mean?*

Me: *Yeah.*

Ridge: *I'm the boss, Addison. Nothing is inappropriate. Come on over.*

Me: *I'll see you in 20.*

• • •

The corporate office of Cole and Spade Hotels was a building that was straight out of a movie. Even walking up to the massive high-rise made me feel important. The exterior was made of blue mirrored glass with a security guard stationed at the front, checking my credentials before allowing me in. The lobby was a mix of plants and marble, gold finishes and elaborate decor, with an incredible scent that hit me the second I came in. The background noise was the sound of a rainforest, playing at just the right decibel while I spoke to the receptionists. There were six—all parked behind a desk that was longer than my entire apartment.

One of the ladies brought me to the elevator, and while she stayed outside, she reached in and waved a fob over the button for the top floor—the level that I assumed housed the partners and the other important people of the company. That small gesture lit the button, and once she moved out of the way, the door closed, and the glass walls of the elevator showed a view of the atrium during the climb. When the door opened, I was greeted by another receptionist, who checked my name tag and then escorted me through a set of locked doors and down a long, wide hallway, eventually leaving me outside Ridge's office.

I knocked on the wood before I opened it.

"Miss Lark," Ridge said, leaning back in his chair with his arms crossed behind his head, eyeing me down as I stepped in and shut the door. "To what do I owe this pleasant surprise?"

His office was bigger than my classroom with two chairs in front of his desk and massive windows that adorned the back, a wet bar in one corner, and what looked like a restroom in the other. There was even a section that had a couch and chairs and a coffee table. As for the artwork, it was everything that embodied my man—masculine, attractive, and extremely powerful.

He sat behind the desk, looking dapper and professional in a black suit, baby-blue tie, crisp white shirt, and a lustful expression that screamed sex.

God help me.

"We need to have a conversation." I set my purse beside me after I took a seat in one of the chairs and clenched my fingers as I held them in my lap. "I figured it was best to have it in person."

"Fuck, you look gorgeous."

His eyes were locked with mine, but I felt his stare on my entire body—a skill I had no idea how he'd mastered, but he was brilliant at it.

"Stop trying to distract me." My voice was low but sharp enough that he knew this chat could go in many different directions.

He smirked. "Why would I do that?"

"Because I'm pissed at you, and you know your words do things to me, and I need you to hold off while I get all my anger out."

A smile pulled at his lips, and he rested his arms on his desk. "And you're mad because?"

I was only trying to play mad.

What I really was, was a storm of emotions that were currently erupting in my chest, forcing tears that I was attempting to hold back. They were feelings that had started at my apartment and built during the entire drive over here.

"Every month, on this day, like clockwork, I get an email, letting me know my student loan payment is due," I said. "And every month, I log in and see a balance that's completely overwhelming and how my payments are barely decreasing. The payoff from the club certainly helped knock some of it down, but the remainder was still extremely painful to look at." I pushed my palm against my chest, the simmering ache almost unbearable. "There *was* a remainder, I should say. Now, the balance is zero."

A day I had dreamed about since I'd started my undergraduate degree, wondering just how many years it would take to pay off, and again when I added a master's degree to my mounting debt.

I was only at the beginning of my payment plan. I had so many more years to go.

The smile didn't fade at all when he said, "Why are you telling me all of this, Addison?"

"Because I sorta went bananas when I looked at my account. I couldn't believe my eyes. I was positive there was a mistake, that I was seeing something that wasn't really there, or that I'd logged in to the wrong account. So, I rushed into Leah's bedroom, pulled her out of a Zoom, and made her confirm that what I was seeing was the truth. And by the smile on her face, I knew something wasn't right. That there was far more to the story than what I was looking at, which took about two seconds to figure out." I recrossed my legs and leaned forward. "I then texted you, and now, I'm here."

"You're here to say what?"

The tears were rimming my eyes, and I couldn't stop them. I wiped my eyelids, trying to come up with something, anything to say, but the words I'd thought of on the way over here were no longer in my head. They'd dissolved. And anything that surfaced in my mouth didn't feel worthy enough to speak.

"Ridge, I…"

"Come here, baby."

He held out his arms, and that was all I needed to see to haul myself up from the chair and rush around his desk and collapse in his lap. My arms circled his neck, my face buried by his throat.

"I can't believe you did this for me."

"I would do anything for you."

That wasn't the first time he'd said that to me, and it wasn't that I'd doubted it before, but every day that passed, he proved it more and more.

Still, paying off my debt was a level I never could have imagined. And I never would have allowed it if I'd been given a choice.

"How do I thank you? How do I even come up with something that's strong enough to say to you or worthy enough to show you how much I appreciate you?"

"This is enough." His voice was so calm.

I gently pounded his chest. "But this"—I swallowed, the spit thickening, my tongue feeling too large for my mouth—"is too much, Ridge. What you did is—"

"Nothing is too much for you."

His arms were locked around me like the mornings when I woke up next to him, every inhale full of his delicious scent.

"I wanted to do this for you, Addison. I couldn't stand the thought of you making payments for the next however many years and having that debt hold you hostage so you could never get ahead." As I lifted my face and gazed at him, he added, "You can look at it that way, or you can look at it as my thanks for being such a wonderful teacher to my daughter. Whatever you want, but I was happy to do it."

I scanned his eyes. I didn't have his talent. I could never see what he was feeling, not like he could do to me. But what I saw behind his stunning cobalt eyes with the navy flecks around the edge was a man who was so kind, attentive, giving, nurturing—and everything I would ever need.

I'd come here to discuss what he'd done, to thank him, to yell at him, but there was something else he needed to know.

Something I had to get off my chest.

Something that finally needed to hit his ears.

"I love you, Ridge."

He slowly licked his lips. "You know, you asked me what would happen when you said those words to me, and I told you, you needed to say it before you found out."

I nodded. "I know."

"Addison..." He unraveled his arms and held my face. Before Ridge, that was a gesture no man had ever done to me. "I love you too."

Hearing him say it to me, feeling that statement move through the air and penetrate my chest, was more than I could handle. All I could whisper back was, "You do?"

"Very much." He kissed me. Slowly. Sucking in my breath and replacing it with his tongue. "Now, go lock the door."

Chapter Twenty-Seven

RIDGE

"Did you get the invitation to the wedding?" I asked Rhett as he sat on my kitchen island, downing his second beer, his legs swinging, the backs of his heels hitting the cabinet beneath him.

I wasn't sure what time he'd left work—or if he'd even come in today—but his suit was long gone, and in its place was a pair of sweatpants, a hoodie, and a baseball hat.

And I also wasn't sure why he'd decided to stop at my place. Addison and I had been in the middle of dinner when he arrived, and he took a spot on the counter. He hadn't moved or said much, and now that we'd finished eating and cleaned up, he was still staying quiet.

"What wedding?" he asked.

Addison was refilling her glass of rosé, and I stood between her and Rhett, admiring the view of my gorgeous redhead before I mocked, "What wedding?" Hell, I knew my brother was in a dark place, but to ask that kind of question meant he was fully checked out. "Brady and Lily's wedding in Edinburgh."

"Oh," Rhett sighed. "That."

My chef had left a container of M&M cookies for Daisy, and with her full glass of wine, Addison was now munching on one. She handed the container to me, and I took one. Then, she offered some to Rhett, and he waved her away.

This wasn't their initial introduction. Over the last few weeks, during the times Addison had been over on weeknights, Rhett had stopped by, unannounced almost every time. I wasn't sure why he popped in; he didn't do much while he was here other than drink beer and stare off into space.

But knowing him, he needed the company.

He needed voices around him, so he wasn't so inside his head—a place that wasn't good for him.

"You're going, aren't you?" I asked my brother.

He took another drink. "I don't know…"

"Don't say that," I shot back. "Brady's a partner, and things are finally good between you two. Don't be that guy, Rhett."

He eyed me down from the other side of the kitchen. "Do me a favor…don't tell me what the fuck I'm doing." He raised his beer like he was giving me a cheers.

"You want me to sit back and watch you destroy a relationship that took all this time to build?" I could feel Addison's eyes on me. "That's not my style. My style is telling you to be there because I know what's best for you. Besides, you have no excuse. Our jet is taking us. We're all staying in our hotel. You just have to show up."

Rhett adjusted his hat and squeezed the visor. "Fuck. Fuck you and fuck him."

"Whoa," Addison whispered.

"Let's tone it down," I warned him. I then gave Addison a look, letting her know I would explain everything later—an explanation I hadn't delved into because it was deep, layered, and it would take a long-ass time to unravel.

"It won't matter if I'm there," Rhett said. He nodded at me.

"You're going." He then nodded at Addison. "And you're going. They won't even notice me missing."

"I'm going?" Addison asked.

Another discussion I hadn't yet had with her, but it was something we needed to talk about for two reasons—I had to pull Daisy out of school for several days, and unless I confessed what was going on to Jana, I couldn't use the wedding to launch our relationship.

"We need to talk about that," I said softly to her.

"Does that mean you're not bringing her?" Rhett huffed, helping himself to another beer before returning to his spot on the counter.

I glanced from him to Addison. "Jana will be there. She was invited. Besides, she's doing Lily's makeup, and Daisy is in the wedding—she and Rayner are flower girls."

"I can't believe you haven't fucking told her," Rhett barked. "What the hell are you waiting for?"

I didn't like his tone.

I didn't like the way he'd worded either statement.

And I didn't like that he was saying all of this in front of Addison. "Rhett—"

"I get it," Addison said, ignoring Rhett's comments and interrupting me. "Don't worry about it."

Her voice was calm, her expression backing up what she'd just said.

But that didn't make things less complicated or make me feel any better about the situation.

I needed to fucking talk to Jana.

She was in town for the next week or so, so I would find a time to go over to her house and explain this all to her. A confession I wasn't looking forward to making, but one that would hopefully alleviate all this stress once it was done.

"And I thought my life was a fucking shit show," Rhett muttered. He took a sip of beer. "It's time you man up, brother."

Is he fucking serious?

"This has nothing to do with manning up," I countered.

"No?" he challenged. "Then, what does it have to do with? You think this is fair to Addison? That she's some secret—"

"She's not a secret. Everyone knows about her, except for Daisy and Jana." My eyes narrowed at my brother. "Do you just want to fight? Is that what this is about? Because if that's the case, I can make that happen, but it's not going to take place in front of Addison."

His legs stilled from swinging. "I can't make myself understand why you've said nothing to her about it. That shit makes no sense to me."

I picked up my filthy martini, but I was too worked up to take a drink.

I didn't know why I wanted to defend myself or why I would even bother, but I still found myself saying, "When Jana's in town, almost every conversation we have is centered around Daisy—her schooling, her activities, her schedule. What am I supposed to do, drop that bomb while she's bragging about the way Daisy is advancing? Hell, I want to. I've tried. I don't want to put this off any longer. But—"

"*I'm dating the teacher* aren't hard words to say, Ridge. You act like you're going to have to confess to fucking murder."

Even his expression was goading my anger. "Rhett—"

"I'm out," he said, jumping off the counter. He set his empty by the sink, stole a cookie from the container in front of Addison, and walked to the door.

I leaned my back against a cabinet, bringing the liquor up to my lips and swallowing until the glass was empty.

"Should I address the elephant in the room?" Her voice was just above a whisper.

I exhaled the burn the vodka had left on my tongue. "Where would you even start? My brother being a fucking asshole? The situation I've gotten us into? The wedding that I want you to attend and…"

She shrugged. "Any of those would work." She shifted her position so she was fully facing me. "I'm not saying your brother is the unfriendliest person I've ever met"—she winced—"but each time I've been around him, he kinda ranks up there."

"He hasn't always been like that."

"What brought it on? Age? Your dad's death? Or I'm not even close?"

I held up a finger, letting her know I needed a second, and I went into the living room to pour myself another drink. Into the mixer, I added vodka and extra olive juice, shaking the shit out of it before I poured the concoction into my glass. As I was heading back into the kitchen, my phone vibrated in my pocket.

It had better be Rhett, apologizing for being such a bastard.

Jana: *Ridge, I have horrible news.*

Me: *What's wrong? Is Daisy all right?*

Jana: *Yeah, yeah, she's fine. I just found out I can't make it to Taylor's concert. The opportunity of a lifetime came my way. One I've been dreaming about since the start of my career. If I pass it up, I'll never forgive myself.*

Me: *I'll take her. Don't even worry about it.*

Jana: *But what about the extra ticket? I don't want it to go to waste.*

Me: *I'll bring Rhett.*

Jana: *Come on. We both know that isn't going to happen.*

Me: *I'll figure it out. Don't stress about it.*

Jana: *I'm sorry…*

"Is everything okay?" Addison asked as I slid my phone back into my pocket.

I heard myself exhale, not even realizing I'd been holding in air or that I'd released it so loudly. "That was Jana. Things are fine.

Anyway, about all of this"—I moved in front of her and cupped her cheek—"I'm going to solve it. Soon. I promise."

Her hand went to the back of mine. "It's okay if it doesn't happen before Brady's wedding. You know my only concern is Daisy. I don't want any of this to affect her. Remember, I was the one who suggested to wait until the end of the school year, so even though Rhett is giving you all this shit about it, I don't agree with him."

I focused on her eyes. "You're so patient, baby."

She gave me a soft smile. "Honestly, I'm slightly worried too. If Jana gets pissed enough and goes to the school board, I don't know what would happen."

"She'd move Daisy out of your class before she went to the school board, but she wouldn't go as far as discussing your personal life with the administration—I guarantee that."

"But how do you think it would look if she moved her out of my classroom? What would she say to the administration to make that happen? Because nothing positive would result from that either." As she filled her lungs, her eyes briefly closed, and the stress appeared— something I hadn't seen until now. "At our school, it's not common for kids to be moved unless it's a student-to-student issue. A teacher-to-student issue would put me under a microscope, and they'd want answers. It's all equally as messy."

Jesus fucking Christ.

Should I have said something to Jana on the first day of school?

Had I made this situation even worse than it needed to be?

"That isn't going to happen either." But as the words left my mouth, I wasn't sure if they were true.

When it came to Daisy, Jana was like me, and there wasn't anything she wouldn't do for our daughter. If this news set her off... I couldn't predict the outcome.

"Ridge"—she held my hand tightly—"can we not talk about this anymore?" Her eyes were pleading with mine. "It's been a perfect night so far—minus the Rhett hiccup. I haven't seen a single storm cloud, only the sun." She paused, which silently emphasized those words. "I'd much rather discuss him than get even deeper into this. My anxiety has peaked. I don't want it to reach a level I can't come back from."

I fucking hated that I had caused her to feel this way.

That her body was stiff, and her breathing was off, and her chest was a bundle of damn tension.

I put my drink down to hold her with both hands. "Of course."

She leaned her chest against me. "Now, tell me why your brother is so grumpy."

Chapter Twenty-Eight

ADDISON

Ridge: *If you're wondering if I got an apology from Rhett this morning, the answer to that would be no.*

Me: *Let's cut him a little slack, okay?*

Ridge: *I'm going to cut you a little slack for saying that, LOL.*

Me: *Now that you explained everything to me and the source of his anger, I have a soft spot for him.*

Ridge: *No. Nooo. And hell no.*

Me: *I can't help it… I'm weak.*

Ridge: *He can be an asshole to me, but to be one in your presence is where he fucked up.*

Me: *But I get why he is one, and all I want to do is give him a hug.*

Ridge: *What am I going to do with you?*

Ridge: *You're a good person, Addison. No wonder you work with kids all day—you're going to make them into the best people.*

Me: *<3*

Me: *Take him out to lunch. Shower him in love. I bet the apology will fall right out of him.*

Me: *You know he's been self-reflecting all night. That's what he does, Ridge. He thinks, and then he overthinks.*

Ridge: *Regardless, I'm pissed.*

Me: *What will put you in a better mood?*

Ridge: *You.*

Me: *Then, come see me during my lunch break.*

Ridge: *Done.*

• • •

Me: *Eating my breakfast burrito as I type this. I love you…you're amazing.*

Ridge: *I couldn't come see my girl and not bring her something to eat.*

Me: *You're just so sweet.*

Ridge: *I need to see you again.*

Me: *You just saw me. ;)*

Ridge: *It wasn't enough.*

Me: *Tonight?*

Ridge: *I have a thing with the guys and the Westons. Let's hope I don't murder my brother while we're out. Alcohol and anger don't mix well.*

Me: *You'd better not, mister.*

Ridge: *Only because you asked nicely…*

Me: *Tomorrow night then?*

Ridge: *Perfect.*

Ridge: *Two more evenings of being kid-free before I get my Daisy back.*

Me: *I know you've missed her.*

Ridge: *For sure, but I've also enjoyed the break and spending time with you.*

Ridge: *Not tomorrow, but the following night, I have dinner with Jana. I asked her to meet me. It's time that we talk.*

Me: *You mean, THE talk?*

Ridge: *Yeah…*

Me: *Whoaaaaaa.*

Ridge: *It needs to happen. The sooner I tell her, the better we'll all feel.*

Me: *Or the worse we'll all feel.*

Ridge: *You're supposed to be the positive one.*

Me: *The sky is suddenly feeling a little cloudy.*

Ridge: *Stop it. I love you. It's going to be fine.*

• • •

The only thing I could do to get my brain off Ridge's upcoming chat with Jana was to bury myself in him. To concentrate on the moment, which would hopefully stop my mind from drifting every time it started. So, that was what I did over dinner when he took me to the most delicious Indian restaurant and in his car during the drive to his house and when we stripped off our clothes in his bedroom and walked naked across his patio to get into the hot tub.

We sat on the same side, but where he faced the view of the Hollywood Hills, I positioned my body toward him, draping my legs across his lap, the jet blowing water against my side, my hands keeping me grounded so I wouldn't sink.

"I'm so relaxed," I moaned.

He brushed his fingers over the top of my hair. "That's all I wanted, baby."

"You never told me how last night went with the guys." I smiled. "Did Rhett behave?"

"Behave? I'm not sure he knows how to do that. But his mood seemed to be slightly better, although the constant booze that we fed him helped."

"Did you have a good time?"

He was leaning his head against the edge of the stone and lifted it to nod. "Half business, half bullshit. That's how it is whenever we hang with the Westons. Aside from me and Brady—because he's working in Bangkok—all the partners are looking for new properties to either develop or renovate. We're expanding so fast, but the need is there, therefore, it has to happen. That's the discussion that took up a lot of the night since the Westons want to put restaurants in all our future hotels."

"With your partners working on-site, that's got to be tough to be away from home for so long."

He rubbed the bottoms of my feet. "If Jana didn't spend a majority of her time on the road, I'd have to do it too."

"I can't even imagine you being away from Daisy."

He exhaled. "I can't either." He stole a glance at the view and gradually looked back at me. "Rowan and Cooper are traveling together, bringing Rayner with them. But when she starts school, it's going to be an entirely different story. One of them will have to stay back with her, and, hell, I don't know how that's going to go." He massaged his palm across my thigh. "Enough about work. Let's talk about you."

I laughed. "What about me?"

"I want to hear how school was today."

I lifted my hand out of the water and waved it at him. "Enough about work."

He chuckled. "Fair." He was now holding the bottom of my chin. "What am I going to do with you this summer?"

"This summer?"

"You're off, aren't you?"

"Yes."

"It would be a crime if we didn't go somewhere during your downtime."

I hadn't put much thought into my summer plans. I was just already really looking forward to the break. As much as I loved my job, by the end of the school year, I needed the summer to rejuvenate.

"The only thing I have on the schedule," I said, "is to go visit my sister for a week—although she'll probably have to work the whole time I'm there."

"Dallas isn't the beach."

"No," I huffed. "It's certainly not. And in the summer, it's extra hot, extra spicy, and extra miserable. Sigh."

"Tell me somewhere you want to go. Somewhere you've always wanted to go."

"*Hmm.*" I rested my cheek on the stone that edged the tub, inches from Ridge's head. "Hawaii?"

"Done."

"Done?" My eyebrows were so high. "You say that like it's the easiest thing in the world."

"Because it is. We have a hotel there—and if you ask Macon, he'll say it's the best resort in our entire fleet." His hand moved to my side. "The hotel is on Kauai, but if you've never been, then we'll need to go to at least one other island, maybe two."

This sounded so dreamy.

So romantic.

I could already see the magic of the beach in my head.

Even though I wasn't allowing myself to fast-forward to tomorrow, the result of his dinner with Jana meant I would hopefully soon get to spend lots of personal time with Daisy. And because of that, I had a question.

"Would Daisy be coming with us?" I asked.

With his free arm, he grabbed the other side of my waist and moved me onto his lap. "You mean to Hawaii?"

"Yes." My legs straddled him; my arms crossed around his neck.

"No, the trip would be just us."

After he kissed me, I said, "I hope you don't think I had an agenda when I asked that question. I wasn't inferring I wanted the trip to be with or without her. I was just curious—that's all."

"And that's exactly how I took it. I know how much you care about her. I also know that if she came with us, the trip would be all about her—as it should be—and we need time alone as a couple."

I took in his eyes first and then his lips. "Hawaii, a beach… Ridge, I'm dying right now."

His hands slid up my sides, slowing when they neared the bottoms of my breasts. The slickness of the water and the smoothness of his skin was the most sensual combination. He cupped each one and grazed my nipples, back and forth, stroking the steam out of me. "Then, you're going to be dying for a long time because I plan to show you every beach in the world."

If I wasn't so tuned in to him, I would have lost focus from how he was touching me. How he was building me toward begging.

"Every beach…stop," I exhaled.

"What, you don't believe me?" The brushing turned to a light pinching, and it was as though he'd lit a match, my entire body ablaze in fire. "I'm not a guy who would ever bullshit you, Addison."

Pants were coming from my mouth. Quiet ones, but deep ones. "I know. I just can't get over what I'm hearing."

He took ahold of my bottom lip, sucking on it, gnawing on it before he pulled back. "We're going to have an incredible life together."

"We already do."

He kissed my neck.

My throat.

Across each cheek.

His hands casually rotated to my back, leading me in even closer, his hard-on grinding into the front of my pussy. "I need you." He used his tip to tap my clit. "I need to bury myself inside your cunt."

He was taunting me.

Provoking me.

"Ridge," I breathed as he returned to my titty, kneading the center, drawing out the pleasure. I reached for his dick, swiping the opposite side that was against me so all of it was getting friction. "What are you waiting for?"

"You."

I was in a maze, lost, hitting walls, desperately searching for an out. That was what it felt like to sit here and wait for him to thrust into me.

Because there wasn't just fire.

There were tingles.

There were internal screams.

There was a need so bad that it was even making my blood pound.

"Me?" I questioned.

"If you want this dick, Addison, then you need to take it. You need to put it inside your pussy. And you need to fuck me."

An order I would gladly accept.

I rose on my knees to position his crown, and then I lowered all the way to his base.

"That's it." He kissed me, his lips rough and needy, his tongue as erotic as his cock.

"Fuck," I cried out as the fullness and pressure registered within me. "Yes!"

"Does that feel good?"

His hands were moving all over me, creating sensations I hadn't anticipated, each one bringing out a short yell or a moan, especially as he began to slip in between my ass cheeks.

An area he hadn't explored.

"Incredible," I exhaled.

"Take more, Addison. Take it harder. Take it faster."

I adjusted my speed, bouncing over him, each dip sending the water splashing over the side of the hot tub. And every time that happened, his hand went closer to that forbidden hole.

"I want this," he demanded.

"My ass?"

"I want to see if it's as tight and wet as your pussy."

My neck was leaned back, my chin almost resting on his nose, so every word he spoke hit my throat. I didn't know how breath could feel like foreplay, but each syllable added to what I was feeling.

"Are you going to give me this?"

I looked at him, still moving, still rocking against him. "I've never done that before."

"A virgin hole." He rubbed my lips with his thumb. "I'll be gentle with it."

I believed he would.

Even if it would hurt.

Even if it would be something I ended up hating.

I'd do it for him.

"It's yours."

He arched his hips, slamming me with several pumps, dragging more screams out of me before he stood and carried me out of the tub, walking us across the patio, and through the sliding glass doors of his living room.

The glass wasn't even closed yet when I heard, "Ridge!"

The voice, a woman's, was one I vaguely recognized. The pitch was loud enough to vibrate through me, the sound startling the shit out of me.

I didn't know where it had come from since my back was to the living room and all I could see was the slider and pool and view of outside.

"Fuck," Ridge groaned in response.

What the hell is happening right now?

I glanced over my shoulder. Jana was standing in front of the coffee table as if she'd been heading for the patio with a sleepy Daisy in her arms. Daisy's eyes were opening, aimed directly at her father.

"Daddy?" She blinked a few times and rubbed her eyelids. "Mommy, are we at Daddy's house?"

My heart didn't just sink.

It dropped out of my body and fell onto the wooden floor beneath us.

Ridge didn't move when he said, "Jana, take Daisy upstairs to her room right now."

Daisy's gaze shifted from her father to me. It took a moment and another gentle rub of her eyes before the recognition passed over her face.

When I saw it, emotion didn't just tear apart my chest.

It completely shattered it.

Nooo.

"Miss Lark?" A second ticked by. "Why is my daddy carrying you?"

Chapter Twenty-Nine

RIDGE

I rushed inside my closet, tossing on a T-shirt, reaching for the pile of sweatpants, where there was a pair of gray ones on top, and stepped into them, pulling them up to my waist. Now that I was dressed, I went back into the bedroom, and Addison was standing by the bed, putting on the clothes she'd stripped off before the hot tub, moving as quickly as I had. With Jana upstairs, putting Daisy to bed, Addison and I had a few minutes to talk until I had to address Jana and deal with the fallout of what had just happened.

"Come here," I said as I approached, holding out my arms.

"I can't." She had just zipped and buttoned her pants and was clutching her stomach. "I feel like I can't even breathe right now." She twisted her wet hair on top of her head and tied it off with an elastic from her wrist.

What I noticed, what drove my hands to her face, was the tears. The second she released her hair, the first one dripped.

I caught it and said, "Addison, I got this. Don't worry."

"It's too late to fix this."

"Fuck that," I whispered, stepping closer to her. "It's never too late."

"Your daughter just saw us naked. With me in your arms. The thoughts that are going through her head right now—"

"Here's the thing about my girl." I aligned our bodies. "Once she's asleep, which I can tell she had been by the way she was talking, things become extremely fuzzy and not easy for her to recall. She'll remember seeing you, most likely, but I doubt she'll remember that you were naked."

With the way we had been positioned, Daisy could only see Addison's back. Her bare ass, her legs wrapped around me—those were details I wasn't even sure my daughter had taken in. Since I'd never turned Addison around, Daisy wouldn't have seen the front of her or any of me, aside from my legs and arms.

And that was if she was even paying attention.

"What about Jana?" Her hands went over her face. "Oh my God, I can't even imagine what she thinks about me right now."

Jana was an entirely different story.

Things had happened so fast that I didn't ask her a single question. I had no idea why she'd brought Daisy to my house, why she'd let herself in, or why the fuck she hadn't called first. We had boundaries established, and she'd crossed mine.

But as the last few minutes ran through my head, two things were certain. Jana had been shocked as hell at what she walked into—I could tell that by the way she'd said my name. The tone and shrillness of her voice. And her expression had told me she wasn't pleased by what she saw.

I carefully pulled Addison's hands away. "I'm going to talk to her now. She needs to understand this—us—and I need to understand why this happened and why I hadn't known they were coming over."

When she nodded, each dip of her head sent another tear down her cheek.

I wiped them away and pulled her against my chest, pressing my lips into the top of her head. "I promise it's going to be fine."

She didn't respond. She just wrapped her arms around me and squeezed. "I'm going to order a rideshare and go home."

"No—"

"Ridge, I cannot be here when you talk to Jana."

The last thing I wanted was for her to go home in the emotional state that she was in, lie in her bed, and fucking stew over this. She was going to blame herself. She was going to lock herself inside her head. She was going to come up with conclusions that she didn't need to make.

I couldn't let that happen.

I wouldn't let that happen.

I would resolve things with Jana, and then I would heal Addison— that was the only outcome.

I pulled back to hold her face. "Then, wait for me in here. I'll talk to her in the living room, and I'll come back once I'm done."

She looked at me as though she didn't know me. "I don't think that's a good idea."

"Why?"

It took her several seconds before she responded, "Because what if she doesn't approve?"

I was right; she was already so far inside her head that she was hitting bottom.

"I don't give a shit what she approves of or not. She's not my mother, Addison. She can't dictate who I see or who I date or who I bring into my life."

"But she can." She bit her lip. "She's Daisy's mom. The weight that she holds"—she took a breath—"is epic, Ridge. Think about it. Really, really think about it."

I understood what she was saying and where those fears could come from.

But even though Jana was her mother, I was her father. I had an equal stake in this. Daisy spent the majority of her time with me, and Jana knew that if I was going to bring a woman around my daughter—and she would soon know that was my plan—then that woman had to have a significant meaning in my life.

By the end of tonight, Jana would know exactly what Addison meant to me and the future I wanted to have with her.

Only then could Jana make her decision.

"Listen to me"—I lowered my face so there were only inches separating us—"I hear you. I know where you're coming from. But I need you to hear me and know where I'm coming from." I pressed my thumbs into her cheeks. "I don't want you to leave. I'm asking you to stay, and I don't ask for much."

"You can't say that to me."

"I just did." I held her hands, and with the tightness I used to clutch them, that was how strongly I stared into her eyes. "I'm confident this is all going to work out, Addison. If I wasn't, I wouldn't have asked you to spend the night." I waited several seconds before I nodded toward the bed. "Wait for me. I'll be back soon." When she didn't move or respond, I added, "Please."

She slowly pulled her hands from mine and went over to the bed, lifting the comforter and sinking beneath it. I walked over and held her cheek, kissing the top of her head, leaving my lips there to breathe her in. My eyes closed the moment I got the smallest hint of her scent.

I left her in the bedroom, shutting the door behind me, and since I didn't see Jana anywhere in the kitchen or living room, I headed straight for the wet bar. I poured vodka onto ice, forgoing the olive juice—it was filler that I didn't need tonight—and I carried the glass over to the couch and took a seat.

Within a few minutes, Jana was descending the stairs. She came over to the mouth of the sectional, her arms crossed over her chest, an expression on her face that was half exhaustion, half frustration. "She's asleep."

I nodded. "Do you want a drink?"

Her arms dropped, and she glanced up at the ceiling, her hands holding the top of her head by her hairline. "I don't know what the hell I want right now. All I know is that what I saw… I definitely didn't want that."

When she finally looked at me, I pointed at a spot toward the middle of the couch. "Sit."

"Ridge"—she clenched her hands as her arms dropped at her sides—"I'm so angry with you right now, I could scream."

"That makes two of us." I pointed again. "Sit."

As soon as her ass hit the cushion, she said, "I'm guessing Addison was going to be the topic we discussed at dinner tomorrow night."

"You guessed right." I took my first drink. "Jana, why did you come here tonight?"

She leaned forward, resting her arms on her knees. "My client called and changed my departure to five tomorrow morning."

"So, you brought Daisy to my house…"

"Obviously."

I huffed. "And did you call to tell me?"

"I called you about ten times. You never answered or responded to my texts, so I just assumed you were sleeping."

"We got back from dinner, and I didn't check my phone, and then we went in the hot tub—"

"I know what happened from there."

"But you came to my house, Jana, without knowing if I was home, and you let yourself in. When it comes to Daisy, we allow leeway, we walk into each other's homes when we know the other person is coming over, but what happened here is not the same situation. This is different."

Her back straightened, and she held the edge of the couch. "I know you're not turning this around like I'm the one in the wrong here."

"But I'm not in the wrong either. I was in my home. I was with a woman. You can't find fault in that."

Her top lip flared. "I can when your daughter sees it."

"She wouldn't have seen it if you hadn't crossed a boundary and brought her in without my knowledge." I took another sip.

"Ridge, I couldn't get in touch with you, and I need to fly out at the crack of dawn tomorrow morning. What else was I supposed to do?"

"You're her mother, Jana. You figure it out. The same way I figure it out when you're traveling and I'm here alone, making decisions for our daughter. I call my mother. I call your mother. I call a sibling. What I wouldn't do is take her to where you are—wherever you are—and expect you to take care of her without letting you know I was coming."

Her mouth opened and closed and then quickly opened again. "I'm doing everything in my power not to scream at you right now."

"You can be upset all you want that Addison is who I was with, but you can't deny that the way you handled this was wrong."

"You're her father, Ridge. If I can't bring her to you, then what the fuck—"

"I didn't say you can't bring her to me. I said you need to speak with me first." I switched the glass to my other hand and wiped the condensation on the leg of my sweatpants. "What if I was away for the night on a work trip? What if I was still out to dinner? What if I was having a ten-person orgy in my living room? What would you have done then?"

She shook her head. "I don't know."

"That's something you should have thought of. You know you can always count on me, but don't assume anything before you walk through my front door." Even though my words had been direct during this entire conversation, I kept my tone even. If anything, it dipped on the softer side.

"We're drifting from the point of all this—"

"There are many points to this. The way you handled tonight was one. The woman I was with is two. Let's talk about her."

Her throat bobbed as she swallowed, and she chewed her thumbnail, her gaze intensifying as she stared at me. "Addison Lark." Her chest rose as she filled it. "Out of all people, you picked our daughter's teacher—"

"I'm going to stop you right there."

"Please don't." Her hand fell onto her lap. "I have boatloads to say on this topic."

"You can say all you want once you understand how things happened with her and what brought us to this moment."

She tucked a piece of hair behind her ear. "I'm not sure I want to even hear those details—"

"You need to hear them. They're important."

She held my gaze for a handful of seconds and then leaned back into the couch, slipped out of her shoes, and crossed her legs in front of her. "Don't make me regret this decision."

I unraveled the story, starting when Addison and I had met at the strip club during Brady and Lily's joint party and how things had gone down that night between us. Hell, I knew Addison's stripping wasn't my information to tell. Addison should really be the one saying this to Jana. But I also knew that Jana had a relationship with my friends and family, and if she mentioned something to them about my girlfriend, there was a chance she could find out anyway.

She was going to hear it from me before that happened.

Once I explained this, along with Addison's motivation to strip and why she no longer worked there, I went on to tell her how I was shocked as hell to find out she was Daisy's teacher—something I'd learned when I followed our daughter to her classroom on the first day of school. I told her that I was the one who had pursued a relationship, how Addison had fought against it for many reasons, and how I'd fallen for her first.

Jana said nothing as I spoke.

She didn't even move.

Only when I finished did I take a drink, holding the vodka in my mouth, assessing what I was about to face.

She held her knees and said with just enough force, "You should have told me."

There they were—the words I'd anticipated hearing.

I slowly shook my head. "Why?"

"Because she's our daughter's teacher...and a former stripper."

"Don't tell me the stripper part bothers you. She was a woman trying to earn money to do something nice for her family since all they'd ever done was sacrifice for her and she wanted to give back. She also wanted to get some of her student loans for her undergraduate and master's degrees paid down. Given that you gave your own parents a gift, Jana, I'd be shocked to hear you have a problem with what Addison did." I deepened my stare, recalling the moment during our relationship that was so similar to Addison's situation. I adjusted my position and continued, "Do you remember how hard you worked for that down payment for their house? You wouldn't take money from me, you wanted to earn it on your own. So, you took job after job to give them that. But you have that option with your job; you can take on all the gigs you want. Addison is on a teacher's salary, she can't make more than she's already making, so she found a second job." I dragged my fingers through my wet hair. "It's not what she wanted, but earning that kind of money, quickly—we both know there aren't many options to do that."

She sighed. "It still wouldn't have been my choice, but you're right, Ridge, I didn't mean to sound judgy, and I can look past that. Her role as Daisy's teacher, however, affects everything—"

"What does it affect? You've said multiple times to me how well Daisy is doing in school. How she's advancing and how much improvement you're seeing. How her reading and comprehension are getting so much stronger."

"Will I be able to say the same if you two break up?"

"That's not happening."

"And if it does?"

"We'll cross that bridge, if it does, which it won't."

A promise I really couldn't make, but one I felt in my heart.

In all these years, my heart had never lied. It had never sent me in a direction it shouldn't—not with Jana, and it wouldn't with Addison either.

"What about when Daisy isn't at school?" she said. "Don't you think it'll be confusing to her when her teacher is spending quality time with her at her dad's house? And how is Addison going to play both roles? Dad's cool girlfriend while disciplining her in the classroom? And do you think our daughter is going to understand the difference between those roles and respect them?"

"Jana—"

"This is a lot, Ridge. It was a lot to walk in on. It was a lot to have Daisy see." She tilted her neck and looked up at the ceiling again. "It's a lot to process since, up until tonight, I was satisfied with the way she's been teaching my kid." She looked at me again. "And, now, I don't know what the hell to think."

"Given Addison's relationship to our family, I understand what that must have been like for you. Certainly a shock, I'm sure. And it wasn't the proudest moment I've had in front of my daughter, but it also wasn't the first time something like that has happened." I watched the recognition come across her face, remembering when a similar situation had gone down when we moved Daisy into a toddler bed and she decided to visit our room in the middle of the night. "The bottom line is, I'm human. We're both human. Human things happen, and they did this evening. And I think Daisy was too sleepy to really understand what she was looking at."

She pulled one of the pillows against her chest. "That doesn't change the fact that she's Daisy's teacher."

"She's a professional, Jana, who's as focused on our daughter as she is on me. Daisy's best interests are all that matter to Addison." I softened my voice even more as I said, "You need to trust that Addison will figure out how to balance these roles and—"

"You want me to trust someone I don't know? Who isn't even related to our child? Because she's your girlfriend? Come on, Ridge. I can't even believe you have the nerve to say that to me."

Mama Bear was still out, but I knew how to handle this side of her.

"Do you trust me, Jana?"

She silently shook her head. "Why are you going there?"

"Answer me."

"Of course I trust you."

"Then, you need to trust that I would never put someone in Daisy's life who didn't want the best for her." I stretched my arm across the back of the couch. "The same way you wouldn't introduce Daisy to one of your boyfriends if you didn't think he would make the best decisions for our daughter. You know, the last relationship you were in, I don't recall us needing a conversation like the one we're having now. Because I trusted you. I trusted your decision-making, and therefore, I trusted him." Before she could chime in, I added, "Don't tell me this situation is so unlike your last boyfriend. They're different people, sure, but ultimately, you were dating someone, and now, I'm dating someone, it's all the same."

She rubbed both hands over her forehead and across the top of her head. "Fuck."

"We knew when we broke up, it wasn't always going to be the easiest, but we've done an impressive job, working together for the sake of our little girl. This is a bump, but we'll get through it." I slid to the end of the cushion and placed my vodka on the table. "But I need us on the same page about this. Because if we're not, it's going to create a mess that neither of us, nor our daughter, needs." I folded my hands together. "I'm happy, Jana. I'm happier than I've been in a long time."

"I know." She lifted my glass of vodka off the table and downed it in one sip, setting the empty back. "I've had my suspicions that someone was in your life. I guess I just know you so well that I could sense it." She tucked the other side of her hair behind her ear. "I never pointed it out. I just kept it to myself, knowing that when the time was right, you'd tell me."

I chuckled. "Hey, I planned to."

"And that does make me happy—although I don't know what that dinner would have looked like. Tonight was a bomb, Ridge. You put a few drinks in me and add that news in, and who knows what would have come out?"

I smiled. "There were many things about our relationship that didn't work, but what we've done so well is put those things aside for our girl. We talk it out when it gets rough. We lean on each other when we have to. We listen to both sides, even when we don't want to. Tomorrow night would have looked just like tonight—two adults with strong opinions because we love our daughter so much and we would do anything to protect her."

Emotion flashed through her eyes. "You're right."

When her arm stretched out toward me, I set my hand on her wrist. "I wouldn't allow Addison to spend any personal time with Daisy until you knew the truth about us." I squeezed her and pulled my hand back. "I'm asking you now to be okay with it."

"Are you giving me a choice?"

I nodded. "Yes."

"And if I'm not okay with it? What then, Ridge?"

I sighed. "I'll cross that bridge when it happens," I repeated for the second time. I looked at the glass between us. "Do you need another drink while you're thinking about it?"

"I need to drive home, so no." She unfolded her legs and moved the pillow back to where it had been. And the words that finally came out of her mouth were, "I trust your decision-making."

I nodded. "Thank you."

Chapter Thirty

ADDISON

I didn't know why I was nervous. Out of all the first-time moments in my life—standing in front of a classroom, walking across a stage to strip—this should have been easy.

But it wasn't.

I was more anxious now as I headed up Ridge's driveway and rang the doorbell than I'd been during either of those two occasions.

Several days had passed since the incident at his house, preparing me for today. Within that span, I'd had multiple conversations with him regarding his chat with Jana. Not only the night it had happened, when we'd stayed awake for most of the evening before I took a rideshare home in the early hours of the morning so Daisy wouldn't see me when she got up, but our chat also continued over the next couple of days. I wanted to fully understand where Jana's head was at, and I wanted to wait to see if she changed her mind about my spending personal time with her daughter.

I just wanted to respect her as Daisy's mother and as a woman.

But it turned out, she stayed firm on her decision.

A week hadn't even passed before Ridge asked if I would come to his house and hang with him and Daisy. I was hoping during that timeframe, any lingering memories she had of that night would fizzle out. Ridge had told me they would, and he was right. She recalled me being there, but that was it. As for her saying anything about it to her fellow students, Ridge had bribed her not to.

As far as I could tell—and I'd know—Daisy had kept our secret.

But I didn't know, if things continued to progress between her father and me—and I hoped they would—if his adorable little girl, who was running toward the front door right now, would be able to keep that secret contained. Ridge's all-glass entrance made it easy to see her coming from the living room, rushing toward the foyer to greet me, her ponytail high on her head and full of curls.

Ridge had told me he was going to prep her a little and tell her I was coming over to play. He'd told me that she said she felt like the luckiest girl in the whole world to be able to play with her teacher at home.

Which couldn't have been any cuter.

"Miss Lark, Miss Lark, you really came." She held the door just wide enough that she could stand in the opening, the grin on her face contagious.

"I did." I ducked down so we were at eye level. "And I brought you a present, but you can only have it under one condition."

Her eyes lit up and widened. "A present?"

As I held it behind my back, I said, "Yes."

"Okay, I promise everything."

I laughed. "Whenever you see me outside of school, you either call me by my real name, which is Addison, or my nickname, which is Addy. But when we're at school, you have to call me Miss Lark. Do you think you can do that?"

She bobbed her head. "I can do that, Miss—" Her mouth formed an O when she realized the mistake she was about to make, and then she giggled. "Addy. I like Addy. It's cute."

"I like it too."

"Addy, does that mean I get my present now?"

I stayed kneeling and smiled. "I went on a walk this morning, and I passed the most beautiful store." Her big blue eyes were getting larger again as I spoke. "I saw these in the window, and because I knew I was coming over here to play with you, I thought you absolutely had to have them." I moved my arm out from behind my back, and I handed her the gift.

She jumped up and down. "You bought me daisies! They're pink! And light pink! And dark pink!"

"Do you like them?"

She nodded. "I love them *sooo* much. I want Daddy to see them. Come on!"

As I followed her inside and shut the door behind us, she yelled, "Daddy, Addy got me flowers. She said I could call her Addy, so don't get mad I'm not calling her Miss Lark. And the flowers are pink, and they're mine!"

When I reached the kitchen, Ridge was at the counter, putting away what looked like the remainder of their lunch, and he smiled the second he saw me. "Addison…"

I winked. "Ridge…"

He left my gaze to look at his daughter. "They're beautiful. You'd better take good care of them." He placed something in the fridge, shut the door, and asked, "Did you thank Addy for the flowers?"

"I don't remember." She turned toward me. "Miss—Addy, did I thank you?"

His smile caused every inch of my body to not only flush, but blush. And if I had to guess, he wasn't even trying to cause this reaction inside me; he was staying completely appropriate in front of his daughter. He just had this effect on me.

I grinned at Daisy. "Not officially, but your excitement made up for it."

"Daisy, you know better than that," Ridge said to her. "What do you say to Addy?"

She rushed over to me and threw the arm that wasn't holding the flowers around my waist. "Thank you *sooo* much. I love them to pieces."

I palmed the side of her head and leaned down to squeeze her. "You're *sooo* welcome."

When she pulled back, she said, "Daddy, I need them to last forever and ever. Because flowers die, and these are too pretty to die."

He chuckled as he walked to the far side of the kitchen and opened a cabinet, taking out a vase that he handed to me. "If you ask Addy nicely, she'll show you how to put the flowers in water so they have the best chance of lasting."

"Will you show me, Addy?" she pleaded.

"Of course. Come here." I brought her over to the sink and set the glass in her outstretched hand. "I'm going to turn on the water and fill it halfway," I instructed so she knew it was about to get heavier. I shut off the faucet when I was pleased with the level and had her set the vase on the counter. "Do you know where your dad keeps the scissors?"

"Over here." She rushed to the island, opened a drawer, and came back. "Can I cut whatever you're cutting?"

"Yes, you're going to do all the cutting." I opened the plastic wrap that was around the bouquet and placed all the flowers on the counter. "You're going to lift each stem"—I placed one in her hand— "and you're going to cut it at an angle." I used my fingers as though they were scissors to show her what I meant.

"Like this?" She positioned the blades exactly where my fingers had been.

"Just like that."

"Ugh," she grunted as she cut the first one. "That was so tough."

I smiled at her. "Now that it's trimmed, you're going to place the flower in the vase."

When she dropped the stem in, the water made a plopping noise, and she giggled. "Pretty!"

I lifted the remaining stalks; there had to be at least twenty. "You're going to do the same thing to all of these."

"Yay!" She took one from my hand and cut it without needing any direction, dropping it in the water and picking up the next. "What if I cut it wrong?"

She was doing the angle correctly, so she must have meant at what point in the stem it needed to be cut.

"It's okay if the stems are different lengths." I had her slice one a little longer. "It'll give the boutique some dimension when it's all done. That means, because the tops of the flowers won't all land in the same spot, they'll almost make the shape of a dome, so you'll get to see the details of every part of the flower."

"Can I see it now?"

I twirled her ponytail around my finger. "You can, but you won't see the full effect until you're done."

As she continued to shorten the stems, she said, "Daddy, does this count as my chores? Because this is hard work. I'm building a dome."

He was sitting on one of the barstools with a tablet in front of him. I didn't think he was actually using it because if he was, I wouldn't be able to feel his eyes. And since I'd been standing at the sink, I'd been feeling them bore through me, my skin remaining hot even though I wasn't looking at him.

"No, little one, you still have to do your chores."

Daisy sighed. "Addy, I have to move so many things from the washer to the dryer once it stops making shaking and spinning. And I have to fold everything when it comes out all hot. The towels are bigger than me! And I fold them into little rectangles and make them in a big pile, and sometimes, the pile collapses, and I have to do it all over again."

"Sounds like you're a huge help," I told her.

"No"—she shook her head—"Daddy's making me do it for Taylor. He says I have to be on my best behavior for her, so I'm trying real hard."

The things that came out of kids' mouths constantly made me laugh, especially in a relaxed setting like this. "Who's Taylor? A friend of yours or..."

"*Swiiift*." She dragged it out for several beats. "I want to go to her concert. It's very important. She sings about me, and I have to hear her sing that song. But not just that song. I know every word of every song, and I can't wait. I told Daddy I'll fold towels for the rest of my life if he takes me."

"She sings a song about you?" I asked.

" 'You're on Your Own, Kid!' " She set another flower in the vase. "She talks about a Daisy, and it's *meee*."

"It's you, huh?" I teased.

"It can't be about another Daisy," she replied. "I'm the *only* Daisy."

"There are millions of other Daisys, honey. I hate to tell you, but you're not the only one," Ridge said. "And I'm not saying that to upset you. I just want you to know there are other people who share your name."

"That's not fair," she whined. "I wanna be the only one."

I set the rest of the flowers on the counter and put my hands on her shoulders and turned her toward me. "There are too many people on this planet to have a name that no one else has, but you know what can make you unique and different from everyone else?"

Her shoulders rose, no longer slumping. "What?"

"Your personality. The way you treat people and make them

feel. The things you can do for this world and everyone who lives in it." I gently tickled the center of her cheeks, and she giggled. "I bet, Miss Daisy, that you're going to do some incredible things because you have the kindest heart, just like your dad, and you're giving and sensitive, and you care so deeply about others."

"I'm all of those things?"

"Yes, you are." I raked back the little pieces of hair that had fallen from her elastic. "So, even though you share a name, it doesn't matter. Because Daisy Cole isn't just going to be a name one day, it's going to be a statement."

She put her hands on her hips. "I know what I'm going to do. I'm going to save the horses."

Her sass made me chuckle. "How are you going to save them?"

"I'm going to let them run free so they're not in barns anymore. I want every horsey in the world to be able to go wherever they want, and I want one outside our kitchen, so when I wake up for school and come down for breakfast, I can feed it carrots outside the window."

"Do me a favor, pumpkin. Don't attempt that when we're at the barn tomorrow. I'm afraid the owner won't be very happy with us." Ridge rubbed his hand over his forearm, drawing my attention to the veins that popped under his skin and the muscle that tightened and the dark hair that covered it.

But what stole my attention right back was Daisy's giggle that turned into a snort.

"Oopsie-daisy," she sang.

I looked back at Ridge, no longer able to contain myself, and I burst out laughing.

"Oopsie-daisy—hands down my favorite thing you've ever said." I hugged her against me.

"Mommy used to say it when I was learning how to walk and kept falling. Now, I say it every time I snort—I don't mean to do it, it just comes out sometimes, and it tickles."

"It was perfect," I told her.

She resumed the cutting, adding each of the flowers to the vase until the only things left were the fallen leaves.

I lifted the glass off the counter and held it in front of her. "What do you think?"

"It's *sooo* pretty."

"I think so too," I replied.

"Where do you want to keep your flowers, Daisy?" Ridge asked. "Do you want them in the kitchen or your bedroom?"

"*Hmm*." She was touching the petals. "I want them next to my bed, so I see them when I go to sleep and wake up."

"Why don't you take them up to your room, then?" Ridge said.

She took the glass from my hands. "Be right back. I'll be super fast."

"No running," Ridge reminded her as soon as she took off.

His eyes then moved to me—I could feel them, sense them—and I turned my head, locking our stares.

"I like this. I like this a whole fucking lot." His eyelids narrowed. "Get over here."

I assumed I had a little bit of time before Daisy returned, so I walked over to where he was sitting and wrapped my arms around his neck and hugged my body against his. "Me too."

"You're so good with her." He gripped my ass, grazing his lips over my cheek. "Which doesn't surprise me at all. You understand kids better than anyone. It comes so naturally to you."

My eyes closed, the sensation of his hand and mouth completely taking over my body. "She makes it easy. She's a good kid, Ridge. In the classroom, at home—overall. You and Jana have done a wonderful job with her."

He turned my face toward him and held it. "I want to ask you something, and I want you to really think about it."

The seriousness of his tone made me say, "Is this about Daisy?"

"No." His stare intensified, shifting from my right eye to my left and back. "Brady and Lily's wedding is in a few weeks. I'd like you to come to Scotland with me and be my date."

It took me a moment before I said, "I—"

"Before you say anything, I know it's not easy for you to take time off during the school year, so I was thinking we could go for just a long weekend. Everyone would already be there, including Jana and Daisy. We'd fly in alone on one of our jets and meet them on Thursday." His other hand rose up my side and rested on the base of my neck. "We'd come back on Sunday. We probably wouldn't get in until late, but there's a bedroom on the plane. You could sleep the whole way back if you needed to."

Brady and Lily's wedding wasn't something I'd even considered going to since, up until the hot tub incident, I'd had no idea when Ridge planned to tell Jana about us. But given that things were still so fresh in Jana's mind, before I even considered, I needed to know her thoughts on this.

"Ridge, how would Jana react if I was there?"

He searched my eyes. "That's what you're worried about?"

I nodded. "Of course. Her feelings will always matter to me, especially because she's going to be attending with Daisy. I wouldn't want her to feel uncomfortable in any way."

"God, I fucking love you." He kissed me deeply. "But I've already given Jana a heads-up. She's fine with it."

It was a relief that he'd thought to ask her prior to this conversation and that he was respectful to her about us. Still, I needed to be assured one more time. "You're absolutely positive there won't be any drama by my presence?" I pressed. "I don't want to cause any type of commotion—"

"If I thought that was going to happen, I wouldn't invite you. I'd never put you in that situation, and I certainly wouldn't bring drama to someone else's wedding." He traced his thumb over my lips. "I want you there. I want you there with me."

I heard the patter of feet on the floor, and I moved to the other side of the island, resting my hands on the counter, trying to calm down my heart and breathing—both affected by everything he'd just said. And even though he was barely within reaching distance, I could still feel him.

On my neck.

On my lips.

I could taste him on my tongue.

"Soon, I'm not going to let you move away," he said, his voice low. "I want my daughter to see the way I love you."

All that did was add to the explosion that was already taking place within me. But it went deeper, his statement churning through my throat to my chest, settling in the base of my stomach that was a mess of tingles, so the only thing I could utter was, "Ridge..."

As Daisy came running into the kitchen, she stopped right next to me, her breath coming out in pants, her ponytail a few inches lower than it had been before. "I showed my pet animals the flowers, and they think they're so beautiful. They say thank you." She smiled and hugged my side, looking up at me. "Want to help me fold towels now? And then we can go to my room, and I can show you all my animals?"

I stole a quick glance at Ridge, whose smile hadn't faded even a little bit. I returned the gesture and glanced back at his little girl. "I would love that."

Chapter Thirty-One

Addison

Ridge: *I just finished putting Daisy to bed, and the last thing she told me was how much she loves you.*

Me: *Awww, Ridge. I love her. We had such a good day together.*

Ridge: *She said good night to the flowers. It was really cute.*

Me: *Thank you for today. I'll never forget it.*

Ridge: *Neither will we.*

Ridge: *You know…you never gave me an answer about the wedding.*

Me: *We got a little interrupted, and then Daisy pretty much owned me up until I left.*

Ridge: *She's as obsessed with you as I am.*

Me: *I wish you could see how hard I'm smiling right now.*

Me: *And I love that you asked me to attend the wedding, and I would be honored to be your date.*

Ridge: *Do you know what I'd give at this moment to put my lips on you?*

Me: *That just means it's going to feel even better when you finally do.*

Ridge: *I love you, Addison.*

Me: *I love you too. Dream about me. xo*

. . .

Ridge: *I don't know what you did to me, but that dream happened, and it was fucking hot as hell.*

Me: *It's not what I did to you. It's that we got interrupted when we were leaving the hot tub, and THAT is still very much on your mind.*

Ridge: *You were going to give me your ass…*

Me: *And you were going to be very gentle with it.*

Ridge: *I still plan to.*

Me: *I didn't have much time to really think about it at that moment. But now, I'm thinking about it. And…whoa.*

Ridge: *Don't overthink it, Addison. I'm going to take care of you. And I'm going to get you to a point where you're fucking begging for it.*

Me: *You think that's possible?*

Ridge: *I know it is.*

Ridge: *Because I know your body. I know what it's capable of. I know how far I can bring you toward pain before it turns into pleasure. And I know this is going to hurt at first, but I also know how good it's going to feel.*

Me: *When?*

Ridge: *When you least expect it…and when I can't wait another fucking second to have it.*

. . .

Me: *RIDGE!*

Ridge: *Yeah? LOL.*

Me: *I just received your package and opened it. Are you nuts? Why are you spoiling me like this? I'm sitting in my room, staring at this giant box, and I'm in complete awe.*

Ridge: *Because I can and because I want to.*

Me: *The dress, the shoes, the bag—they're all so stunning. And the fact that it's from you and Daisy made me all swoony. I can't wait to wear them to the wedding, Ridge. <3*

Ridge: *When I told Daisy you were coming and that I wanted to get you something to wear, she insisted on going shopping with me. She helped me pick it out. Everything was approved by her.*

Me: *How did you even know my size?*

Ridge: *Baby, I don't forget details, not when they're about you.*

Me: *My mind just exploded, in case you were wondering.*

Me: *I just tried everything on, and I'm going to send you a pic. Wait until you see how it looks. It's like this dress was made for me.*

Ridge: *No, don't. I want it to be a surprise when I see it on you in Edinburgh.*

Me: *I love that. And I love you. Thank you for giving me the most gorgeous dress that has ever been on my body and shoes that I'm dying over and a bag I can't stop staring at.*

Me: *You know, you're lucky you cut off all the tags because I know everything is designer, and if I found out how much you'd spent on it, I'd make you return it.*

Ridge: *Do you think this is the only time I'm going to do something like this? I've told you before, this is only the beginning…*

• • •

Ridge: *I've been staring at my phone all morning, waiting for you to text me. I'm on fucking pins and needles over here, Addison. Tell me the meeting with your principal is over.*

Me: *Sorry, it just ended. I popped into his office during my lunch break. That was the only time he had available today.*

Ridge: *And?*

Ridge: *If you tell me he has an issue with us and your job is in jeopardy, I'll go into his office myself and have a chat with him.*

Because you're not losing your job over us dating—I'm telling you that right now.

Me: *He was pleased that I came in and discussed things even though I'm not contractually obligated to tell him anything. He just appreciated the transparency in case something does come up, that way, he's prepared and not completely taken off guard.*

Me: *The only thing he did say was that if things end between us and either you or Jana wants her moved to a different teacher, then he would address things then. A plan would then be made and followed. Aside from that, he was pretty indifferent about our situation.*

Ridge: *That's never going to happen.*

Me: *Daisy changing classrooms?*

Ridge: *Us breaking up.*

Me: *Melting. <3*

Chapter Thirty-Two

RIDGE

I'd told Addison to dress comfortably; the flight to Edinburgh was going to be a long one. But when the driver took me to her apartment to pick her up and she walked out to the SUV, wearing yoga pants, a sports bra, and a zip-up sweatshirt that hung off her shoulders, revealing her bare stomach, I knew I was going to have a hard time keeping my hands off her. There was something about an athletic look on that woman that I just couldn't get enough of.

Hell, I couldn't get enough of her period.

And now that the secret was out and Jana was cool with it, I could spend much more time with Addison. Many of those occasions involved Daisy, where Addison would come over in the evenings to have dinner with us and on the weekends when we spent time at the barn. A few nights ago, she'd gotten on one of the horses, and I watched her ride with my daughter, the two of them laughing and smiling.

It'd brought me so much fucking joy.

I knew Scotland was going to be no different. An experience I was really looking forward to, especially getting Addison all to myself for this entire flight until we landed and the chaos of the long weekend started.

As soon as she climbed in, I pulled her toward the middle, holding her body against mine while we rode to the airport. My lips found the side of her head, and I breathed her in.

"I can't wait to see you in that dress."

She turned her head toward me. "It makes me feel like a princess when I wear it. I hope they're getting married in a castle. That would be so fitting."

I ran my thumb over her cheek. "They love Edinburgh so much that they bought a house there, and that's where they're getting married. The wedding is going to be small and intimate. Nothing like you're imagining. Immediate family, the partners, and a handful of friends."

"That's exactly what I would want. A wedding that's just for the bride and groom. That sounds absolutely perfect."

I let out a small moan when I took in her lips. "Tell me what else you'd want."

She playfully hit my chest. "Taking notes?"

"Maybe."

She rested her arm over my shoulders. "You couldn't possibly be any more perfect." She leaned her head back and released a long exhale. "Let's see... I'd love to get married on the beach. My bare feet digging into the sand with daisies weaved in my hair. My sister and Leah on my side—that's it—and a dress that I'm unafraid to get wet, so I can walk through the lapping waves. Music and dancing all night long."

"Easy requirements."

"That's me though." She combed the back of my hair. "I wouldn't want anything that's over the top or stuffy or in a ballroom so large and filled that it would take all night to speak to everyone." Her eyes closed. "I want to be able to see the sun as it sets and not notice a single cloud in the sky." When her eyelids opened again, her smile was reaching them. "And after the sun sets, I want to be able to look up and see the stars. I don't want anything covering them. I want to smell the salt and feel the breeze across my face."

"While I'm twirling you around in the sand…"

She nodded. "Every word of that."

I kissed her, tasting the desire on her mouth, one so thick that it matched mine, and I pulled away when I felt the SUV come to a stop. "We're here," I whispered.

She glanced toward the windshield. "Can't say I've ever done anything like this before." She huffed. "Normally, my seat is in the last row, hugging the wall of the restroom, and every time the toilet flushes, my seat vibrates."

"This isn't all that different. Just a few less rows and a bigger restroom."

She whipped her head in my direction. "Right. The similarities are endless." She laughed. "You're forever trying to make me feel better about everything."

"And I'll never stop." I opened the door and stepped onto the tarmac, the jet less than ten yards away, and I held out my hand for her to grab. "Come on."

Once her feet hit the pavement, I brought her over to the stairs, where I shook hands with the pilots. And while the driver brought our luggage to the back of the plane, I escorted Addison up the steps and into the main lounge.

"Sit anywhere you want," I instructed.

There were sections of couches and seats, and she chose the middle, taking up one side of the love seat, leaving plenty of space beside her for me to occupy.

Our flight attendant immediately approached and said, "Hello, Miss Lark"—she then glanced at me—"and Ridge, it's nice to have you both on board. What can I get you to drink?"

"Extra-dirty martini for me." I put my arm around Addison's shoulders. "A rosé for my lady."

Addison added, "Thank you so much."

"I have all your requests in the fridge," the flight attendant said. "I'm happy to serve you whenever you get hungry, so just please let me know. In the meantime, I'm going to bring out some snacks you can enjoy during takeoff." She disappeared into the galley.

"Your lady?" Addison smiled.

I kissed the corner of her mouth, a few inches above her grin. "Do you have a problem with that?"

"Not at all. I thought it was cute. But I'm curious what your requests were…"

I chuckled as I pulled back. "Did you think I wasn't going to pick out what we're eating for dinner? You know me better than that."

She shook her head. "If you tell me we're having ramen, I might die a little."

I cupped her face, positioning my lips in front of hers. "Who would serve ramen during a flight when there's a chance we could hit turbulence? A bold move that could turn into a disaster."

"Italian, then? Steak?" She smiled harder. "Sushi?"

I pressed my nose to hers. "You know me… I'm a fucking bold one."

"We're having ramen, aren't we?"

"I told the flight attendant that she needs to consult with the pilots before she serves us dinner to ensure we'll have a solid fifteen or so minutes of smooth air."

She laughed. "Only you."

"No, it's more like, only *for* you."

"God, I love you, Ridge Cole."

"No, baby, I love you more."

The flight attendant returned with our cocktails, and during her second trip out to the main cabin, she brought a tray of fruit and another that was full of cured meats, cheese, crackers, hummus, and guacamole. She made sure we had napkins and utensils and told us that the pilots were doing the final checks and we would be taking off within the next ten minutes.

I rolled up a piece of prosciutto, paired it with a slice of cucumber, and dipped it in some hummus before I held it in front of Addison's mouth.

"No raspberry?" She winked and nodded toward the tray, which had no melon or cantaloupe on it, only fruit that had a tart flavor.

"That's for the next round," I told her. "The first one needed to go with the hummus, and raspberries don't work with hummus."

"Fair." She took it in her mouth, covering her lips with the back of her hand. "Delicious."

I held my glass in front of hers. "To our first trip together."

She finished chewing and clinked her wine against my tumbler, taking a sip. "This moment needs to be documented." She reached into her back pocket and pulled out her phone, holding it above us. When she finished taking the selfies, she flipped through them and showed me her favorite. "I think it's time."

"For what?"

She was smiling so big. "To make us social media official. Cheesy, I know. I don't post a lot at all, just important moments in my life or places I go and things I find beautiful." She paused. "Like right now."

"What makes right now so special?"

A shyness started to creep through her expression. "We're no longer in hiding. Everyone in my life, including my job, knows about us, and the same is true for you. So, I get to tell you how much I care about you, and it doesn't matter who hears. I get to show you how wild I am for you, and it doesn't matter who sees."

"Are you going to feel that way in Scotland?"

I watched her think about my question, gradually nodding. "When we were leaving the barn the other day with Daisy, you held my hand and wouldn't let me pull it away. And when we took Daisy out to dinner a few nights ago, you kissed my cheek after dessert. So, yes, I would reach for your hand at the wedding, and I'd give you a peck on the lips, and I'd dance with you, and I wouldn't be afraid if she saw."

An answer that not only had my dick raging hard, but they were words I felt inside my chest.

"Post the photo, Addison."

She hit the screen several times and slipped her phone away. "I tagged you."

My pocket vibrated, and I took out my cell, seeing the notification on the screen. After a few taps, I was looking at the picture. She hadn't written a caption; she'd just put a red heart emoji.

I screenshot the post, cropped the pic, and uploaded it to my own account. But instead of a red heart, I used the sun emoji. "And I tagged you."

Her eyes widened. "You posted it?"

"Sure did."

She shook her head, her smile not fading at all. "I might have stalked your profile the other night when I couldn't sleep. You know, going all the way back to your very first post."

"See anything interesting?"

"Aside from how much of a badass you are." She tapped my chest. "I loved the photos you posted of Daisy—and I love that you never show her face, just the back of her or the top of her head. Like she's there, but not there."

"I have such a public account, keeping her private but present is important to me."

"And the photos of you with celebrities and athletes and business executives. Ridge, you have one fabulous life."

"Well, you do know most of it is for show and encouraged by our in-house publicist."

"Makes sense." She shrugged. "So do all the shots of the different hotels you've visited. It makes your followers want to check them out and live a life like yours."

I brushed the hair out of her eyes before I held the side of her face. "Most of those are just some good Photoshopping."

She stared at me. "You're kidding me. They're not all real?"

"Some, but not all. We're staying at the Edinburgh hotel while we're there, so that'll get posted, but Dublin will get posted, too, and that's not on the itinerary." I turned to my side, leaning against my shoulder. "Pre-Daisy, all the pictures are real. Post-Daisy, my priorities have changed a lot. It's not that I'm not dedicated to the company. I give it everything I have. But since becoming a father, my role as an executive has shifted." My hand lowered to her side. "And it'll shift once more when I become a father again."

Her mouth opened, and a single laugh came out. "What are you saying?"

"We've talked about kids."

"And I've told you how many I want, but, mister"—she blocked the crotch of my jeans with both hands—"we're not starting that project today."

I laughed. "You're going to be my wife before that project starts. Cool?"

"Very, very cool."

"But I've been dreaming about you being pregnant. Watching our baby grow inside you. Feeling it kick. Resting my face on your belly every night so I can talk to it before we go to sleep and tell it I how much I love it." I spread my fingers to her navel, the tightness of her yoga pants allowing me to feel the flatness that was there now. "That's what I want, Addison."

"Dear God, I hope my ovaries aren't listening to you right now... even though they're exploding."

I leaned forward so our faces were close together. "I hope they are listening." My thumb slowly brushed over her lips. "But there's going to be an order here—engagement, wedding, baby—and I promise I'm going to follow it."

"You have no idea what you're doing to me." There was emotion in her eyes as she looked at me, as she held me, as she extended her leg over my lap as though she couldn't get close enough.

"You've done the same thing to me." I turned her face toward the window as we began to speed down the runway, aiming her toward the clouds. "I see our future, Addison. I see it every time I close my eyes. The life we're going to build together and the family we're going to have." I rubbed my teeth over my top lip. "When I saw that breathtakingly gorgeous redhead on the stage, shit, I knew I had to have her. I knew she had to be mine. And there wasn't anything I wouldn't do to make that happen."

Her arms went around my neck, and our bodies aligned, and she hugged me. I rubbed her back as I buried my face in a nest of her locks, her vanilla-latte scent wafting from them.

"I've been thinking about your dress," I said softly.

"Yeah? Why?"

I pulled back and said, "It's perfect, but I think there's something missing from the outfit." I reached into my pocket and pulled out the small box that I'd put there before I left to pick her up.

She glanced from the box to me. "Ridge...is that..." She cut herself off to take a deep breath.

"When I propose, it's not going to happen on a plane on our way to someone else's wedding. I'm going to be on my knee, and that moment is going to only be about us." I placed the box in her hand. "Open it."

Her eyes were already starting to fill with tears. "You're spoiling me again."

"And nothing makes me happier." I nodded toward her hand.

She pulled at the pink ribbon that surrounded the small white box and lifted the lid. Her mouth opened the second she saw what was inside. "You didn't…"

I reached inside and lifted the necklace from the holder, setting it in my hand. The design was dainty and so small that it got lost on my palm. "I got in touch with Brady's jeweler, and I told him I wanted him to make me a sun. This was the third mock-up; each one I made smaller until I felt like it would sit perfectly under your throat. And the rays, we changed those too. At first, they were squiggly, but I wanted them straight with three diamonds on each one." I opened the clasp and wrapped the chain around her neck, hooking it before I set it on her chest. "Now, when I'm not with you—and I don't plan for that to be often—I'll always be there. You won't have to look at the sky. I'll be right there, on your body, where I'm meant to be."

She lifted it off her skin and squeezed her fingers around it. "I've never loved anything more." The first tear rolled over her eyelid. "I lie. I have. And that's you."

Chapter Thirty-Three

ADDISON

"Look at my girl," Rhett said as he stood beside me in the back of Brady and Lily's Edinburgh home. His elbow was resting on the corner of my shoulder—a position that was more out of convenience than endearing—and the two of us were facing the grass, where Ridge and Daisy were dancing to the band. "She's going to be one hell of a heartbreaker when she gets older."

Daisy was in a light-pink dress that matched Rayner's, who she'd pushed down the aisle while sprinkling flower petals. And of course, there were daisies weaved into her hair and along the edges of her dress.

A wedding that had been perfect in my eyes—small, special details that stood out because nothing was too elaborate to overshadow them. And now that the ceremony was over, the backyard had been transformed into a magical, twinkling starlit paradise, where everyone was either dancing or drinking or eating.

I grabbed his fingers and squeezed them. "As long as her dad never gets that title, Daisy can break all the hearts she wants."

"Ridge? Shit." He sighed loudly. "You've got nothing to worry about there. I'd be the first to tell you you're fucked, but you're not. That motherfucker is crazy for you. That man has one mission, and it's to make you his wife."

A conversation that lined up with the one we'd had on the plane on the way over here.

But we had plenty of time for that to happen—I wasn't ever going anywhere, and neither was Ridge.

I turned toward Rhett, taking in his profile. His black hair and beard, eyes that were ice blue—a reflection of his personality at times. What caught my attention the most was the tattoo on his thumb. It was the face and mane of a lion.

I reached for his other hand and held his thumb so I could get a better look at it. "It's beautiful and so fitting."

When we locked eyes, he stared at me silently for a few seconds. "He told you everything, didn't he?"

I nodded.

"Don't look at me like that, Addison. I know what you're thinking..."

"You're misreading my expression, Rhett. What you're seeing is how blown away I am by you. You're just misunderstood—but not by me. I get you. But by everyone else." I offered a simple smile. "You're inspiring—I hope you know that."

He whistled out a mouthful of air. "Hell, I know who to call the next time I need a little pick-me-up. How about I phone you instead of guzzling a whole bottle of whiskey? Can you be my phone-a-friend?"

I laughed. "Asshole."

He pretended to punch my shoulder. "You know something? I like you. You're fucking perfect for him. A little spicy, a little sassy, and a whole lot of kindness. You're just what he needs."

I glanced toward the dance floor. "He's everything I need. If you had asked me if something wonderful could build from where we met, I would have told you you're nuts. And here we are—he saw past all of it."

"That's because Ridge was a stripper in college."

I craned my neck back. "He was?"

"He didn't tell you? He used to dress up as a cop and do bachelorette parties." Within a few seconds, his balled-up fist was covering his mouth, and he was laughing behind it.

"Dick." I slapped his chest. "I've never been more thankful to have a sister and not a brother. I wouldn't have survived your kind of teasing every day."

"Ah, but you just inherited yourself a brother, Addison." He clenched my shoulder before he released it. "Another sister too." He nodded toward Rowan. "I'm going to go get a drink."

As I watched him walk away, I realized the power in what he'd just said. Ridge's family was becoming mine, and that meant Rhett would hopefully be in my life forever, and so would Rowan. She was standing on the other side of the lawn with Cooper, who was holding their little girl. I needed to spend some more time with Rowan. The past two days, since we'd arrived in Scotland, had been full of wedding festivities and sightseeing, and Rowan was a bit limited with what she could do because of Rayner.

With Ridge and Daisy still occupied by the music, I set my destination on his sister, smiling to everyone I passed on the way. This wedding had introduced me to so many of Ridge's friends and colleagues. There were the Daltons—the group of lawyers who the Coles and Spades hired for business and personal affairs and hung out with regularly. There were also the Westons, who were friends and business associates. And then there were the Spades, who I got to really know, along with all of the incredible women they were dating, engaged to, and married to.

A group that seemed large due to their personalities, but one so tight and loyal, and they had welcomed me with open arms.

I was just walking around one of the tables when I noticed Jana. She was sitting halfway between where Rowan was standing and I was heading, and it seemed, due to the way she was positioned, she was watching Daisy and Ridge dance.

We'd been in each other's presence multiple times over the last couple of days, and during every instance, she was cordial. She didn't embrace me with a hug, and neither did I, nor did we go out of our way to speak to one another, but when words were exchanged, the mood wasn't stormy.

There were things I felt I wanted to say to her.

Things I felt I needed to say.

And I felt it was my responsibility to make the effort. Even though I didn't technically do anything wrong and I hadn't purposefully set out to date a student's parent, I couldn't help but feel it was my place to break the official ice.

So, instead of going over to Rowan, I stopped at Jana's table, waiting for her to notice my presence and look up at me. I'd expected the nerves. I just hadn't anticipated them coming on so strong.

I attempted to calm my voice when I said, "Do you mind if I sit?"

"I was just going to go get a cocktail"—she adjusted her hat—"but sure, take a seat."

I pulled back the chair and carefully scooped the bottom of my dress before I settled on the cushion. "I've been wanting to talk to you. I don't totally know what to say about all of this—my head is a cluster of thoughts—but I feel like you should at least hear things from me even if you've heard them all from Ridge." My head was so jumbled that words were flying out and I couldn't stop them. "As Daisy's teacher—I don't know—I feel it's important."

Jana's stare wasn't hard, like I had anticipated. It also wasn't warm and fuzzy. But she looked at me with respect, with eyes that didn't feel as if they were judging me.

I waited for her to say something, and when she didn't, I continued,

"I want you to know that all I ever wanted to do was be a teacher. I have this immense love for children and the desire to educate them and mold them—that's the biggest, most vital part of my life." I folded my hands in my lap and immediately unfolded them. "When it comes to your daughter, she's my only focus. To be everything she needs as an educator. Regardless of what happens or what's happening in my personal life, her schooling will always come first to me."

"I just worry." She traced the outer edges of her lips as though she was wiping away any smudged gloss. "I worry about everything if I'm being honest. If something goes wrong with you and Ridge, Daisy is the one who will suffer."

I stole a quick glance at Ridge and was surprised to find his eyes already on me. I didn't keep my gaze on him for long. I wanted to give Jana the full attention she deserved, but in Ridge's expression, I saw that he was appreciative that I was speaking to her.

As I stared back at Jana, I said, "And I can completely understand where that worry would come from. I realize giving you my word doesn't mean much. You don't know me at all; therefore, you don't know how I'm a woman who stands by my word, but I promise you, Jana, nothing will interfere with Daisy's learning. She will receive the best education that I'm physically and mentally capable of giving." I set my hand on the table, rubbing it over the cloth to work off some of the sweat. "You know, before I left for this wedding, I had a meeting with the principal of my school. Did Ridge tell you?"

She shook her head.

"I'm not required to tell the administration that I'm in a relationship with Ridge despite him being a parent of a student. Still, I told my principal anyway. I just didn't want there to be an issue at any level, and I wanted him to be aware of the situation in case something did happen and you or Ridge wanted to transfer Daisy to a different classroom."

Her stare grew as she watched me.

"The last thing I would want was for anyone to be caught off guard—like the night that went down at Ridge's house." My hand flew to my chest, my heart pounding as I thought of that evening. "The principal assured me that if either of you ever wants to change classrooms or anything like that, he will work with you to make it happen. I just want you to know you have options."

She rubbed her hands over her bare arms. "Thank you for doing that."

"Of course. Like I said, Jana, Daisy is my priority. Always."

She glanced away, and I followed her stare around the backyard, even up at the sky, before it returned to me.

"I've had some time to reflect on everything I said to Ridge that night after I put Daisy to bed and we hashed everything out. I realize now how unprepared I was for that conversation. I was shocked by what I saw. I was angry as hell at him for not telling me. My head was full of assumptions, and none of them were accurate." She broke eye contact again to look toward the dance floor. "I couldn't understand in that moment why he hadn't told me, but I do now."

"We talked about it often," I admitted. "He wanted nothing more than to come clean. It was eating away at him."

"I'm sure it was." Her gaze dropped to my necklace and lifted again. "He's not the kind of guy to withhold information of any kind. He's not secretive or sketchy or anything like that. If anything, he's probably too honest."

"I need to tell you"—I took a deep breath—"that I'm horrified by what you walked into that evening." I pushed harder against my chest. "If I could change anything, it would be that."

She slowly nodded. "I'm just glad Daisy doesn't remember any of it."

"Same." I winced as it replayed in my head.

She had a long fishtail braid that hung to her chest, and she began to play with it. "When Ridge told me about your other job, I want you to know, there was a moment when I didn't think too highly of you. I'm not sure if he told you that part or not."

"He didn't."

And I wasn't sure how I felt about that.

When Ridge had recapped their talk, he'd glazed over Jana's reaction to me stripping and said it wasn't what they really focused on. But hearing that she hadn't thought too highly of me made me glad he hadn't told me.

Was that fucked up?

I didn't even know at this point. I just knew that had to have been an extremely difficult line for him to walk when things were already cluttered and a bit chaotic.

Her chest rose and fell a few times. "I shouldn't have done that. I should have understood why you took on that job and where you were coming from because I'd been there too." She spread her lips wide, a modest smile without showing any teeth. "Ridge reminded me of that and what I'd done to come up with the down payment for my parents' house. Our choices weren't the same, but that doesn't make yours bad. You did what you had to do, and that wasn't easy."

I lifted my hand off the table and put it back on my lap, linking my fingers together. "I want you to know it's something I still struggle with. I never in my life ever thought I'd get on a stage and take my clothes off, but what's weird about the whole thing is, I don't regret it. Because had I not done it, then I wouldn't have gotten to see my parents' faces when my sister and I gave them their gift. That's something that meant absolutely everything to me."

And maybe, had I not stripped, then I wouldn't have connected with Ridge—a detail I wasn't going to mention, but I was sure she was thinking that too.

"Girl, I wouldn't have done it." Her hand went to my arm, and I was surprised by the warmth of her skin. "I'm saying, I wouldn't have the nerve or the confidence to follow through."

"Years of cheerleading helped, but, yeah, I'm with you. It wasn't easy—that's for sure." Her fingers left me, and I let several seconds of silence pass before I said, "I want you to know that when it comes to Daisy and her education, you can come to me and talk to me about it. If you're not comfortable doing that, I understand that, too, but I'm here and I hope at least a small part of you knows that."

She nodded. "I do."

I went to stand, and she set her hand on my shoulder and stopped me.

"I need to ask you something." Her gaze returned to Daisy and Ridge. "Taylor Swift is Daisy's idol, and going to her concert is all she talks about. I don't know if Ridge mentioned it, but I'm not able to go—a work thing came up, and it's a dream gig that I just can't miss."

I waited for her to look at me before I said, "He didn't tell me."

"When I told him I couldn't attend, he said he was going to bring Rhett." She rolled her eyes. "We both know Rhett would rather stab his eyes out than go to that concert."

I laughed. "Truth."

I could see the hesitation in her gaze, the build-up, the courage that moved through. "Will you go with them?"

A question that definitely wasn't easy for her to ask. In fact, I bet it was harder than I could even imagine.

I put my fingers on top of hers. "Yes. I would love to. Thank you, Jana."

She gave me a slight nod and pulled her fingers away, and I took that as my cue, leaving her to go to the dance floor, where Daisy was turning in circles with the help of Ridge's hand.

"Everything okay?" he asked as I joined them.

"Better than okay."

He put his arm around my shoulders and kissed the side of my head. "Damn it, you amaze me."

"It was something I had to do, Ridge. She's Daisy's mom."

"Some women wouldn't, and some women couldn't—and then there's you." His eyes dipped down my body. "The most beautiful woman here, looking positively stunning in that rose-gold dress."

I gave him a smile and an air kiss, and I grabbed Daisy's other hand. "Look at you with all the moves," I said to her. "Who knew you were such a good dancer?"

She held up her other arm. "Twirl me, Addy."

"I have a better idea." I scooped her up in my arms, her six-year-old body almost too big to hold the way I wanted, but I found a way to make her fit against me, and I held one of her hands and turned with her. "Tell me when to stop, okay?"

"Faster, faster."

She laughed as I picked up speed, and during one of the rotations, I noticed Ridge had his phone in his hand and appeared to be taking pictures of us.

Daisy gave him a huge grin before she said, "Stop!"

I slowed and began to swing us instead.

That was when she cupped her hands over my ear and whispered, "You're my daddy's friend, aren't you?"

"Yes, I am. Why?"

She continued to whisper, "I wish you were his girlfriend, not his friend."

I let out a small laugh that I could no longer contain. "Do you think I should ask him to be my boyfriend?"

Daisy's nod was exaggerated.

"Will you help me ask him?" I said to her.

"Yes!" She looked at her father and waved him over. "Daddy, come here!"

Ridge put his phone away and put one arm around Daisy and the other around me. "What can I do for you ladies?"

"Daisy has a very important question to ask you," I said.

He looked at his daughter. "And that is?"

Her grin was so wide as she wiggled in my arms. "Will you be Addy's boyfriend?"

Ridge chuckled.

"It was Daisy's idea," I told him, smiling. "And since it was, I thought she should be the one to ask you."

Ridge leaned into Daisy's ear and whispered something I couldn't hear.

Daisy giggled just before he pulled away, and she put her hand on Ridge's chest and another around my hair.

"Tell her," Ridge nudged.

"Daddy says yes."

"And what else did I say?" Ridge pushed.

"That he loves the both of us very much," Daisy sang.

Chapter Thirty-Four

RIDGE

It was one thing to be in love with a woman. But it was a whole other thing to see that woman love your daughter, to watch her treat your little girl with patience and tenderness and respect, the way Addison did with Daisy. Witnessing them together, circling the dance floor at Brady and Lily's wedding, was a feeling that had never entered my body because I'd never been with a woman, aside from Jana, who had a relationship with Daisy.

I wouldn't allow it.

Until Addison...

She was the exception when it came to everything.

And Daisy was enamored with her, so much so that, because the two of them had been having such a blast together, Daisy started to cry when it was time for them to leave. It was late, and our girl needed to go to bed. All the drivers were outside Brady and Lily's house, waiting to take the guests to the hotel for the night. And even though we promised Daisy that we would have breakfast with her in the morning, many tears were shed, and arms were outstretched for hugs that she didn't want to end. I knew the second Jana got her into the car, a full-on meltdown would go down with screams and sobs, triggered by Daisy being overtired. And minutes later, I also knew she'd be asleep, and Jana would have to carry her up to their room. So, I asked Jana if she wanted me to ride back with them and help out. Jana appreciated the offer, but told me that she'd manage just fine.

I just hoped Addison's level of sleepiness wasn't the same as Daisy's. I planned to do everything in my power to keep her awake for as long as I could. Because tonight wasn't going to end without my tasting her. Without putting my lips on every inch of her body.

So, the first thing I did when we got back to our suite room was draw her a bath. I added in some bubbles and oil—luxuries I'd had my assistant request before we checked in—and as I started to walk out of the bathroom, she was standing in the doorway with a grin on her face.

"A bath?" She casually crossed her arms over her chest.

"I thought you could use one. It's been a long day."

"That it has." She shifted her weight, assessing my expression. "Are you going to join me?"

When I reached her, I gently turned her around, placing her back to me. I found the zipper of her dress that was hiding beneath a fold of the fabric, and I lowered it. As it got to her waist, freeing her from the top, I helped her step out of it. She looked at me from over her shoulder, wearing nothing but a pair of heels and a strapless bra, which I unhooked and let fall to the ground.

"I see you're not wasting any time."

I ran my hands up her sides and turned her around. "I waited an entire ceremony, reception, and a ride back to the hotel—what is that, fifteen or so hours?—to get you naked. It's more than fucking time."

She set her arms on my shoulders and stepped in closer, giving me a breeze of vanilla. "Are you sure you want me in the tub?"

"I want you relaxed."

"You're telling me your tongue can't do that?"

I chuckled. I fucking loved when she talked dirty to me. "Baby, you're going to get my tongue, don't you worry." I held her chin and gave her a slow, steady kiss before I took her hand and walked her over to the tub, helping her step in. "I'll be there in a second." I nodded toward the water. "Get started without me."

As she sank into the water that had pooled in the bottom, I took her dress into the bedroom and hung it in the closet before I stripped off the sections of my suit. Once it was all off, I rejoined her in the en suite. Her legs were extended to the other side of the tub, her feet crossed, her toes wiggling along the lip. Her arms were behind her head, and the bubbles were just starting to seep over her chest, her long hair floating on both sides of her face.

"Addison..." The view was making me speechless. The way hints of that gorgeous body were revealed through the different breaks in the bubbles. How every time she shifted, I could see a flash of her chest or a peek of her hip or nipple through the water. "You have no idea how beautiful you look."

"Every time you say that to me, it feels like the first time all over again."

"And every time I say it, I mean it more." My head shook as I took her in, and I backed up to the counter between the sinks, leaning against it. "I've never met anyone who can look more breathtaking with each day that passes. But you, Addison...you do. The proof is in front of me right now."

Her eyes fluttered closed. "Get in here."

I gripped the edge of the counter. "What are you going to do to me in that water, baby?"

She let out a small laugh. "Now, those were words I thought you were going to say to me."

"What do you want me to do to you, Addison?"

She glanced down my body until she was focused on my hard-on. "I want that."

"You're going to get plenty of that." I pumped my shaft a few times.

A coyness began to filter into her expression. "I think there's something else we've discussed."

"And that is?"

She nipped her lip. "My ass."

"What about it?"

"Well, the last time it was supposed to happen, we got interrupted. There are no interruptions tonight, Ridge."

"Are you telling me I can have it?"

She unraveled her legs and tucked them in closer. "Is that what you want?"

I chuckled. "You can't answer my question with a question—it doesn't work that way." I went to the side of the tub and knelt down, holding her chin between my fingers. "I asked if you were going to give me your ass."

She continued to play with her lips, using her teeth, her tongue, until she finally said, "I gave it to you once before. That hasn't changed. It's still all yours whenever you want it."

"But tonight—is it something you're up for?"

"If anyone in this world can make me want it—now, before, whenever—it's you."

That was a challenge I'd accept.

And one that made my dick throb even harder.

She was giving me anything I wanted, whenever I wanted it.

There was truly nothing sexier.

"*Mmm*," I moaned.

I stood and stepped into the warm water, sliding her forward so I could position myself behind her. My legs stayed on the outside of hers, and while her head rested on the bottom of my throat, my arms crossed over her chest, the hardness of her nipples pressing into my forearms. I kept my arms still for several seconds, and then I slid them forward and back several inches, giving those hard buds a tease.

Within a few strokes, she was pressing her back against me. Not just the top, but the bottom as well, which was aligned with my hard-on. And every time she bore down, my tip ground into her.

"Goading the fuck out of me, I see."

"Really?" she challenged. "Keep playing with me, mister, and you'll see what else I do to you."

I chuckled again and uncrossed my arms, my fingers crawling down the center of her chest, between both of her tits, and across her flat stomach until I reached the start of her pussy.

"Ah," she moaned.

I'd only grazed the very top, a spot that couldn't even give her an orgasm. She was just that tuned in, anticipating what I was going to do to her next and how it would feel.

But I didn't go there right away.

I brushed my fingers over the entire space, toward the inside of her thighs and around each angle, my fingers rocking back and forth between her legs and her pussy before I eventually found my way to the center.

"Ridge," she exhaled, her back arching straight into my cock as I traced down her clit. "Yes."

I was giving her the lightest pressure as though it were the very tip of my tongue, and I was using it to whisper across her. But it was enough to get things churning inside her—and they were.

Her moaning gave that away.

The slight movement of her hips did as well.

And then there was her breathing, the way it would hitch every time I moved less than an inch, resume back to normal, and halt the second I lowered again.

"I wonder how wet you are…"

I wanted nothing more than to dip in and feel for myself. To experience the tightness of her pussy as it clenched my finger, her attempt at trying to keep it inside her because she wanted more.

But I was saving that. I was making myself beg for it, just like I was making her.

"Do you want me to tell you?" She turned her head so her face was pointed up at me. And while she waited for me to respond, she pushed even harder, her back circling my shaft.

I tapped her clit with the pad of my thumb. "Fuck yes." I repeated the identical action a second time. "I want to hear all about it."

She drove the side of her face into me and arched. "Ridge, I'm dripping." She gasped. "For you."

Her lips touched the side of my chin, and I felt each breath she took.

"You want me?"

"Yes. But…"

"But what?"

"I need you too."

There was a difference, and my desire built as I heard I fit somewhere in between.

"What do you want me to do to you, Addison?"

She exhaled. "I want you to make me scream."

There were many different ways I could do that. One that I knew would work almost instantly was using my finger, and it was the easiest, given the way we were reclined.

I bent my hand around her, going past her lips, and rubbed around the outside of her pussy. "Like this?"

"Fuck," she groaned and gripped my wrist, trying to push me deeper. "Give it to me."

The pleading was so fucking hot.

But it wasn't enough.

I needed to know she would do absolutely anything to have me.

So, I stayed there, circling, waiting, and after each pass, her moans got louder. Her movements turned stronger, the water rolling past the edge of the tub and overflowing onto the floor.

"Ridge, I can't wait. I need—"

I was inside before she even finished her sentence.

"Yes!" she shouted.

Damn it, she was right; she was dripping. The wetness soaked into my skin, and as her voice filled my ears, she told me just how badly she wanted this.

"Baby…" All I wanted was to make her feel good. To know I was the reason for her moans. To have her so worked up that she would do anything to have me.

And she was there—at the peak.

I gave her only one finger, slipping it in and out, turning and tilting to reach her G-spot. Every time I hit it, she would buck against me, driving my hard-on into her back.

"Ah!" She sucked in some air and lifted her arms, wrapping them around my neck. "Ridge!"

"God, I fucking love your pussy."

Not just the feel, the smell, and the taste of it—three things I lived for—but the look of it too. The perfect folds and the softest skin and the way her clit was hidden, like the most beautiful present was buried beneath.

She placed her heels on the top of the tub, her knees bending, giving me all the access I needed.

"You want to come?" I rasped in her ear.

"Please." Her exhales were even pleading with me. "Please, Ridge."

"Let me hear it." I picked up the speed only a tiny bit. "Let me hear how much you want it."

She released my neck to hold my wrist again, pushing on it, digging her nails into my skin. "Make me come. I'm begging you. Let me have—" Her voice cut off when I pulled my finger out, dragging it up her clit and stomach, between her tits, and stopping at her neck.

"It's time to get out of the tub."

She was panting.

Each breath caused a wave of water to slap against the rim. "What?"

"Do I have to carry you to the bed?"

It was clear she didn't understand why I'd left her hanging like that when she was on the verge of getting off. But my reasoning made complete sense, and she would see that soon enough.

"Carry me?" she responded. "You're serious...aren't you?"

"Dead fucking serious."

I slid out from beneath her, stepping onto the floor as the water and bubbles trickled off me, and I held out my hand, helping her onto her feet. Once she was standing in the tub, she released my fingers and wrapped both palms around my dick.

"Is this what you want?" She began to pump me faster.

"That's not why I stopped, Addison. This isn't about me, it's about you."

"Then—"

"Get over here."

I pulled her into my arms and lifted her out of the water, waiting for her legs to circle my waist before I carried her into the bedroom. As soon as her back hit the mattress, I kept her on the edge of the bed and ducked my head, kissing down the same path that my fingers had taken many times tonight.

I started between her tits, pausing to give each of her nipples a lick, a tug, a fucking bite. All that did was earn me a scream, so I repeated it all over—lick, tug, bite for each one—before I moved to her stomach, kissing across her ribs and around her belly button. With her knees bent, her legs automatically spread, falling open against the bed as if she were getting herself ready for my face.

But I took my time getting there, pressing my lips on the sides of her pussy and down her thighs and over the middle until my nose was resting on the top of her clit.

I left it there, inhaling her.

My eyes then closed, my mouth opening to take in even more of her scent. "Fucking home," I whispered, but loud enough that she could hear me. "I missed this."

She dived her fingers through my hair, twisting the locks while I breathed over her. The air was hitting right where I wanted, the spot where she was throbbing. And with each breath I took, her legs seemed to get wider, spreading further over the bed, her fingers digging in harder as they continued to run through my hair.

"I know you want it," I said.

But what I wanted was her so fucking wound up that her body would truly take whatever I gave it. And what I planned to do wasn't going to be easy on her. It wasn't going to feel good at first. But if I could get her in a place where her head was focused on only one thing, then it would be much easier on her.

I looked up from between her legs, past her curves and her tits, and locked eyes with her. "But I'm just savoring you, baby."

With her lips parted, her expression was ravenous, the heat even reaching her stare. "You're killing me."

"Good."

My nose lifted, and my tongue, pointed at the tip, licked the whole length of her clit. I went slow, wiggling between her lips, giving her the amount of friction she needed.

"Ridge! Oh my God!"

Fuck, she tasted good, and with her scent wrapping around me, that made me want to stay there until the morning. But if I spent much more time here, my girl would be screaming, and I couldn't have that.

Not yet at least.

So, every time she began to lift off the bed and jerk her hips upward, against my mouth, I would lower my speed or pull completely away and replace my tongue with my lips instead.

It was torture.

I knew that.

And I could hear what it was doing to her. The anguish in her voice, in her breathing, in her fucking movements.

Just when she thought I was going to give in, the entire process would start over. I didn't even give her a finger—it would be too much at this point. It would get her there far too fast, possibly to the point where I couldn't bring her back, and I couldn't let that happen.

"What are you doing to me?" she cried.

The question I'd been waiting for her to ask.

I glanced at her face again. She was sitting up, resting on her bent arms, gazing down at me.

Feral as all hell.

"I'm making you beg for it."

She licked her lips. "Haven't I already done that?"

I used my thumb to flick her clit. "No."

She jumped from the pressure, and when she saw that I wasn't going to give her more, her head shook. "I haven't?"

"No, you haven't begged me to fuck your ass, Addison."

The realization came through her eyes. "That's what you're waiting for?"

"In part, yes." I dropped my finger past her pussy, and when it reached her ass, I touched the rim of that forbidden hole. But I didn't stay still. I moved around it. "The other part is that I needed to get you ready for this."

"I'm ready."

I let out a chuckle. "Yes, I think you might be."

"I had a feeling this was going to happen here, and I brought something to help us." She pointed at the closet. "It's in the front pocket of my suitcase."

She went to move, and I stopped her.

"I'll get it. Stay there."

I walked to the closet and located the pocket, reaching inside, and when I felt the cold plastic, I pulled it out and carried the bottle back to the bed.

"You certainly came prepared." While I opened the bottle of lube, I aimed my tip at her pussy and plunged inside.

"Ridge!"

"Fuck," I moaned.

I needed this for me.

I needed it for her.

But I only gave her a few quick pumps of my shaft before I pulled out.

"You're so fucking mean," she hissed.

I laughed as I squirted some of the clear gel onto my finger and spread it across my dick and around her ass. "You might be saying that again very soon, but I promise I'll change your mind."

"In case you were wondering, Leah bought that for us."

I tossed the bottle onto the bed and slid her back a few feet, so her head was closer to the pillows, and I positioned myself between her legs. "Hold on—Leah bought it?"

She smiled. "I might have filled her in on your dream of doing this."

"So, that was her gift to you?" I laughed.

She returned the gesture. "What can I say? I have a good bestie."

"Yes, you do, and you're going to thank her because I was going to use my spit, and I assure you, you'll like this much better." I lifted her legs and held them around me, making sure she kept that position before I released her and pointed my crown at her ass. "I need you to relax for me. That's the only way this will work."

"Are you about to split me in half?"

"For only a second. You'll get used to it quickly. I promise."

To keep her mind focused, I rubbed her clit, strumming it like she was music. Her moans were quiet, but they were present, even while I pressed into her.

"Wow, you weren't kidding," she said softly.

She was so fucking tight; I didn't know if I'd fit.

I needed a new plan.

So, I backed up, and I coated the gel around my finger, eventually breaking through and pushing in.

"This…" Her head tilted, and her back arched. "Okay… I can do this."

Her breathing confirmed what she'd just said, telling me she could handle this, and that was why I continued to go in further. I didn't hurry the process. I couldn't do that with this. There were steps, and if I didn't follow them properly, this would be the last time I'd ever have her.

That wasn't going to happen.

Therefore, I went slow as hell, listening to every sound she made, to every breath she took, preparing her, spreading her. And when I was sure she could take more, I moved faster, going all the way past my knuckle until my whole finger was in. But the entire time I was doing this, my thumb was stroking her clit. She needed the combination. And I was right because she began to moan.

As soon as my ears heard that noise, I gently pulled out and aimed my cock at that tight fucking hole, swiping her clit while I inched my way to my crown. "Breathe, Addison."

God-fucking-damn, this felt good.

Tight.

Wet from the lube.

A suction cup that was swallowing my dick and not letting it go.

Meanwhile, she was gripping the blanket on both sides, her teeth gnawing away at her lips.

"Can you tell me how you're feeling?"

"I can't talk yet."

But I knew if she was hurting badly enough, she'd tell me to stop, and she hadn't.

Her legs weren't caving inward either.

Nor did I hear the sounds of extreme pain, and I knew them—I'd watched a child being born.

"Breathe," I repeated. "Once I'm all the way in, it'll get better, it's just going to take a second."

Her eyes locked with mine.

"Are you all right?" I asked.

"Yes."

"Can you handle more?"

As she nodded, I grabbed the bottle and added some extra lube to the rest of my shaft, fingering it all the way around so even the slightest shift forward would get inside her.

"I'm almost there," I said.

There were only a few inches left, but I didn't want to just give them to her and rush through it, even though I was fucking dying to sink myself fully inside her. I kept up the same speed, and I gradually worked my way there.

And when I arrived, giving her the stillness I'd promised, I said, "I need you to breathe for me, baby." I gave her clit more pressure, my thumb rubbing back and forth, never tiring and never stopping. "I'm going to stay just like this until you get used to me. I want you to tell me when you're ready."

Her hands flattened against my thighs, her palms slick. "I think I can feel you all the way in the back of my throat."

"Honest answer—but even though I'm big, I'm not *that* big." I chuckled.

As I watched her chest rise and fall, her eyes close, I tried to ignore the fact that her ass was pulsing around me, tightening, tugging on me without even moving.

That it wouldn't take more than a few strokes and I'd be coming.

She felt that fucking good.

"Will you go slow?" she asked.

Her words brought me back, her eyes now open, her hands turned and gripping my legs.

"Of course, baby."

"Then, I'm ready."

If this were her pussy, I would have reared back and slammed into her. But I had to remind myself that this experience wouldn't be anything like that. This was a crawl—turtle speed, like she would say. And this was her first time, so a wrong move, and it would be over.

So, regardless of what I was feeling, of what I wanted, I would make every second of this about her.

I licked my thumb, getting the pad nice and wet, and I returned it to her clit, bearing down to add more friction. Only then did I pull myself back, dragging out of her, going as far as the center of my dick before I slid in again.

"Addison, I can't even describe what this feels like."

"Ah," she sighed—a sound that was more pleasure than pain. "It's getting better."

I could tell by the way her legs were positioned—how there had been a slight shake to them before and that wasn't the case anymore. And her hands—she wasn't squeezing me; she was simply holding me.

"Within a few more strokes, it's going to start feeling good," I told her.

But that was up to me and the intensity in which I used and the power that I needed to reserve so I didn't have her yelling in a way that she'd hate.

"I'm not sure I completely believe that—" Her voice cut off, and her fingers bore down on me.

I halted. "Are you all right?"

"I…"

I reached for her face and pointed it toward me. "You…what, Addison?"

Her lips opened, and a deep moan came out of them. "I believe you."

"Baby…" I groaned. "You want it, don't you?"

Her nails found me again. "Don't stop." Her hand was on my wrist, a place she'd gripped many times tonight. "Make me come, Ridge."

I could make this last all night.

That was how fucking amazing it felt.

But all it would do was force her to resent me.

So, I'd get my baby to come so fucking hard, and then I'd take care of her.

To do that, I found a quickness and momentum that she could take. With each punch, my balls banged against her, tightening, sparking as my orgasm started to lift through my body.

"Fuck," I growled. "I'm going to fill your fucking ass."

She pushed down on my thumb. "Harder."

I listened, I watched, assessing what she needed, and I gave it to her, accelerating, grinding her clit.

"Ridge!"

I didn't know how, but she was wetter, narrowing around me. And when that happened, things started to move. Not just between us, but within me.

"You'd better fucking come," I warned.

I saw the second it happened within her body.

Her legs lifted; her hands slapped my thighs. Her mouth opened, and the loudest scream came out of it. "Ah! Yes! Ridge!"

Those noises she was making were from me.

From my fucking dick.

From how goddamn good I was making her feel.

As the shudders slammed through her, her ass became even

snugger. I knew, at that point, she could take a little more power, so my blows turned short but sharp, and they sent me straight over the fucking edge.

"Addison"—I drew in air, shocked from the intensity that I was feeling and from the pleasure spreading through me—"your ass is fucking milking me."

Within a stroke, I reached the edge, where I dangled for a single second before I was sent straight over.

"Oh my God!"

The words had been spoken in her voice, but I swore they came from me.

Each time I drove back and slid in, more cum shot from my tip.

And each time, a blast of tingles ricocheted through my body.

And each time, what made the feeling even greater was hearing her moan, her breath, her screams that always ended with my name.

I slowed once the sensations died down within the both of us and I was fully empty. As soon as I was out, I leaned down and pressed my lips to her clit. My thumb had spent so much time there; I wanted to make sure she wasn't sore. I kissed each of the places my hand had swiped, slowly working my way up her body.

My mouth then went to her cheek, her chin, and hovered above her lips. "Baby…" I exhaled. "You're fucking amazing. I hope you know that."

"I didn't think I was going to survive. I certainly didn't think I was going to enjoy it."

"And you did?"

She scanned my eyes, a smile moving across her face. "Far more than I'd ever thought I would."

"Wait until the next time. It's going to blow your mind." I gave her most of my body weight, my hands cupping her cheeks. "I love you, Addison."

"You should."

I laughed, and she did too.

"More than I could ever tell you and more than I could ever show you," I said. My palms went beneath her back, and I lifted her off the mattress. "I'm going to take you in the shower so I can wash you and heal you a little."

"And then you're going to put me to bed?"

"Yes." I kissed her again. "And I'm going to hold you until tomorrow morning."

When I went to pick her up, she squeezed my wrist. "Ridge…" There was emotion in her eyes—I could see it growing; I could feel it. "I love you more."

Chapter Thirty-Five

Addison

It didn't matter if I was on a stage, in my car, or in the middle of a bar; when I heard music, a pulse moved through my body, and all I wanted to do was dance. For most of my life, that music had come from the radio or some type of streaming site. I just didn't have the funds to attend concerts even though I would have loved to.

So, when Jana had asked me to take her place and go with Daisy and Ridge to see Taylor Swift, I hadn't thrown my arms around her and told her how excited I was, but I'd wanted to. Nor had I told her that this was a dream opportunity, and never had I thought I would get to see one of my favorite artists live, but I wanted to do that too.

As the date of the show got closer, I couldn't contain the flurry in my body. Daisy and I had made a countdown calendar, and every day, we would cross off a box, jumping in anticipation that we were one night closer. Poor Ridge had to hear about it relentlessly, and he was getting it from both sides since Daisy was talking about it nonstop, whether she was in class or at home.

But it wasn't just the buzz of going and all the chatter that surrounded the event. It went far deeper than the three of us showing up to the stadium to watch the concert. When it came to this performance, every detail mattered. This was a gala of eras, and we needed to pick our favorite and roll with it. So, in addition to the countdown and the constant Taylor talks, we had to plan our outfits. That took multiple trips to the mall and hours spent in Daisy's room with a glue gun and glitter and lace.

The best part about creating this masterpiece was that we got to do it together and bond over it.

From head to toe, our girl sparkled. There were jewels and glitter on her pink Chucks, her white socks were trimmed with lace, her baby-pink skirt had several layers of tulle beneath it, and her silver sequined top had *Swiftie* in the middle, decorated with even more glitter. But it wasn't just the ensemble that mattered. Hair and makeup were just as important too. So, while I got her ready, we FaceTimed with Jana. I wanted Jana to give me some tips on how to do Daisy's makeup and how to create the heart around her eye so it would stay the whole night without smudging. I knew Jana was upset that she couldn't be here, and I wanted her to feel as though she was part of the big event even if she was far away.

Once Daisy's face was completed, I put some pink studs in her ears and checked her nail polish, every nail done in a different pastel, to make sure none of it had nicked. And the last piece was a headband of daisies that I secured across the center of her forehead and tucked through the locks of her hair.

I took a more subtle approach, settling on a jean skirt and a T-shirt that I'd knotted at my waist with *1989* printed in the middle and knee-high cowboy boots. I wore my hair down and curled and had glitter on my eyelids and my lips in a glossy pink.

As for Ridge, we couldn't let him show up in the polo he'd paired with cargo shorts. He needed to not only act the part, but look it too. So, right before we left the house, Daisy handed him our gift. I couldn't believe she hadn't blown the surprise, but she'd kept her lips sealed, and Ridge was shocked when he opened the box. We'd had the T-shirt made a few weeks prior—in pink, of course—with the words *Swiftie by Choice* in the center and *(my daughter's fault)* beneath.

And because Ridge was such a good sport, he smiled as he put on the shirt and told Daisy it was the best gift she'd ever given him. I couldn't stop laughing from his teasing glare as we made our way to the car, still giggling as we got out and walked toward the stadium.

As Daisy walked between us, holding my hand and Ridge's, he said in a low voice, "Admittedly, I've never been so fucking happy to have a day arrive. I don't think I'd have survived if I had to make another friendship bracelet."

I pointed at his hand, a wrist that was adorned with a slew of beads and sayings, and I air-kissed him. "You're truly the best dad ever."

"I know." He nodded toward Daisy. "Look at her."

Even though I did, I didn't need to. I could feel the energy through her fingers. There was nothing in this world that she wanted more, and Ridge was giving it to her.

But what Daisy didn't realize as we walked into the arena—and I only did because Ridge had told me—was that the seats he had purchased were VIP, which meant we were standing directly in front of the stage. We weren't rows back; we were hugging the long T that cut through the floor like a massive runway. There wasn't a section in the entire stadium that could bring us closer to Taylor. If she walked by our area—and she would—we would be able to see every freckle, every one of her hairs that went from straight to curly throughout the night, every sequin that had been stitched into her outfits.

Since the stage was taller than Ridge, Daisy was forced to look up. But when she did, watching the clock on the giant screen in the back that gave a countdown of how much time was left until the show started, there were tears already filling her eyes. Her small pink-covered feet were hitting the ground every time she jumped. Her lips weren't just pulled wide, but there was a look of awe in her expression, a level of elation that I wasn't sure I'd ever felt.

"Daddy, there's only a minute left! Taylor's coming! Taylor is *cooooming*!"

The music that had been playing quietly in the background started to get louder. A hum was moving its way through the crowd. The anticipation was so thick that I wouldn't be able to feel the sun even if it could penetrate through the roof of the stadium.

Ridge lifted Daisy into his arms and put her on his shoulders so she could see the stage better. Her eyes began to drip, her bracelets glowing from the lights as she held up her arms.

While I focused on Daisy, my feet couldn't stop moving; the dancing had started even if the concert hadn't.

I could just feel it.

And I wanted it—the music, the entertainment, the love that these two brought to my life.

Ten seconds.

"Look!" Daisy screamed. "It's almost time!"

I waited until there was movement in my peripheral vision before I stole a peek, and Taylor's dancers were now on the stage with large feathers in their hands, like the tails of a peacock. Ridge was feeling the beat, too, swinging Daisy back and forth, the movement only adding to her elation.

And it was the heaviest I'd ever seen it—on her cheeks, in her smile, in her wiggling body.

She didn't shift her eyes from the stage.

She didn't lower her arms.

Nothing, not even a storm, could get her to look away.

"Daisy, is this everything you wanted and more?" I asked.

She didn't even give me a glance when she nodded.

That was the moment when I realized what tonight was really about. This had nothing to do with Taylor or music or the energy I felt inside the stadium. Sure, all of those things were present, and I couldn't wait to sing and dance and feel the vibrance of every era that Taylor brought us through. But the real meaning of tonight was the love of a little girl and what it was like to watch this through her eyes. Ridge's attempt to make her pay off the cost of the tickets by doing chores around the house was insignificant. He was teaching her life lessons and values that would carry on long past this concert. What really mattered was that he was giving her this moment.

A moment neither of them would ever forget.

And I was lucky enough to get to witness it.

I heard Taylor singing, but my stare wasn't on the stage.

It was on Daisy.

And when she reached the first chorus—a routine I'd seen many times online and that was good enough for me—I couldn't drag my gaze away from our little girl. Despite the tears that were streaming their fastest, there was no sadness in those beautiful eyes that looked so much like her father's; there was no wavering as she held her hands in a heart.

This was love.

And I'd never felt it deeper.

For just a second, my stare lowered, and it locked with Ridge's gaze.

He wasn't concentrating on the performance either, although that didn't surprise me.

He was focused on me.

He ran his thumb under my eyes—a move that confused me at first until I realized Daisy wasn't the only one crying. I was too. And once he dried the bottom of both eyelids, he pulled me against his side, and I clasped on to Daisy's ankle, and I gripped Ridge's waist.

"You're my *Miss Americana*," he said, referencing the name of the song Taylor was singing.

I laughed out loud at his expression and from the fact that he knew the song because Daisy wouldn't let him listen to anything except Taylor.

"I'll gladly take that title," I told him. "But you better not be my *Heartbreak Prince.*"

Epilogue

RIDGE

As I reached across the small bit of sand that was between our lounge chairs and dived my fingers into the back of Addison's hair, I couldn't stop staring at her. It wasn't her bikini that captured my full attention—although, fuck, that certainly didn't hurt. Her body was magnificent, and there were days when I still couldn't believe it was mine. But what I really couldn't stop gazing at was her expression. Since we'd arrived in Kauai, it covered her face every time she glanced at the ocean and when she ran to the water to dip her bare feet in the waves and as she gazed up at the sky. During those occasions, when her head tilted back and she looked up, her hand automatically went to her throat, circling her fingers around the sun that dangled beneath it, and I fucking loved that.

I saw every one of those moments because I couldn't keep my eyes off her.

But what this trip made me realize was that her smile had very little to do with the ocean or the sand or the waves or the sky.

Her smile had everything to do with me.

She turned her head toward me, the grin already present, but it grew as our eyes connected. "Your phone doesn't exactly make the best background music for the beach. It hasn't stopped ringing since lunch. Is everything okay?"

My cell was lying on the chair next to me, and I picked it up and turned it on vibrate. "I should have muted it this morning. I'm sorry. I'm sick of hearing it blow up."

"Are you sure it's nothing important?"

"Shit no, it's not important. Well, at least in my opinion. Rhett would disagree, and so would Brady. They're filling in for me on the last-minute renovations at our Beverly Hills and Malibu hotels, and they're calling because they have endless questions. I made it clear before we left for Hawaii that they'd just need to figure it out." I shook my head. "And, obviously, they can't."

She took a long, deep breath. "That's ballsy, don't you think?"

"Because Rhett's going to murder me?"

She exaggerated her nod. "Exactly that."

"Probably." I ran my hand over my head and looked up at the clouds. "I'm actually surprised he hasn't flown here yet to choke my ass out."

"The day isn't over, there's still plenty of time for that to happen."

I laughed. "Truth."

"I bet Rowan is ready to murder you too. You know Rhett is complaining to her about you, and the two of them are ganging up behind your back and planning your death."

"I'm positive that's happening as we speak." I sighed. "Hell, Cooper's probably dying for me to come back, too, so he can stop listening to her complain about me."

Addison turned on her side, tucking her arm behind her head to use it as a pillow. "What about Macon? I know you mentioned he and Brooklyn might be coming out here to join us, but they wouldn't know until last minute. Have you heard anything from him?"

"He texted me this morning and said he couldn't make it work.

He found a piece of land in Croatia that he wants to look at for a new hotel. He and Brooklyn are flying there instead."

"I bet she's bummed, not about Croatia—that's amazing—but about missing an opportunity to come here and see her family. I know she loves spending every second she can with them."

"Don't worry, I'm sure the trip to Croatia is a compromise, and after heading to Europe, they'll come straight here."

Her exhale was loud and lengthy. "You Coles and Spades live quite the life."

"And you're going to become one soon, so you're going to know firsthand just how that life is."

Her face blushed, which happened every time I mentioned that she was going to become my wife.

"Besides, without Macon and Brooklyn here, I get you all to myself."

She put her hand on my chest. "I don't hate that idea at all."

"I didn't think you would." I lifted her fingers and kissed them. "Have you heard from Leah?"

She groaned. "Yes. She's bringing the last of her things to her new apartment, and she hates me for not being there to help carry all the boxes. But she recruited some people from work to assist with the heavy lifting, so even though I'm not there, she's got it covered."

My brows rose as I took in her face. "Why is she moving boxes? I paid for a moving company to take her things."

"She canceled the movers you'd hired." Her smile told me everything I needed to know even though she continued, "She wouldn't let you spend a dime on her, but she appreciated the offer and that you were willing to do that because you'd stolen me away from her. She said you owe her a million cocktails instead."

"Jesus, you two are cut from the same fucking cloth."

"And now, you know why she's my best friend—we not only have everything in common, but we also share a brain." She paused. "And

I'm really going to miss her"—she put her hand up—"not enough to leave your house and move back in with her. Just miss her in a way that I won't get to see her every day." She flicked her bottom lip with her teeth. "I wouldn't change anything about living with you and Daisy. I absolutely love it."

"Now that I have you in my house, I can't imagine living there without you." I felt my gaze deepen. "Neither could Daisy."

"You don't have to imagine it. It's never going to happen." She pushed her hair back despite several of the pieces staying and teasing the corners of her eyes. "Heck, it was hard enough to leave for the week that I visited my sister. How many times a day did we talk while I was gone? At least three million?"

I chuckled. "Just about."

She raised her hand to my cheek. "You're stuck with me."

I kissed the back of her hand, and then I used mine to brush across her forehead and down her cheek to her chest, where the sun necklace sat. "You know, you're carrying a huge responsibility on your shoulders for the next school year."

"How so?"

"With Daisy moving on to second grade, you're going to have to watch her teacher like a hawk and make sure she's giving Daisy an education that meets your standards." I gave the necklace a shake and pulled my hand back. "You need to be my eyes and ears at that school."

She put her hand on top of mine. "Mrs. Larson, Daisy's new teacher, already knows what our girl needs. We've talked extensively about it." She squeezed my fingers. "Don't worry, she's the best second-grade teacher we have at our school."

I let those words simmer. "Is it a coincidence that she was assigned to her, or did you have something to do with it?"

"You mean, innocent ol' me, work the system and get Daisy the top teacher? I would never." She winked.

I laughed. "Does that mean you had Jana do your dirty work and had her shoot off an email to the administration and specifically ask for Mrs. Larson? Or..."

"Would it surprise you to hear that we double-teamed the administration and both Jana and I made the request?" She bit her lip.

"Not even a little."

She bent her arm to prop herself up a little. "Jana texted me about options for the next school year, and I told her about Mrs. Larson. We thought it would be best if she reached out, and I backed up her request by working some magic in the administrative office."

My head slowly shook. "You girls are a lethal duo."

"We get what we want. What can I say? I just love that we got what's best for Daisy."

"Remind me to never go to battle against the two of you at the same time—I'll be fucked."

She laughed. "Come on...we're not *that* bad." She paused. "Okay, maybe we are."

When we finally quieted, I said, "Honestly, I'm just glad the two of you can have conversations about Daisy and she's comfortable reaching out to you."

"Since Brady and Lily's wedding, things between us have warmed up a lot—you know that. It makes me so happy that she trusts me and she trusts my decisions." She adjusted the top of her bikini. "I don't know if we'll ever meet up for drinks or anything like that, but who knows? Wilder things have happened."

"Like?"

She thought for a moment. "Like how the man who hired me for a whole shift at the strip club is now my boyfriend who I'm living with."

I pushed the stray hairs away from her eyes. "Who's going to become your husband."

Her smile got even larger. "And that."

"And who loves you more than anyone in this whole fucking world."

Her eyes fluttered closed. "Mister, there's someone who comes in a close second and would fight you if they heard you say that."

"Your sister? Your mom? Dad? Leah?"

Her eyes opened, and she held my hand to her face. "Our Daisy."

Our Daisy.

She was right about that.

I took in her eyes, her nose, her lips, and then I glanced up at the sky one last time. It was a cloudy afternoon, the sun only peeking through the open spots between the thick, billowy ones.

In those spots, where the rays were the strongest, he was there.

I couldn't see him.

But I could feel him.

And I knew he was watching me, listening, present in every way that he could be, so I silently said, *Dad, I'm loving big. I'm loving hard. I'm loving unapologetically. Because you're right; being in love is the greatest blessing in this world.*

I looked at Addison and silently added, *I'll never be alone again, Dad. I promise.*

Acknowledgments

Nina Grinstead, at THE END, right before I made the final edit, you sent the simplest text: *I've got you.* <3 But those words, Nina, aren't simple at all. They're exactly what I need—you know that; you always know. But it doesn't end at THE END because I believe in my whole heart that this is just the very beginning. For the both of us. To a million more moments of you holding my hand under the table. Because those are my favorites. I love you. To the moon and back.

Jovana Shirley, before I started writing this, I looked back to see how many books we'd done together, and I was speechless at the number. So many track changes—ha-ha (no, but really, LOL)—so many stories you've helped me weave together, so much love and encouragement from you. You know how I feel; there's no one better, no one more trustworthy than you. I mean that with my whole heart. At the end of every book, I always write, I can never do this without you, and I mean it more and more each time. Love you so, so hard.

Ratula Roy, how will I ever thank you for being honest with me one hundred percent of the time; for not sugarcoating a single thing you say to me; for giving me the hard truth, even when I don't want to hear it; for giving me the motivation when you know I'm lacking it; for finding the words when I can't; for holding me together when I'm falling apart; for letting me fall apart because you know I need it? For understanding me when I don't understand myself. I hope you know I can't be me without you. I love you more than love—and I'll never stop saying that to you.

Hang Le, my unicorn, you are just incredible in every way.

Judy Zweifel, as always, thank you for being so wonderful to work with and for taking such good care of my words. <3

Christine Estevez, you've been the most wonderful addition to my team. I appreciate you so much.

Nikki Terrill, my soul sister. Every tear, vent, virtual hug, life chaos, workout—you've been there through it all. I could never do this without you, and I would never want to. Love you hard.

Pang, I treasure you. In all the ways. And I'm so, so lucky to be able to work with you.

Sarah Symonds, I love you, friend, and I miss you terribly.

Brittney Sahin, months later and I'm saying the same thing all over again: I survived another book because of you. Endless thank-yous. Forever. Love you, B.

Kimmi Street, my sister from another mister. Thank you from the bottom of my heart. You saved me. You inspired me. You kept me standing in so many different ways. I love you more than love.

Extra-special love goes to Valentine PR, my ARC team, Rachel Baldwin, Valentine Grinstead, Kelley Beckham, Sarah Norris, Kim Cermak, and Christine Miller.

Mom and Dad, thanks for your unwavering belief in me and your constant encouragement. It means more than you'll ever know.

Brian, my words could never dent the love I feel for you. Trust me when I say, I love you more.

My Midnighters, you are such a supportive, loving, motivating group. Thanks for being such an inspiration, for holding my hand when I need it, and for always begging for more words. I love you all.

To all the influencers who read, review, share, post, TikTok—Thank you, thank you, thank you will never be enough. You do so much for our writing community, and we're so appreciative.

To my readers—I cherish each and every one of you. I'm so grateful for all the love you show my books, for taking the time to reach out to me, and for your passion and enthusiasm when it comes to my stories. I love, love, love you.

AMARA
an imprint of Entangled Publishing LLC

Printed in Great Britain
by Amazon

47314218R00192